The Divided Realms
BOOK 1

Captured

MAGGIE L. WOOD

The Divided Realms, Book 1: Captured
Text © 2011 Maggie L. Wood

Published by Lobster Press™
1620 Sherbrooke Street West, Suites C & D
Montréal, Québec   H3H 1C9
Tel. (514) 904-1100 • Fax (514) 904-1101 • www.lobsterpress.com

Publisher: Alison Fripp
Editor: Mahak Jain
Editorial Assistants: Simon Lewsen & Ryan Healey
Proofreader: Catherine Knowles
Graphic Design & Production: Tammy Desnoyers
Cover Concept: Vo Ngoc Yen Vy
Production Assistant: Vo Ngoc Yen Vy

 Canadian   Patrimoine   We acknowledge the financial support of the
Heritage   canadien   Government of Canada through the Canada
Book Fund for our publishing activities.

Library and Archives Canada Cataloguing in Publication

Wood, Maggie L.
      Captured / Maggie L. Wood.

(The divided realms ; 1)
Previous title: The Princess Pawn.
ISBN 978-1-77080-071-7

      I. Wood, Maggie L. Princess Pawn. II. Title. III. Series: Wood, Maggie L. Divided realms ; 1.

PS8595.O6364C36 2011   jC813'.6   C2010-906523-9

Printed and bound in Canada.

To Scot, my very own knight in shining armor.

– Maggie L. Wood

Acknowledgments

I would like to thank everyone at Lobster Press for giving me a second chance with this series, for your excitement and enthusiasm, for making me feel like part of the team, and for getting back to me within an hour of my sending an email query. You have all been such a pleasure to work with! And I would also like to thank my innovative editor, Mahak Jain, who has somehow managed to teach this old dog some new tricks. Thanks, Mahak, for all your insightful comments, excellent suggestions, and infinite patience. You rock!

THE DIVIDED REALMS
BOOK 1

CAPTURED

∽ MAGGIE L. WOOD ∾

Lobster Press™

CAST OF CHARACTERS

THE GALLANDRIANS:

Aleria Farrandale: Queen of Gallandra

Ulor Farrandale: King of Gallandra

Alaric Farrandale: Heir to the throne of Gallandra and son to King Ulor and Queen Aleria; husband of Princess Diantha

Willow Farrandale: Princess of Gallandra and daughter to Prince Alaric and Princess Diantha, also known as Willow Kingswell on Earth.

Varian Farrandale: Prince of Gallandra and younger brother to King Ulor

Sir Baldemar of Tamarvyn: Mage knight to King Ulor

Lady Merritt du Aubrey: Lady-in-waiting to Queen Aleria

Brand Lackwulf: Squire to Prince Alaric

Malvin Weddellwynd: Mage apprentice

Gemma Fletcher: Servant girl from the city of Graffyn

THE KELDORIANS:

Morwenna Somerell: Queen of Keldoran

Tarrant Somerell: King of Keldoran

Diantha Somerell Farrandale: Heir to the throne of Keldoran and daughter to King Tarrant and Queen Morwenna; wife to Prince Alaric

Sir Lachlan Montrose: Mage knight to Queen Morwenna

Lord Garnock of Grisselwait: Commander in King Tarrant's army

THE CLARIONITES:

Cyrraena: Faerie Queen of Timorell and guardian to Mistolear

Nezeral: Faerie Prince of Clarion, from the House of Jarlath

PROLOGUE

Cyrraena Silvenfrost, the faerie queen of Timorell, stared at the bright little head poking through the swaddling blanket. She touched the babe's soft, springy curls, careful not to let emotion cross her face. The humans, one a king, the other a nurse, were eyeing her with doubt. She couldn't let them see any indecision. Especially now, when all their hope rested in the small bundle she cradled.

She looked away from the sleeping infant and scanned the gloomy faces around her. King Ulor's dull gaze troubled her the most. He'd already lost too much for a human. His wife. His son. The child's mother. And now Willow, the child herself – his only granddaughter. What if he couldn't bear the grief? And, more importantly, what if he couldn't keep the opposing forces at bay until Willow's aging process completed itself?

Cyrraena held the baby out to Nurse Beryl. The time for second-guessing had passed. Nurse Beryl's practiced hands embraced the child. She'd been nursemaid to the royal family for most of her life and had fought vehemently to accompany the tiny princess. Again, Cyrraena wavered. Nurse Beryl was competent, but she had just passed into her sixtieth year. By the time of Willow's return, Beryl would be well into her seventies. If something should happen to her ...

But no. Cyrraena clenched her jaw, studying the hard-eyed nursemaid. The little woman was glaring at her. Her impertinence didn't upset Cyrraena – it calmed her instead. The nursemaid would make sure the infant princess remained unharmed. She would safeguard her with every ounce of her short-lived human soul.

Cyrraena motioned to her attendant, who stepped forward and placed the gift into her outstretched hand. The pendant, a fragment of smooth white enamel fashioned in the shape of a swan, had been given to Princess Willow at her christening. As the child's nethermother, Cyrraena had the right to bestow on her a magical virtue. She had chosen wisdom. It was an attribute, she knew, notoriously iffy for its time frame structures. But Willow would need wisdom if the humans were to succeed in Mistolear's battle ahead. She sighed, closing her fingers around the gift. She hoped fifteen years would be enough time for Willow's virtue to bloom.

A leather-gloved hand brushed her arm. "Your Majesty?"

Cyrraena looked at the sad face of King Ulor. "The crystal, then," she said, "is it ready?" He nodded, his eyes still bleak. She gestured for him to begin the process.

He handed a crystal globe to Nurse Beryl. "Everything is

ready," he said. "When the portal closes, you will find yourself inside the lodging house." He pressed the child closer against the nurse, his hand lingering on the babe's soft nest of red curls, then he stepped away.

"You may touch it now," he said, nodding to the bright crystal.

Nurse Beryl hesitated. Her forehead furrowed in consternation, then smoothed out. She touched the glowing crystal.

The old nursemaid and the infant princess disappeared almost instantly.

CHAPTER 1

"Abby, wait!" Willow coasted her bike to a stop. "Please, can I just talk to you for a sec?" Abby gave her a stony glance and kept right on walking, knocking into Willow's three-speed with a disinterested hip check.

Willow used her foot to balance herself. She froze in surprise before pedaling after Abby. "Abby, listen. I can explain about this morning. If you'd just –"

"You know what, Will?" Abby stopped midstride and turned to face Willow. Her thin, wind-whipped hair blew angrily around her face. "I don't care about your explanation. Because *nothing*," she snapped, "could excuse what you did today."

"What are you talking about?" Technically, Willow hadn't really *done* anything. That was sort of the problem – she was supposed to meet Abby at lunch to work on their worm project. Except Willow didn't show up. "I mean, I *am* sorry about ditching you at the library today. I really am. But you don't have to make a federal case out of it."

"I'm not talking about the library."

Just then a school bus rumbled past them. The groan of its shifting gears filled the tense silence.

"Hey Abi-whale!" someone yelled. "You should be wearing a sign!"

Willow winced. Another shout drifted over Hewitt Street before the bus disappeared. "Yeah!" someone else shouted. "Danger: *Wide Load!*"

Some of the anger seeped out of Abigail's face, leaving her looking sad and defeated. "At the cafeteria you didn't say anything. You just sat there while those morons made fun of me." Her eyes misted. "I thought you were different," she whispered.

Willow's heart sank. "Abby, I ..." Abby turned around and walked away before Willow could figure out how to finish that sentence. Willow started to coast after her, feeling mean and guilty. But she braked when she heard someone shout her name.

"Hey, Will!"

She turned to see Dean Jarrett sticking his head out the window of Rick Burke's red Camaro. "Forget Guinevere!" he yelled. "Think French maid!" Then both he and Rick made hooting noises and gunned the Camaro.

A hot blush swept over Willow. Dean was talking about the costume she was going to be wearing at Melissa Morrison's Halloween Party. He was also the reason Abby was angry at her. She waved at him. He'd swiveled his head around to watch her.

When Willow looked back at Abby, the other girl was already halfway down Hewitt Street, her black clarinet case bouncing vigorously against her leg. Willow sighed and started to pedal in the other direction. She tried to rationalize the situation, tried to convince herself that she hadn't done anything wrong. Abby was just being too sensitive. After all, Dean Jarrett teased everybody. He didn't mean anything by what he'd said at lunch. It was just the way he was. If Dean and she ever had a chance to be alone together – the thought made Willow flush again – she could ask him to go easy on Abby.

Leaves rained down from the oak trees that lined both sides of Meadow Brook Street. She plowed through them, eager to get home and try on her Guinevere costume again. She propped her bike against the faded red bricks of her tiny bungalow, not noticing at first that every window in the house was tightly curtained and the front light was on. As she walked toward the doorstep, though, the living room blinds started to do a nervous little flutter-dance. And then, a few seconds later, the light flicked off and on, off and on, as if someone were sending out a coded message.

Willow dropped her book bag in panic and raced up the front doorstep. Nana must have had a relapse. She jabbed her house key into the lock, praying that everything would be okay.

Suddenly, the key flew out of her hand.

"Princess, you've returned!" Her grandmother pulled open the front door and grabbed Willow's wrist. "Make haste!" she said, glancing about. "We haven't a moment to spare."

"Nana, what ...?" was all Willow managed to get out before the old lady yanked her inside the house.

"The summoning!" Nana whispered breathlessly. "It's come, Your Highness. It's finally come!"

Willow took in her grandmother's appearance. The frazzled hairdo. The too-bright eyes. The blouse with the buttons popped off. Willow's eyes trailed down Nana's long black skirt. It was on backwards and the zipper gaped open.

Nana turned and began pulling at Willow's arm again. "Must ready ourselves. Must ready ourselves. So much to do. So much."

Alarm filled Willow. She'd been right. Nana *was* having another relapse.

"Na-na," Willow made her voice soft and musical as if she were speaking to a child. "Slow down." She put an arm around the little woman and gently rubbed her shoulders. "Why don't we sit a minute? Besides, I don't even know what a summoning is. Aren't you going to explain it to me?"

Her grandmother stepped back and blinked at her, clearly startled that Willow needed an explanation.

Willow squeezed Nana's shoulders again. "Listen, you sit right down here, okay?" She led her grandmother over to the couch by the fireplace.

Nana sat down and Willow wrapped her in a knitted afghan. "There. Feel better?" She brushed hair away from the old lady's eyes, looking anxiously into her face. Nana seemed a bit better. Her breathing was deeper and she didn't look so agitated.

"Should I light a fire?" asked Willow. That would do the trick. Her grandmother loved fires. Nana nodded and Willow grabbed a matchbook from the mantel and knelt down by the fireplace. She lit a match and held it to the packaging of the store-bought fire log.

Nana's dizzy spells and memory lapses had started last year. At first, she forgot small things, like her doctor's name or his office's street number. Then she forgot they owned a fridge and stored food in the snow. Or she thought the remote control was a telephone and tried to make calls with it. The full-scale delusions didn't start until late in the spring. The doctor did all kinds of tests, but didn't get any concrete results. All he could say was that Nana was probably in the early stages of Alzheimer's.

Willow sighed. For a full month now, her grandmother had been acting normal. She'd begun to hope that the doctor had been wrong. No dizzy spells. No blackouts. And no delusions about living in a castle and being a nurse to some medieval princess.

Willow grabbed the poker and jabbed the fake log with its sharp point. Right now, her grandmother probably thought she was the fireplace servant or something. When Nana was in her castle-fantasy mode, she had a lot of servants: a cook, a maid, a gardener, a whole squadron of armed guards, and a kitchen boy named Gwaine. Did kitchen boys light fires?

She sighed again and gave the log another jab, trying, at the same time, to push aside her fears. What if Nana had to go to a hospital or a nursing home? What would Willow do? Nana was all the family she had. She'd probably get stuck in a foster home.

"Gwaine," Nana said, "the fire looks fine now. I need you to go and fetch the princess. And no dallying in the kitchens either."

Willow rolled her eyes. She'd been right. Kitchen boys did light fires. She stood up and walked out of the living room, waited a second, then came back in. When Nana was like this, it was better to humor her. If you tried to explain reality, her eyes would just glaze over like tinted windows. Couldn't see in. Couldn't see out.

Nana leaned over to a table beside the couch and reached for her favorite ornament, a delicate, gem-cut crystal resting on a golden stand. "Princess, look," she said, "the crystal has begun the summoning spell. We must prepare. I don't know how much time we'll have before the spell reaches its peak."

"Where does the spell take us?" Willow asked.

"Why, to Mistolear, of course, Your Highness."

Mistolear! Willow felt a wave of childhood nostalgia. She

stared at the couch that had been her pretend princess carriage and the chair that had been her magic horse, Moonbeam. Nana had been inventing Mistolear for her ever since Willow could remember, making up thrilling adventures about knights and princesses and faeries and magic. Heck, for the first six years of her life, Willow had actually believed she *was* a princess trapped in an alternate dimension by an evil faerie lord. But crabby Mrs. Letton, her first grade teacher, had squashed that fantasy.

"Princess." Nana offered up the crystal. "Keep watch, my lady. I'm too old."

"What, uh ... should I do with it?" asked Willow, taking the crystal and holding it up to the light. The globe looked the same as it had the last time she had looked at it. She shifted it around in her hand. The way the light reflected colors into it was pretty, but it wasn't glowing. "Keep it with you, Princess. That's all. Just keep it with you. And when it glows, we'll touch it together and ... and go back home." Nana smiled vaguely and lay back against the couch cushions.

Willow tucked the afghan up around her grandmother's chin. "Don't worry," she whispered. "You rest. I'll take care of it."

She bent down to kiss a wrinkled cheek. "I'll take care of everything."

Willow set the last pot to dry in the dish rack and peeled off her rubber gloves. She wondered if she should call Dr. Pembleton. In the spring, when Nana's spells had worsened, Dr. Pembleton had asked Willow to document Nana's behavior and keep him informed of any new developments. But Nana had been doing so well lately that Willow hadn't spoken with him in over a month.

She found Dr. Pembleton's doodled-on, dirt-smeared business card. It was taped to the wall beneath the telephone. Nah, there was no sense in calling him now. He wouldn't be there at night and she'd just have to listen to his answering service telling her that he'd get back to her in the morning.

Willow sighed and sat on one of the wobbly kitchen chairs. She leaned an elbow on the table and stared at the crystal sitting on top of her school books. She'd been about seven when she and Nana had started playing that summoning spell game. Touch the crystal. That's all you did and you'd be magically whisked away to another world.

Another world. She reached out and ran a fingertip over the stone. It'd be nice to be someplace else. Someplace where no one ever got sick and your best friends didn't get mad at you.

The stack of unpaid bills on the edge of the table caught Willow's eye. Despair swept over her. Nana had always been vague about finances, but they'd managed somehow. Lately, though, Nana had been letting things slip and Willow couldn't help but note that some of the envelopes were marked

"Second Notice."

She fingered the pile of bills. What if Nana didn't actually have any money to pay the bills? No money meant no way of looking after themselves. And what if Nana needed to go into a nursing home? Who would pay for that?

The clock over the sink chimed ten times. Willow shook off her gloom. She still had math homework and a writing assignment to do. Cheery thoughts of nursing homes and illness would have to wait until later. She scooped up her books and carried them along with the crystal into her bedroom. Across the hallway, she could hear Nana's chainsaw-snoring. She grinned, closing her door against the rattling, staccato sounds. Her tiny grandmother could saw logs with the best of them.

Willow's homework desk was cluttered with teetering books, discarded computer printouts, and her new, slightly used Toshiba computer – a spiffy laptop she'd bought with a whole summer's worth of babysitting money. She tossed the printouts – rejects from an essay she had written for Melissa Morrison – into the makeshift recycling box beneath her desk, setting the crystal and her homework in the newly cleared spot. Algebra, she decided, placing the heavy math book on the floor, could wait. Mr. Rosen's writing assignment had to be more interesting than solving quadratic equations.

Willow settled into her desk chair and typed *A Ghost Story by Willow Kingswell*. She stared at the working title that

Mr. Rosen had given them. Her plan was to do something weird with it. Like write about ghosts that haunted nail polish or purple shoelaces. Bizarre things that nobody would expect.

She started writing. *Once there was a ghost* ...

She stopped, peered at her first sentence, and deleted it. *A ghost once lived in a ...*

No, that wasn't right, either. She deleted the words again. Blank space filled the screen, mirroring her blank mind.

Willow played with the mouse, circling it around and around the empty page, until it hovered over the START button at the bottom of the screen.

She might as well get in a quick game since she obviously wasn't going to be finishing any homework. A few clicks later, an ancient-looking chessboard filled the screen. The three-dimensional playing pieces were in the same positions they'd been in when she'd saved the last game.

Willow frowned at the screen. Things were not looking too good for her White guys. Her king was in check from a Black knight and soon to be in double check from Black's sneaky, marauding queen. She looked around her players. There were still a few moves open. She dragged her bishop over to E4, watching as the bishop raised his magical staff high in the air and nuked the Black knight with a lightning bolt. The knight's armor made clanking sounds as he fell to his square and disappeared.

A box at the bottom right-hand corner of the computer

screen indicated that it was White's move again. Willow squinted at the words. It was disconcerting how fast the computer made its moves. When she and Nana played, they took minutes, not seconds, to make their moves. She clicked the REDO button for a replay of Black's last maneuver. A pawn had stepped forward, opening up an attack route for Black's bishop.

Willow stared at the screen, her mind as empty of strategy as it had been of story ideas. She rubbed her temples. Her head was too plugged up with worry – that was the problem. Worry about Nana, worry about herself, and worry about the future.

Her fingers slid from her temples down into her hair, curling around a thick red strand. Memories she'd been trying to suppress suddenly washed over her. Smoke. Flames. Carpet blazing, the fire edging dangerously close to the curtains. The last time Nana had been stuck in castle-fantasy mode, she'd almost burned the house down trying to cook food in the fireplace.

Maybe it was her fault, Nana being sick again. She'd lied to Nana and told her she was going to Melissa's Halloween Party before she'd even been invited. And so poor Nana had spent hours last week hunched over the sewing machine, making Willow her Guinevere costume. It must've been too much for her.

She wiped her eyes and swiveled in her chair. The red gown hung from a hook on the wall beside her bed. Nana had been so excited about making it for her, as if Melissa's party were a royal ball or something.

Willow stood up and pulled off her jeans and hoodie. She took the costume from the hanger and slipped it on, shivering as the cool silk lining pressed against her warm skin. When she had the buttons done up, she walked over to the full-length mirror and stared at herself. The costume clung to her skin, giving faint curves to her lean body. She slid delicate fingertips over the soft, ruby red folds. The color deepened her hair to a shiny copper. She felt beautiful in it. Like a real princess.

It needed something, though. Willow turned from the mirror to her bureau, where an old metal jewelry box sat beside her three chess trophies. She opened the dented lid and took out a necklace. Light flickered along the thick gold chain and the delicate white enamel swan that dangled from it. She carefully clasped it around her neck. The swan was an heirloom. Nana had said it belonged to Willow's mother's family and had been passed on to the eldest daughter for over a century. Willow's mom had been its last owner.

Willow drifted over to the mirror and studied the smooth enamel feather bumps and the delicacy of the swan's gold sculpted bill and feet. A tiny crown hung from its neck, attached to a thick gold chain. She traced a fingertip along the sharp edges of the crown, trying to imagine her mother wearing the necklace.

Nana's crystal and the swan in its battered jewelry box were the only things that had survived the house fire that had killed both her parents when she was a baby. No photographs, no bits of clothing, no special ornaments, nothing else existed – except for these two mementos.

Sometimes, when she wore the necklace, Willow pretended to have conversations with her mother. Right now, though, she didn't want to think about a woman she couldn't remember. She wanted to fantasize about romance and happy endings. She wanted reality to disappear. She closed her eyes and imagined strong arms wrapping around her, keeping her safe and secure.

After a few seconds, a ragged sigh escaped her lips. It wasn't going to work tonight. There were no white knights on chargers coming to her rescue.

Or, for that matter, falling in love with her at Halloween parties.

She turned abruptly from the mirror and plopped back into her desk chair. Truth was, the only one who'd *ever* come to her rescue was Abby. Willow's face burned. God, she'd been such a jerk today. She should have gone after Abby. Abby had sat in doctors' waiting rooms with her, had helped clean up the smoke damage from Nana's fire, had even brought groceries over when Nana had been too delusional to get money from the bank. And Abby had been there for her whenever Willow had needed someone to talk to.

Willow gritted her teeth, a new sense of resolve sweeping through her. Forget Dean. Forget the stupid party. She knew what was really important to her now and it wasn't some insensitive boy or a bunch of snotty popular girls. Tomorrow, she was going to apologize to Abby and beg to be friends again. And first thing in the morning, she'd make that appointment with Dr. Pembleton. Whatever it took to keep Nana out of a nursing home and Abby as a friend, she was going to do it.

Feeling better about things, Willow turned off her laptop. She might as well get to bed early. She shouldn't risk Nana waking up first and trying to cook pancakes in the fireplace. She rubbed at her neck and yawned. A light glinted before her. Willow blinked at it, then shielded her eyes as the light flared to a blinding white.

Heat seared her face. "Jeez!" she yelped, twisting her head. She moved away from the desk, squinting back at the glare. The dazzling light exploded again and then mellowed to a steady glow.

Willow's eyes widened at the light's unexpected source. *Nana's crystal.* She wheeled her chair back to the desk. This couldn't be real! The glow was just a part of Nana's dementia.

So why am I seeing it too?

Gingerly, Willow touched the stand on which the crystal globe rested. It was burning hot! She snatched her hand back. What had Nana said before? Something about touching the crystal. They both had to touch it together. She pulled her fingers into her sleeve and picked up the stand carefully.

Willow glanced at her alarm clock. It was past eleven – time for her to check on Nana anyway. She stood up and carried the crystal across her bedroom and into the hallway outside Nana's closed doorway. Hesitating, she studied the crystal's brightly lit facets. Could something scientific explain this? And what if showing it to Nana caused another relapse?

That was a risk Willow couldn't take. She headed back to her bedroom, but the feeling of unease growing inside her turned into foreboding. She couldn't quite put her finger on it, but she knew something was wrong. Then it hit her. The quiet. What had happened to Nana's chainsaw-snoring?

Blood drained from Willow's face as she bolted for her grandmother's bedroom. She opened the door, holding the crystal out like a flashlight. The room was dark and eerily silent.

"Nana?"

No answer. Willow darted over to the bed, setting the globe on the nightstand. Her grandmother was lying on her side, looking comfortably asleep.

"Nana?" Willow whispered. She gently shook an exposed shoulder. "Nana? Are you awake?" No movement. Not an eyelash flutter, a sigh, or even a breath.

A terrible thought took hold of Willow. She flung back the blankets and felt Nana's thin chest for a heartbeat. Nothing.

"*No!*" She raced to the phone in the hallway and dialed 911 as quickly as her trembling fingers could push the buttons. "Hello! Hello! I need an ambulance! *I need an ambulance!*"

"Okay Miss," the lady on the phone said calmly, as if she hadn't heard a word. "Take a deep breath and tell me what the problem is."

Willow took a deep breath and tried again. "My grandma's not ... my grandma's not *breathing*."

"What's your address?"

"T-Ten Twelve M-Meadow Brook Street." Willow's voice sounded thin and childlike. She released her breath in ragged shudders.

"It's okay," said the dispatcher. "You just sit tight. An ambulance will be there in just a few minutes. What's your name?"

"Willow."

"Okay, Willow. You're doing real well there. Do you know what happened to your grandmother? Did she fall or anything like that?

"No. I – I just went in to check on her. I thought she was asleep."

"Are your parents there?"

Willow hesitated. Would they take her to a foster home right now – *tonight* – if she told them the truth? "They – they're out."

"Do you have their number? Do you want us to contact them?"

"No. No, it's okay. I'll – I'll do it." Before the woman could ask any more questions, Willow hung up the phone. A tight ache gripped Willow's heart and a harsh, accusing voice pounded in her head. *This is your fault. You should have called Dr. Pembleton when you had the chance.*

The phone rang. Instead of answering it, Willow stumbled back into her grandmother's room and took Nana in her arms. "I'm sorry!" she cried. "I'm so sorry!"

Willow felt as if hours passed before she finally let go of Nana. Where was the ambulance? Why hadn't they come? Willow shivered when her fingers grazed Nana's cool skin. More tears spilled down her cheeks. She wiped at them and pulled herself to her feet. She knew the ambulance wouldn't help anymore. It was too late.

In the dim light, she could see the crystal's soft, burning-ember glow. Anger exploded inside her. That stupid crystal! It was a part of Nana's delusions, a part of what set off her relapse.

Willow reached for the globe, ready to fling it into the garbage. But before she grabbed it, she curled her hand into a fist and slammed it into the wall. Everything – her fear, her worry, her exhaustion – came crashing in on her. She barely felt the ache in her knuckles. "Okay, Nana," she yelled. "If you're going to leave, then I'm going to leave too!"

It was a crazy, straightjacket kind of idea, but it reeled inside her head. She stormed across the hallway into her bedroom. *Everything* was a mess. She whipped her head around to look at the clutter – chess trophies, textbooks, photographs, knickknacks. None of it mattered. She stomped to the closet and threw some clothes into her backpack. Her gaze fell on her laptop.

She sat on the edge of the bed, hugged the computer to her chest, and stared at the girl in the mirror. The desperate eyes, the wild hair, the red gown swirling around her feet.

Willow got back up and trudged into Nana's room. The silk rustle of her gown sounded loud in the peaceful quiet. Nana looked asleep. Willow scowled at the crystal. A siren wailed down the street as she reached down, ready to finish what she had started.

CHAPTER 2

"Well, here she is. How was the portal, Your Highness? Not too bumpy, I hope."

Words. Willow could hear words. Someone was speaking to her. She tried to focus but everything around her was spinning. She stumbled forward.

"Hold off, Lady Merritt. The poor girl's not yet got her sea legs."

Strong hands grasped at Willow, saving her from a face-first sprawl. Her cheek pressed up against smooth leather, and she felt herself being lifted and set on a chair. The room careened like a Tilt-A-Whirl ride. Willow clutched at her laptop, trying to anchor herself.

"Is she hurt?"

"No, no. Just a bit dizzy. She'll be right as rain in a moment."

Those voices again. Willow squinted, struggling to see where they had come from. Dark shapes hovered around her. "Wh-who's there?" she asked.

"It's an odd thing that she's holding. What do you make of it, Sir Baldemar?"

"An object from Earthworld, no doubt."

A gentle hand lifted Willow's chin.

"Look at her, Milord. She has the look of her mother."

One of the dark shapes was beginning to take form. Willow could make out a young brown-haired woman dressed in blue. She patted Willow's arm and smiled at her.

"Are you all right now?" the woman asked. "Can you speak?"

Willow squeezed her eyes shut and opened them again. The strange woman was still there. She tried pinching herself next, but that didn't work either. The dream was actually getting clearer.

"Sir Baldemar, what is she doing? Do you think perhaps she's cold?"

Willow heard a low chuckle. "No, Milady. I uh – I believe the young lady is trying to wake up."

"Wh-who are you people?" Willow finally managed. "*Where am I?*" Her eyes scanned the high, curved ceiling and then the walls. A gold and purple cloth covered most of the space in front of her. The tapestry was shaped like a shield and had a large swan embroidered at its center. It reminded Willow of a coat of arms she'd once seen in a book.

"Didn't Nurse tell you?" The brown-haired woman's eyes opened incredulously. "Where is Nurse Beryl, anyway?"

Nurse Beryl? Beryl was Nana's first name. Beryl Kingswell. "You mean my grandmother?"

"Yes. Where is she? Why did she not come through the portal with you?"

Willow looked up at the ceiling, blinking away tears. "Nana's dead," she said flatly.

A heavyset man with lank brown hair and wrinkled robes appeared from the shadows. He moved slowly toward Willow, stooping so that he could grip her shoulders. "My dear Willow," his voice rasped, "you have our deepest sympathies." The flickering torchlight danced in his sad, wet eyes, making them gleam like blue icicles.

Willow squinted at him, ignoring the thin tear stream that trickled down his cheek. For some strange reason he seemed to be glowing. A purple light surrounded him like a halo.

"It was not meant to happen this way," he muttered. "The faerie queen made promises. She pledged me your safety."

Willow stared at his bleak, unfamiliar face. Alarm jerked inside her. "Who are you?" she asked, shrugging his hands away. "And my name. How do you know my name?" She looked wildly around the room, clutching her laptop to her chest. "Where am I?"

The man everyone called Sir Baldemar stepped forward. Willow gasped. He was glowing too, only his color was a deep midnight blue. It made him look like a tall, wide-shouldered phantom. Before she could scream, he pulled a gold medallion from his shirtfront and held it up. "Be still," he said. The words rumbled from his chest like a loud purr. A weight pressed down on Willow. She sank back into the chair, weak and light-headed.

"Now, then." Sir Baldemar dropped the medallion beneath his shirt neck. "I think it's time we explained things." He bowed low to Willow. "Princess Willow," he continued, "you are now in Carrus, the capital city of Gallandra, in the lower magical realm of Mistolear. This gentleman to my left is your grandfather, King Ulor Farrandale, high king of Gallandra." The stocky man with the sad, glowing face and blue icicle eyes nodded at her. "And this," Baldemar tilted his head slightly toward the young woman, "is Lady Merritt du Aubrey, lady-in-waiting to the queen. And I," he bowed low again, "am Sir Baldemar of Tamarvyn, your grandfather's humble mage knight."

Willow leaned back in the chair, rubbing her fingers across the top of her computer. So she was having a dream about Mistolear – now it was all making sense. Ladies-in-waiting, the king of Gallandra, and his humble mage knight. They were perfect. Exactly how Nana had described them.

"Willow, do you understand what Baldemar is saying?" asked the King Ulor dream figure. "Do you understand that I am your grandfather?"

Willow smiled at him and decided to play along. After all, it was only a dream. She nodded.

"Do you know who you are? Do you know that you are Princess Willow Farrandale, heir to the throne of Gallandra?"

Princess Willow Farrandale, heir to the throne of Gallandra. Willow liked the sound of that. It had real snob appeal. She imagined the popular Melissa Morrison and her friends bowing to her. *Yes, Your Highness. No, Your Highness. Can we kiss your butt, Your Highness?*

"Princess Willow, did you hear what the king said?"

Lady Merritt's voice cut into Willow's daydream. Could you daydream in a dream? She'd never had a dream inside a dream before.

"Princess? Princess? Sir Baldemar, I believe your calming spell has been too effective. Look at the child. She's practically in a stupor!"

"Well, perhaps it would be best if we let her rest for now," said the king. "She will need her strength tomorrow."

"Very well, Sire," said Lady Merritt, helping Willow stand. "I'll escort Her Highness to the prince and princess's old chambers."

Willow, her laptop cord dangling against the skirt of her Guinevere gown, smiled and followed the woman obediently.

⌇

Flowers. Something smelled like flowery perfume. Willow sniffed at her sheets.

Phew! They reeked of it. She turned onto her back and rubbed her eyes, trying not to let the strange dream she had last night bother her. In her dream, Nana had died and Willow had been beamed into Mistolear like some character in a Star Trek episode. But she was awake now and everything was normal again.

She'd better get moving. The dream had felt like a warning and she had to call Dr. Pembleton today. Willow ran her fingers through her hair and sat up. That was weird. Her room was still dark.

She squinted in the dim light. Her mouth dropped open. She was buried under a bulky mound of blankets, totally naked, in the middle of an enormous four-poster bed.

Willow kicked the woolen covers away. She wrapped a sheet around her shoulders and crawled across the mattress, pulling back an inch of the heavy bed curtains. A brick wall and a shuttered window came into sight.

She stuck a bare foot onto the chilly stone floor and crept, shivering, over to the window. Hinges creaked as she drew back the shutters. Cold air rushed over her, turning her breath into frosty white puffs. There was no glass. Just a big open space.

Her stomach flip-flopped as she glimpsed the high stone walls and cone-tipped towers that encircled an outdoor courtyard. She squeezed her eyes shut, counting down from ten. The ripe smell of churned soil and farm manure drifted in with the cold air. A dog yelped and then she heard indignant pig squeals. Children's raucous laughter echoed up to her.

Willow covered her head with the sheet and plugged her

ears. "Da, da, da," she hummed loudly. "I'm awake!" She lowered the blanket and opened her eyes. Nothing had changed. The dog being chased by the dirty kids, the scrawny chickens, the bleating goats and sheep, the hairy little pigs, and the six women in the white-veiled nun costumes stirring huge vats of soapy, steaming water – they were all still out there.

Willow closed the shutters and backed away from the window, her heart thumping wildly. She gnawed at the inside of her cheek and turned around slowly. The shadowy room with its canopied bed came back into view. It was furnished with an elaborate chest, a desk and chair, tapestries, and a large fireplace filled with glowing ashes.

Was this real? Had she actually traveled through time and popped into an alternate universe or another dimension or something?

Or ... she pinched her arm really hard to test her next theory ... had her daydreams finally gone psycho on her? Was she becoming as delusional as Nana? A red thumbprint appeared on her forearm. The pinch definitely hurt.

Willow jumped at the sound of a light tap on the door. A pretty brown-haired lady poked her head around the doorway. She looked familiar, like from a dream ...

"Princess, you're awake. Did you sleep well?" She breezed into the room in a bejeweled red and black dress, the most spectacular outfit Willow had ever seen anyone wear. A short, plump woman followed her, carrying towels and a water basin.

Speechless, Willow stared at them and nodded.

"I am Lady Merritt," said the brown-haired woman, giving her an elegant curtsy. "We met last night, but I fear Sir Baldemar's spell may have been too strong for you to remember a thing. The king," she prattled on, ignoring Willow's bewilderment, "has sent me to help you get ready for breakfast." She unfurled a cream-colored dress. "The seamstress used your garment for measurements and altered some extra gowns for you. And these," she held out a pair of matching slippers, "should fit as well, as you seem to have taken after your grandmother in both height and hoof.

"Now," she continued, "we'll assist you in dressing and take you to the king."

Willow watched as the shorter woman bustled behind a tapestried dressing screen then reappeared a few seconds later without the water basin and towels. "Will you be needing any help with your bath, Princess?" the woman mumbled. She took a quick peek at Willow and then looked away uncomfortably.

"Uh ... no," said Willow, finally snapping out of her daze. "I think I can manage." She ducked behind the screen, clutching the sheet.

She plunged her hands into the water basin and splashed hot rose-scented water over her face. She had to pull herself together here. There *was* a logical explanation for all this and she was certain it *didn't* include a crystal ride to Gallandra.

A thin white dress came flying over the screen. "Your shift, Highness."

Willow pulled down the flimsy material and held it in front of her. What was this supposed to be? Underwear or something? It looked like a sleeveless nightie.

Reluctantly, she dropped her sheet and stepped into the shift. Since she didn't have regular clothes, and her feet were turning blue, now was not the time to complain.

The shorter woman, who seemed to be some sort of servant, came around the screen and laced up the dress Lady Merritt had brought for her. The woman fitted pointy slippers on her feet and then smoothed out her hair with a silver comb.

Willow raised huge, floor-touching sleeves and looked at herself in a gold-framed mirror. "I look ... I look ..." she started.

"Like a proper princess," finished Lady Merritt.

No, that wasn't what Willow had in mind. She glanced at the servant woman and Lady Merritt and then back at herself in the mirror. Had it escaped everyone's notice that she was glowing? Willow squinted in confusion at the thick glass. Her hair looked like a red neon sign and her face and neck were emanating a vampirish shade of pearly white.

"What's wrong with the mirror?" she asked, twisting her body to the left. The glow twisted with her.

Ignoring the question, Lady Merritt came up behind Willow and placed a band around her head. "To complete your attire," she said, smiling. She gave Willow a pat on the shoulder. Willow stared at the thin gold circlet, all concerns over her strangely glowing skin evaporating. Her fingertips explored the crown's sharp pearl-topped spikes.

"Your mother wore this. In fact, this was your parents' bedchamber. Your nursery was through that door there."

Willow forgot to breathe. Blood pounded in her ears as she remembered what Nana had told her – her parents had been killed in a house fire.

"Are you well?" asked Lady Merritt. "You look a mite pale."

Willow shook her head. "It's just ... I thought ..." She continued to gaze at the circlet, her fingers now following a trail of sparkling diamonds. For a second, she was ready to believe this wasn't a dream. "Is my mother alive?"

"Well, I – I –" Lady Merritt's mouth opened and closed like a gasping fish. "N-no, dear," she finally stammered, "I thought you knew. She was captured a few days after your birthing."

"Captured?" said Willow. "You mean, like, she's a prisoner somewhere?"

Lady Merritt shook her head. "I'm sorry. I shouldn't have said anything. Come now." She squeezed Willow's fingers and smiled kindly. "The king, your grandfather, is waiting for us. He'll answer all your questions and concerns." She turned toward the servant woman, ordered her to tidy up the room, and then led Willow down the long hallway.

Willow followed after her. There had to be a logical explanation. This *couldn't* be real. She was *not* a Mistolearian princess. She did *not* time travel. Even if the skirt dragging along the floor and the crown pinching her scalp said different.

"This way," said Lady Merritt. She took Willow's arm and steered her down another hallway. She stopped in front of an imposing door guarded by a sword-carrying man. "We have arrived," she announced. She waved her hand at the man in a curt, shooing motion and waited while he opened the door for her.

As Willow passed him, she noticed that he gave her an odd look, as if she had a wad of green spinach stuck between her teeth.

"Lady Merritt," said a deep, raspy voice. The purple-glowing man she had met last night rose from a chair and came toward them. He seemed to be in good spirits, Willow noticed, and a little better groomed than he was the night before.

"Thank you for taking care of the princess," he said. "She looks lovely."

Lady Merritt nodded and gave a quick curtsy. "Thank you, Your Majesty. It wasn't difficult. The princess has Your Majesty's good bones. And the queen's marvelous height." Her voice broke. "Queen Aleria would have been so pleased to meet her."

King Ulor's face sagged at the mention of Queen Aleria. Willow frowned. If the king was supposed to be her grandfather, then Queen Aleria must be ... *her grandmother*? But then – who was Nana?

The king managed a tight smile as he ushered Lady Merritt into the hallway. Willow stared after him, taking in the crown, the purple robes, and the ruby-studded ring circling his index finger.

"Well, my dear," said King Ulor when he returned to Willow. "What do you say to some food and a bit of wine to break your fast?" He offered her his arm.

"I think there has been a mistake," Willow replied. She had to get this straightened out now, before things got too complicated. "I'm not your granddaughter. That's impossible."

King Ulor dropped his arm. He gave Willow a long, sorrowful look and then reached out to touch the curve of her cheek. "There has been no mistake, my dear," he said gravely. "You are, indeed, my granddaughter."

"But I can't be. Look, my parents died in a fire when I was a baby. And I don't have any other relatives except my real grandmother and she's ..." *What? Sick with Alzheimer's? Dead in her bedroom?* Willow could no longer distinguish reality from dream. She blinked back a sudden rush of tears and turned away from the king. "I want to go home," she whispered. "I *have* to go home."

King Ulor patted Willow's shoulder. "I am truly sorry about Nurse Beryl. Was she ill? The chessboard gave us no indication that something was wrong."

"She probably had Alzheimer's or senile dementia or something like that." Willow wiped at her eyes and tried to get her emotions under control again. She turned to the king. What was that he'd just said about a chessboard?

"I am not familiar with this ... Alls-himers." King Ulor stroked his beard and frowned.

"It's a disease that damages your brain," said Willow. "Makes you forget things."

"Ah." The king nodded. "The memory sickness. Yes, we have such things here as well."

"Umm ... Your Majesty?" No, that didn't sound right. Too formal. "Uh ... Sir?" she tried again. "You said something about a chessboard. How could a chessboard tell you about Nana?"

King Ulor drew in a deep breath. "Ah, the chessboard. I was hoping to eat first. But I can see that you'll need to see it for yourself – *if* I am ever to persuade you to call me Grandfather." His eyebrows arched slightly.

Willow felt her face redden. "Sorry, I didn't mean ..."

King Ulor shook his head and waved her apology aside. "No, no. It's quite all right. There's no shame in caution. I'm sure if I were in your place, I would find myself thinking the same way." He strode over to the fireplace and stopped before a gigantic brass candlestick. Wrapping his hands around its midsection, he blew out the thick candle and then slowly tilted the candlestick backwards.

Willow watched bug-eyed as a section of stone slid to the side. Her heart pounded loudly in her ears. She knew what was in there. The candlestick. The hidden tunnel. It was all the same. Exactly like Nana's Gallandrian story. The one about the king's secret room and a magical chess set.

King Ulor relit the candle and wriggled it from the stand, then turned back to Willow. "Well, come on, then," he said, smiling resignedly. "Best to get it over with."

The passageway led to a musty corridor. Willow lifted her skirts with one hand and used the other to guide her down the rough steps. She stopped for a moment when she saw her skin's pearly glow brighten in the darkness.

Up ahead, King Ulor was rounding a corner, the candle-light and his purple glow disappearing along with him. Willow dropped her hand and hurried after him. She'd have to figure out why she was glowing later.

King Ulor stopped in front of a low wooden door. He handed the dripping candle to Willow, then reached for a key that hung from a chain beneath his robes. Unlocking the door, he gestured for Willow to go ahead of him.

Willow ducked through the doorway into a dark room. King Ulor took back the candle and used its flame to light torches along the wall. Slowly, the light revealed a circular chamber with a vaulted ceiling. She gasped when her gaze fell on the floor. It was right there. Exactly as Nana had described it. A chess set the size of a coffee table sitting on top of an elaborate marble pedestal.

Willow's scalp prickled as she moved closer to the chess set. She reached out to touch one of the pieces, a tall, slim bishop. A tiny man-face was sculpted onto the surface of the stone chess piece. A tiny, perfectly carved man-face.

"You do, of course, know how to play," said King Ulor, startling her.

Memories of Nana's chess set and of endless hours spent learning and playing passed through her mind. She'd learned chess the way others learned piano. Practice. Practice. Practice.

The king stared at her a moment, then glanced down at the board. "Ah, I see the change now," he said, lifting a White pawn piece. "Nurse's piece has become the blacksmith's son." He set the pawn down again. A troubled frown creased his brow as he studied the chessboard. Lamplight flickered behind him, casting shadows that blackened his purple glow. "And how would you move," he asked, "if you were playing White?"

Willow's thoughts came into focus again. Chess was solid. Logical. Something she could hold on to and understand. She studied the board, testing possible moves, and it didn't take long to figure out that White was in deep trouble.

His queen and half his pieces were gone. And what was left of his army was hopelessly bunched in the right-hand corner.

Both these guys must be idiots, she thought. Neither one had castled his king and Black was wasting his queen in a useless back rank position, when he could've used her to finish the game a long time ago.

Willow fingered the back of White's far-right pawn. It was

the only pawn with a clear path. "I'd either try to queen this pawn and checkmate the Black king, or I'd sacrifice it and use the rook to checkmate."

She dropped her hand and looked to see if the king accepted her line of reasoning. She knew neither ploy could really work. Black was still too strong. He had all his pieces, except for his far-end pawns. And his bishops and knights were just too well placed. White would need a bona fide miracle to win.

King Ulor was silent. He rested his thumb and forefinger on top of the White king as if planning his next move, then lifted it away from the board and held it out to Willow.

Willow watched in horror as he turned the piece so that it faced her. It was like one of those moments in a horror movie when you see someone from the back and you just know that when he turns around he's going to have blood-dripping fangs or no eyeballs.

She gaped. *King Ulor's face was carved into the chess piece.* He handed her the piece. She clenched her fist around it.

"Look at it," he urged. "You must look at it."

Willow's fingers slowly uncurled from around the piece. She held it closer, touching the rounded forehead, the long straight nose, and the pointed beard. It was him, all right. Even the small eyes and lips were his, all carved with incredible precision.

"Didn't Nurse tell you about the Game? Didn't she tell

you *anything* about who you are?"

Willow shook her head, but at the same time she knew that Nana *had* told her. Not in a direct way. Nana had known she could never do that. But in other ways. Ways that wouldn't make Willow feel like some kind of mental case.

That was what the stories and role-playing games were all about. The costumes. The chess. Even her summer riding lessons, which had seemed so extravagant.

She remembered Nana teaching her chess and weaving the game into an elaborate story. Two kingdoms turned into chess pieces by an evil faerie prince. One kingdom in need of a new queen. Her head pounded as if someone were flicking a finger under her skin.

"The image is mine, Willow," said King Ulor. "And this one," he picked up the far-right pawn, "is yours."

Willow stared at the face carved into the stone chess piece. Her face.

"We've been placed under a Game spell," he continued. "A very powerful one, which, I am afraid, we are in grave danger of losing."

Willow's insides felt like mush. Traveling through time or dimensions, or whatever she had done, must take a lot out of you. She blinked at King Ulor. He looked concerned. She started to speak, to say something about Nana's chess lessons, but her legs trembled and swayed, and then she buckled like a rag doll.

CHAPTER 3

Willow opened her eyes. Everything appeared fuzzy around the edges. Her lids fluttered shut, then opened again. Lady Merritt's face floated over her, a small frown puckering her mouth. She dabbed a wet cloth to Willow's forehead. "There, there, dear. Don't try to rise yet. I fear you've had a bit of a tumble."

King Ulor, his face also worried, appeared behind Lady Merritt. "Is she well?"

Ignoring Lady Merritt's protests, Willow pushed away the wet cloth and sat up, gingerly massaging a sore spot beneath her circlet. "I'm okay, I just fainted. I feel fine now." Not exactly the truth. But it got them to stop hovering.

"Here, drink this," ordered a gruff voice. Sir Baldemar, the man Willow had mistaken for a phantom the night before, held out a golden goblet.

Willow accepted the drink and tried to look past the blue glow to his rugged face. Her opinion didn't change much. He still looked as if he could scare the heck out of little kids on a dark night. She took a big gulp from the goblet and began to cough and sputter as the clear liquid burned its way inside her.

Lady Merritt leaned her forward and began whacking her back. "No, dear," she said between whacks. "Illysian wine." *Whack!* "Has to be sipped." *Whack!* "Not gulped."

Willow sat up, trying to smother her last coughs. For such a fragile-looking woman, Lady Merritt could deliver some pretty solid back whacks. "Thanks. I think –" she coughed "– I'm okay." She took a delicate sip from the goblet and wiped at her damp lap.

Lady Merritt smoothed out her skirts. "Shall I tell Cook to bring up some breakfast now?" she asked the king.

King Ulor nodded. "Yes. That's just what the princess needs. Some sustenance."

A giggle escaped Willow. *Some sustenance.* Sounded like something Sylvester the Cat from *Bugs Bunny* would say. Only it'd be a spitty *thome thusenance.*

King Ulor gave her another concerned glance. "Come sit. We have many important matters to discuss."

Ha! Important matters! Now *there* was an understatement if she'd ever heard one. Willow took another mouthful of wine and realized the stuff wasn't half bad. Sort of had a fruity taste. Like Kool-Aid with a kick.

"Best not to drink any more on an empty stomach," warned the blue-glowing man. "It will muddle your head."

"Yes," agreed King Ulor. "Especially if you aren't used to it. Come now." He took Willow's hand, giving it a grandfatherly pat. "Sit by the fire with me."

Willow clung to his arm, letting him guide her to a chair. She sank onto it and ran her hand under the circlet again. She was suddenly very hot.

"Perhaps some water would be more to your liking," said King Ulor, noticing her discomfort. Immediately, Sir Baldemar handed Willow a cup.

Willow hoisted up her voluminous sleeves and sipped the cold water. The chess room was starting to come back to her. The magic game. The girl-faced chess piece. She didn't know when she would wake up from this dream, but so far had gathered that for whatever reason these people had sent her away, they now wanted her back.

There was a short rap at the door and a guard entered, ushering in three servants who placed bread on the table and served plates of bacon and bowls with cheese and fruit.

Willow thanked the wine server, who was staring at her slack-jawed, and reached for her water again.

"Okay," she said after the servants left. "Why does everyone keep looking at me like that?" She held out her hands. "Is it because I'm glowing like a lightbulb?"

King Ulor picked up a bread loaf and tore it in two. "No, it's not the glow," he said. "Everyone who is a chess piece in the Game has it, so they're quite used to that. I'm afraid it's more, uh ... well ... You were just a baby when they last saw you. And now here you are, four months later, a fully grown young woman."

Willow gaped. "What did you say? Did you say ... *four* months?"

The king, his goblet halfway to his lips, froze. Slowly, he returned the goblet to the table. "Yes," he said. "Fifteen weeks, to be exact."

Willow could feel her head starting to spin again. But how could that be? She'd lived with Nana for as long as she could remember. Fifteen *years*. Not fifteen weeks!

"Are you ..." she paused, finding it hard to get the words out. "Are you saying I've only been gone from here for fifteen *weeks*?"

The king looked confused, then waved to Sir Baldemar for help.

"Yes," Sir Baldemar said matter-of-factly. "You were born a bit over three months ago. Your mother, the princess Diantha, was captured two weeks after your birth. Your father, Prince Alaric, and grandmother, Queen Aleria, were captured three days after that. And then you were sent to Earthworld with your nurse to age. You see, the faerie queen cast a spell so that for every year you spent on Earth, only a week would pass in our Mistolearian realm."

King Ulor's hand reached out to touch hers. "We had no choice. You are Queen Cyrraena's chosen netherchild and the only one who can stop this Game."

Fifteen weeks.

She felt a feathery touch across her knuckles and then a squeeze. King Ulor was still holding her hand, trying to pull her thoughts back to him.

"At present," he said, "we are under siege from King Tarrant's army." He paused and looked uncomfortably at his hands. "I had better explain things more fully. You see, Tarrant Somerell, King of Keldoran, is your mother's father. Your maternal grandfather. His capital city of Tulaan is the back rank of the Black team, as my capital city of Carrus is the back rank for White. The Keldorians attack us because they believe we have captured your mother, the princess Diantha."

There was that word again. *Captured.* She had a sneaking suspicion that when they used the word "captured," they meant something entirely different from what she thought the word meant. Willow withdrew her hand from King Ulor's. "What exactly does that mean? Being *captured.*"

The king pointed to a desk where Willow could see a normal chess set sitting on top of some books. "The game – would you bring it here?" Sir Baldemar set the chess set between them.

"In an ordinary game of chess, capturing is done like so." King Ulor moved the White queen down a clear file and knocked her into a pawn. Willow nodded. She knew how to play chess. "Well," continued the king, "capturing in our magical Game is somewhat similar. If a player on the opposing team kills or 'captures' one of us, we are also removed from the Game." He picked up the Black pawn and placed it along the sidelines of the chessboard.

Willow nodded again. The way the king had explained it made her think of Nana. Nana had taught her chess that way, by making believe the pieces were real people. "So then, the players that are captured, are they ... are they dead?"

King Ulor didn't answer right away. He looked forlornly at the chessboard. "We think so," he finally said. "When we're captured, we change into one of these." He held up the sidelined pawn. "The rules were never made very clear, and we've only just started to play, but ..." He took a deep breath. "When Queen Aleria, your grandmother, saw your mother as a chess piece, she didn't see a life force."

"No life force?" What did he mean? That her mother was dead? Willow's heart tightened. The seed of hope that had sprouted there withered. She trembled. Jeez, what was wrong with her? She'd believed her mother was dead for fifteen years now. So why did the thought suddenly hurt so much? She shook her head and reminded herself this was all a dream.

Except ... what if it wasn't?

"I am sorry, dear." King Ulor patted her shoulder. "I wish I could give you more hope. But it is, I believe, better to be prepared for the worst."

"But how could the queen know? I mean, what if the captured players just went someplace else?" Willow figured anything was possible in this crazy place.

King Ulor sighed. "It's possible. But not probable." He replaced the pawn on the chessboard and picked up the White queen. "The Game spell is just like real chess. The queens have all the power."

A chill prickled Willow's neck. *The queens have all the power.* She remembered Nana saying those exact words.

"Queen Aleria has all the magic of Gallandra inside her. She can heal. She can conjure." King Ulor placed the queen piece back on her white square. "*And* she can see auras of the life force. So, you are correct. If Aleria didn't see your mother's life force, then your mother is either dead or she is not inside the playing piece."

Another spark of hope flared in Willow. She tried to smother it. This was ridiculous. Her mother was dead and had been for years.

Feeling slightly more composed, she buttered a slice of bread and looked from King Ulor's purple glow to Baldemar's blue one. "So let me see if I have this straight. You're saying that you guys, my father's family, and the Keldorians, my mother's family, are under some kind of spell that forces you to play chess. Only *you're* the chess pieces, right?"

Both King Ulor and Baldemar nodded.

"So right now, you guys, the White side, are losing." She remembered what King Ulor had said about being under siege from King Tarrant. But it didn't make sense. Hadn't she seen kids and animals playing in the courtyard this morning?

"Where is this Keldorian army, anyway? I thought you said your castle was under siege."

"Well," admitted King Ulor, "they did breach our city gates a few days ago. But the castle walls are a different matter. They're twice the thickness. And with no magic in their siege machines, we have at least another fortnight to put your plan into action."

Willow blinked at him. "My plan?" She didn't remember making any plans.

"To queen the pawn and checkmate the Black king."

Willow snorted. "You can't be serious." She'd suggested queening the pawn earlier, but only as a joke. She didn't really think that would work.

"You see," said King Ulor, lifting a White pawn and moving it down to Black's back rank, "if you, as a pawn, can get *here*, you will become a queen, just like in an ordinary game of chess. But queening in this Game means more than just extra movement ability. You will have immense magical powers that will allow you to stop King Tarrant from winning." He smiled at Willow and squeezed her fingers. "It's your challenge, my dear. We're all counting on you."

Willow's eyes widened. What was he saying? Did he actually want her to try and *capture* her own grandfather?

"But we, of course, don't want you to harm the Keldorians," King Ulor added quickly. "We only want you to prevent them from attacking us." He took a long sip from his wine goblet. "You see, your other grandfather is, I fear, a bit hotheaded. He believes we are the ones who killed his only daughter – who was a Black pawn in the Game – to keep her from being queened. Utter nonsense. We all loved Diantha dearly. No one here would have harmed a hair on her head."

"However," interrupted Sir Baldemar, "she was, nevertheless, captured." He gave Willow an assessing gaze. "We suspect enemy spies from the south may have tricked one of our players into harming her in some way and planting a bloody knife as evidence. Or," a hard glint appeared in his eyes, "we may have a traitor here in the palace."

"In either case," continued King Ulor, "we must get you to Keldoran so you can put a stop to King Tarrant's war, and then we can all decide what to do about Nezeral."

Click. Click. Click. The pieces fell into place. Willow's stomach sank like a rock.

Nana's faerie tales, she realized, never *were* faerie tales, not in this world, anyway. They were, each and every one of them, absolutely *true*. The one about Nezeral came flooding back.

Nezeral had come to Mistolear from another realm. He wasn't a mortal man. Nana had called him *fey*, saying that his blood was of the ancients, and that unlike humans, he could live forever.

"He came here, didn't he," she said, "because of King Tarrant?" She needed to be sure she wasn't just making things up.

Both King Ulor and Sir Baldemar nodded. "You know of the summoning then?" asked King Ulor.

Willow rubbed at a throbbing temple. "I think so. King Tarrant was dying, right? I think he had lung fever. And didn't one of his mages break some kind of magic law?"

"Yes, it's all true," said King Ulor. "Nezeral is a Dark faerie from Clarion, which is another realm, just as is Earthworld. However, Clarion is an upper realm, and both Mistolear and Earthworld are lower realms."

"And the realms are not supposed to be together, right?" added Willow, remembering one of the laws of summoning. "Beings from the upper realmworlds aren't allowed to mingle with beings from the lower." Nana had never said why this was so, but if Nezeral's little *Game* was any indication, Willow could see why that particular rule was in place.

"The clause to that law, of course," continued King Ulor, "is that if an upper realm being is summoned or invited to a lower realm, he may choose to come. The great difficulty is that he also may choose *not* to leave."

And from Nana's story, Willow knew that Nezeral had chosen to stay. True, he had healed King Tarrant, but then he'd started making outrageous demands. He'd ordered Diantha to become his consort, even though she was already engaged to Prince Alaric. And then he'd commanded the king to hand over all his lands and wealth. When King Tarrant refused, according to Nana, Nezeral had offered him a sporting chance.

Pick a game, he'd said. *If I win, you cede to my demands. If you win, I return to Clarion.* King Tarrant, who was a brilliant chess player, picked chess. But he was tricked. Once begun, King Tarrant was doomed to lose, as the chess game was rigged by one of Nezeral's spells.

Once King Tarrant lost, Nezeral restated his initial demands, but the king, backed by his wife, Queen Morwenna, refused. It was just the excuse Nezeral needed. With his awesome powers, he changed both the Keldorians and the Gallandrians into battling chess pieces.

The rest of the story gripped Willow. She could hear Nana's lilting voice telling it to her as a bedtime tale:

The moment the Game spell took effect, all magic was gone from the land, taken from mages and healers and given to the queens. But neither Queen Aleria nor Queen Morwenna would use their powers to attack the other. They refused to play the Game, and instead, continued with their lives and allowed their two children to wed. All went well for the first year. The queens learned to use their powers and went about their kingdoms helping the sick and needy, casting the crop spells and teaching people old ways of threshing, brewing, and baking that didn't require magic.

When their granddaughter, the infant princess Willow, was born, both kingdoms celebrated with two days of feasting. But on the fourth day, a terrible tragedy occurred. The princess Diantha was found lying in her chambers beside a bloody dagger, her body turned into a Black pawn. Rumors spread quickly, and before King Ulor could send word to Keldoran, King Tarrant had already been informed of his daughter's death. He was told that the Gallandrians had murdered her to insure that she would never reach the back rank of the Game, and thus never be queened. He immediately sent an army to attack Gallandra. Queen Morwenna tried to stop him, but it was no use. King Tarrant was like one bewitched.

Queen Aleria and Prince Alaric, on their way to explain to the Keldorians what had happened, met Tarrant's forces, were captured and transformed into chess pieces. King Tarrant ordered King Ulor to hand over the child or go to war. King Ulor tried to reason with him, but to no avail. In desperation, he was forced to send his newborn granddaughter and her nurse to another realm ...

So there you had it. Willow gulped, fighting to maintain her calm. She was a four-month-old infant princess from another realm, trapped by a psychotic immortal into being a player in a magical chess game, *and* according to some faerie queen, the only one who could break the spell. Nothing crazy about that.

The king clasped one of Willow's hands. He pointed to Sir Baldemar. "Baldemar here," he explained, "is a mage knight. Do you know what that is?"

Willow nodded. In Nana's stories, a mage knight was a very powerful man, skilled both in weaponry and magic.

"Well then," went on King Ulor, "you would also know

what a capable protector he is, so you will have no need to fear for your safety."

"My safety?"

King Ulor smiled encouragingly. "The Keldorians," he explained, "are laying siege to the front of the castle, so most of their attention is directed on our north wall. There is, however, a secret postern gate that will allow you and Sir Baldemar to escape unnoticed.

"Varian has been notified by messenger bird ... Varian is my younger brother, Prince Varian Farrandale. His lands are in Torinth, bordering Thorburn Wood. He will be meeting up with you with a contingent of knights and will accompany you and Sir Baldemar the rest of the way to Keldoran." King Ulor unclasped Willow's hand and leaned back heavily in his chair. "Of course, getting King Tarrant to treat with us will be the hard part. The man's part mule, you must know. But," he leaned forward again, a bright gleam in his eye, "don't worry about that, my dear. Once he catches sight of you, looking for all the world like your mother, I am sure he will see reason. Come now, then, enough of this serious talk. Shall I take you for a tour around my castle?"

Willow didn't answer right away. She was still trying to process all this new information. "Ah, you know," she finally replied, rubbing at her temple, "I have a bit of a headache. So if you don't mind, I'd just like to lie down."

"Of course," King Ulor said, helping Willow to her feet.

"We'll call Lady Merritt to escort you back to your chamber. And don't worry about how you'll get to Keldoran. Plenty of time for all that tomorrow."

A wry smile twitched onto Willow's face. *Right*, she thought, *plenty of time for all that tomorrow. That is, if I'm not too busy fighting pirates with Peter Pan or slaying witches with Dorothy.*

CHAPTER 4

The fire was beginning to thaw the numb chill that had taken hold of Willow. She edged to the far side of the mattress, trying to avoid the drifting smell of food.

She didn't want to be warm, didn't want to eat, and did *not* want to feel better.

Lady Merritt had just been in and had given her the duty-of-a-Gallandrian-princess speech. And then the servant woman had delivered the eat-something-you'll-feel-better one. All afternoon the two of them had been pleading with her to speak to King Ulor, to eat something, or to at least try on the jewels and gowns that they'd been attempting to bribe her with. It wasn't going to work. She could not be bought, bullied, or shamed.

She took a deep breath and squeezed her eyes shut again. "I am not in Gallandra. I am on Earth. I am only sleeping, and when I open my eyes, I will be awake and in my own bed." But when she peeked out with one eye, the bright purple and gold of Princess Diantha's bed canopy came into view. "*Damn!*" she muttered, striking her fist against the mattress.

"Damn! Damn! Damn!" Ever since her conversation with King Ulor and Sir Baldemar, a kind of desperate panic had set in. If this were all true, if it wasn't a dream, then Nana really was dead. And Abby was at school today, presenting their worm project on her own. Willow's chest hurt. Oh God, what would Abby think when she found out about Nana, and when Willow never showed up at school again – ever? *She'll think I ran away.* No, no, no! This time Willow pounded her head. *"Wake up!"* she yelled. "Wake the hell up!"

But nothing happened. She was still here lying on the canopied bed. Her toes were still cold and her belly still hungry – two things she should *not* be able to feel in a dream. *No*, she insisted to herself. She didn't care what her senses felt. The sooner she accepted that none of this was real, the sooner she'd wake up. She stretched her legs and her bulky skirt over the bed and stared down at her slippered feet. Maybe she was wrong about the sense thing. Maybe instead of ignoring her senses, she needed to use them to find something that didn't fit with Nana's stories.

Her eyes turned to the wide-open window at the foot of her bed. Lady Merritt had said the glass in the window disappeared when the magic disappeared, so that now they were forced to use wax-dipped fabrics as coverings instead. She went to the window and pressed a cloth corner between her fingers. Crumbly pieces of the colorless wax broke off and fell to the floor.

Willow gazed at the cloth as she gouged another wax chunk. Well, that was one big thing that didn't make sense. If there was no magic in this world, then how could the magical crystal have brought her here in the first place? And how come Sir Baldemar was able to use his medallion to perform his healing magic?

A sudden draft blew cold air around her face and neck. She dropped the window cloth, turning back to the warmth of the room. Maybe what she needed was to get away from everything. If she could find someplace that seemed reasonably normal, *then* her mind might release itself from the dream. She'd wake up in her own room and Nana would be there, Abby would meet her at school, and everything would be fine. She crept to the closed door and pressed her ear to the wood.

There was a guard outside her room. She heard his armor rattling every time he opened the door for the servant or Lady Merritt. He was still out there. Or someone was. She could hear feet scuffing against the floor. Willow suppressed the urge to scream and stomped back to the bed, angrily kicking over a stool in her path. Something white and gold flew from the stool and landed on the carpet with a soft thud.

Her swan necklace. The last time Lady Merritt had been here, she had seen the necklace and explained that the faerie queen had chosen Willow as her "netherchild" and "gifted" her with the powerful fey emblem.

Willow scooped up the necklace, smiling sardonically.

Hey, maybe my faerie godmother will help me. Wave her magic wand and send me back to Earth. She flopped onto the edge of the bed and leaned against the pillows.

According to Lady Merritt, this scenario hadn't been far from the truth. It had been Queen Cyrraena's idea to send Willow and Nana to Earth in the first place. She had cast the spell that allowed Willow to age so quickly and she'd been the one to pick Willow as Mistolear's champion in battling Nezeral. Queen Cyrraena was supposed to be some kind of guardian for Mistolear. But to Willow, Queen Cyrraena sounded mental. After all, why would anyone in their right mind pick a baby to be a champion?

Willow dangled the swan at eye level and frowned. So why hadn't Nana ever mentioned the faerie queen or the gift? Back home, Nana had shelves overflowing with books on faerie and Celtic legend. So it wasn't like she hadn't had the opportunity. Willow sat back up again. But maybe Nana hadn't known about the pendant, or maybe she'd forgotten because of her dementia. Willow sighed and dropped the chain over her head. She supposed she'd never find out now.

A pleasant heat engulfed her. Her eyes drooped and a lazy soaking-in-a-tub feeling swept over her. From a distance, she could hear voices outside her room and then the sounds of the guard clanking away down the hall. A soft knuckle-rap to the door broke through her trance and she opened her eyes. Volts of electric energy charged through her.

What the ...? She yanked the hot necklace out of her bodice. The swan had done something to her!

The knock came again, louder this time. "Princess, are you awake? Princess ...?"

"Um, yeah. Yeah, I'm awake." *Very awake.* She dropped the now tingling necklace back down her bodice and stood up. "You can come in."

To Willow's surprise, a teenage boy entered the room and gave her a curt bow.

Willow gaped. She couldn't help it. And not because his skin was glowing red either. But because of his short, tight-fitting chain mail, thigh-high leather boots, and gold-plated sword. It was as if he'd stepped out of her imagination. Granted, his hair was dark brown instead of blond and his black eyes raked fiercely over her, but still, there he was, just as she had imagined him – her knight in shining armor. A knight who was now stooping before her on one knee, his long hair falling romantically over his shoulders.

She blinked several times, waiting for him to speak or stand up. But he didn't move a muscle. "Er, hello," she said. "Can I help you?" He glanced up, confusion written all over his black eyes. She was obviously breaching some form of princess etiquette.

"Rise up," she tried again, using what she hoped was a princess-like voice.

He stood up, hesitated a moment, and then closed the

door behind him. Then he walked toward her, his grim face filled with determination.

Willow stepped backwards. She had just clued into the fact that she was alone with an armed stranger with apparently no guard outside her room.

The guy went for his sword, suddenly whipping it out of its scabbard and holding it high above her.

Willow gasped, but before she could scream, he dropped to one knee again, the sword dropping with him, its sharp tip grazing the stone floor.

"I, Brand Lackwulf," he began loudly, "son of Cedric Lackwulf, lord of Rueggan, and squire to Prince Alaric, do solemnly swear to serve and protect thee, Princess Willow, heir to the throne of Gallandra and Keldoran, for all thy days." He paused for a moment, leaning forehead to sword pommel, and then said dramatically, "I pledge thee my loyalty, my sword, and my life."

Limp with relief, Willow gaped at the top of his bowed head. *I'm alive! He's not going to kill me.* She heard a creaking sound and saw a boot tip jiggling up and down. He was waiting for her to say something.

She tried "You may rise" and "Arise, Sir Knight," but all she earned was a glare. "Please get up. I don't know what to say" only got her a tight-lipped frown.

"Look, Brand or Cedric or whatever your name is," she finally hissed, "tell me what I'm supposed to say and *I'll say it!*"

"*Arise Sir Brand. I accept thy oath of fealty,*" he snarled.

Willow repeated his words and tried not to look nervous when he stood up and angrily plunged his sword back into its scabbard. He turned and the sword tip swung out, knocking over a big candleholder at the foot of her bed. Willow bit her bottom lip to keep from smiling.

"You'd better not be mocking me, Princess," he warned, straightening his sword with furious dignity. "To make fun of a knight's fealty pledge is a grave matter."

Willow frowned. Cute or not, his tone – condescending and disdainful – irked her. And – *fealty pledge*? Willow's temper flared. He had nerve. He was the one who'd burst in here and scared her half to death, and now he was saying *she* was at fault? She'd tell him what he could do with his *fealty pledge*!

Brand dropped his gaze and fiddled with his sword pommel. "I gave my squire's pledge to your father," he said softly. "You are the first to have my knight's."

Willow's sharp retort died on her lips. She could see that this fealty thing was a big deal for him. "Well, I really wasn't making fun of you. Where I come from there aren't any knights or squires or kings or anything like that. Nobody makes ... fealty pledges."

He glanced at her, his face lit with interest. "Sir Baldemar told me of your Earthworld. That it has no magic. How might one live without magic?"

His way of speaking sounded all noble and Lord-of-the-

Ringish. "I don't know," said Willow, smiling. "How *might* one live without TVs and phones and video games?"

Brand looked blank. "Tee-vee?" He didn't try to repeat phones or video games. "What is tee-vee?"

"Never mind," said Willow, shaking her head. "It's not important." She shifted her gaze around and smoothed out her velvet skirts. "Um. You wanted to talk to me about something, though, didn't you?" She figured the king had probably sent him to bring her down for dinner.

Brand surprised her by taking her hands in his. "Princess, nobody knows of our meeting, and what I am about to say to you must be kept in the strictest confidence."

Willow stared at his large, rough hands, which glowed a bright rosy pink. A commingling, she realized, of his red glow and her white one.

"Do you understand, Princess?"

Willow nodded. She didn't really. She was mesmerized by how small her fingers looked against his.

"I know the king has shown you the Game and told you of his plans to send Sir Baldemar to Keldoran with you. But did he tell you what position Sir Baldemar plays?"

Willow let her hands slide from Brand's. Just when the dream was getting good, he had to go and mention the dumb Game. "No, I don't know his position." She felt anger begin to creep through her. Was that all anyone cared about – the stupid Game?

"Sir Baldemar is the king's last rook. His last bishop lies abed with a fever. And I am the last knight." Brand took a deep breath and sighed. "You saw the Game. You know what will happen if he sends his last rook, don't you?"

Willow saw the pieces in her mind's eye. The rook and bishop were all the king had left for protection. Use the most powerful one to guard a pawn and the game would be over in a few quick moves. "Yeah. But what difference does it make? He'll just lose the Game sooner, that's all."

Brand stared at her in disbelief. "How can you say that? We have to play! We can't just give up." His nostrils flared and then his eyes suddenly narrowed. "You don't know what will happen if we lose, do you?"

Willow folded her arms across her chest and pursed her lips.

"You don't know, *do you*?"

Willow *was* curious what would happen when the Game ended. But, while Brand had to be the handsomest boy she had ever met, he was quickly becoming the most irritating. She didn't need *him* to explain the Game to her.

Willow sat on the edge of her bed. "To tell you the truth, I don't really care." In the iciest voice she could muster, she added, "You can go now."

Brand folded his arms and eyed her contemptuously. Finally, he shook his head. "What kind of a princess are you? To allow your own kingdom to fall to ruin, when it's in your power to save it." He stomped over to the bed and hauled her to her feet. "Your father would be ashamed of your cowardice. But I don't care and you *will* hear my words!"

Willow punched Brand's chest with her free hand. "Let go of me, you jerk! Who the heck do you think you are, anyway?"

Brand grabbed both her arms and pinned them to her sides. "No. Now listen to me. If the Game is lost, the losers become chess pieces. *Permanent* blocks of marble. Do you understand? *We cease to exist!*"

Cease to exist? Willow gulped and shook her head. "Look, twenty-four hours ago, I didn't even know this place existed. I didn't know about the game. About being a princess. About my parents. Nothing." Brand looked surprised but didn't say anything. She sniffed and blinked hard. She was *not* going to cry in front of this jerk.

"You people are total strangers to me. Yet you *all* expect me to just jump right in and save you. Well, maybe I can't. Or maybe I don't want to. All I really want to do is just leave here." She brushed past him, heading for the door. She'd had it with this place, and she was going to find the king and that Baldemar guy and *make* them send her home.

"Princess ... wait." Brand reached out and held on to her arm, gently this time. "I am sorry. Sir Baldemar said you would be trained. That you would be ready."

She stopped and turned, not sure if he was being sincere or if he was just trying to butter her up.

"But there *is* no way to leave," he said. "You *do* know that, don't you?"

Blood drained from Willow's face. She hadn't considered the possibility that maybe she couldn't go back. Panic prickled down her spine.

"I mean, until Nezeral is defeated, there is no way you can return to Earthworld – or any other realm, for that matter."

She began to breathe again. Maybe Brand was just trying to scare her. So that she would go along with whatever it was he'd planned. She eyed him suspiciously. "And why can't I?"

"*You* left the linking crystal in Earthworld," he said, sighing as though only a complete idiot would do such a thing. "And unless Queen Cyrraena sees fit to make us a new one, no one can go anywhere."

It was true. The crystal had been sitting on the night table, and instead of picking it up by the stand so that she would have been carrying it, she'd only touched it. She glared at Brand and crossed her arms. "And how do I know you're not lying? Just so I'll do what you want."

Brand's eyes glittered and he lowered his voice. "Very well. Come with me, then. We'll go down to the great hall and *you* can ask the king for yourself."

Willow didn't like his smug smile. People who knew they were right and you were wrong smiled like that. "Okay, so let's say I believe you. What am I supposed to do? You got a plan any better than King Ulor's?"

"Yes, I do." Brand stopped smiling. "That's why I am here. I will take you to Keldoran myself. If Sir Baldemar is here to protect the king, you and I shall have a much better chance of making it across."

Actually, his plan *was* better, thought Willow. At least with a rook and a bishop – albeit a sick one – the king might have a slim hope. And maybe the other side would be so engrossed in trying to trap him that they wouldn't notice an advancing pawn.

"So, okay," she said, "let's say I go with you. What happens if I do get to Keldoran? I'm supposed to get powers, aren't I? What happens then? Are you expecting me to use them to capture my mother's family?" The king hadn't expected her to, but she didn't know what Brand had planned.

"No, of course not," he snapped. He ran his fingers through his hair and looked less sure now. "We are going to find Nezeral. It's *him* we want. He isn't invincible, you know. He must have a weakness. We just have to find it."

Willow snorted. Yeah right! Find the weakness of an all-powerful immortal being. No problem. Piece of cake.

Brand clenched his jaw and deep dimple grooves appeared along each side of his mouth. She'd ticked him off again, apparently. She shook her head. She and this teenage wannabe-hero were supposed to set off and destroy an evil faerie prince? The whole darn thing was just so hilarious, she started laughing. She couldn't have stopped if she had tried. Her laughter turned into gasping hiccups and streaming tears and then she fell to the floor with a thud, clutching her stomach.

"Princess, are you well?" asked Brand. He hunkered down beside her, patting her shoulders, trying to calm her. She supposed he'd never seen a princess sitting butt-first on a floor before, laughing like a fool. Especially about a minute after she'd been close to tears. *Butt-first!* The image only brought on more gales of laughter.

"Oh gods, I am sorry," he mumbled. "I didn't mean to ... are you well?"

The laughter was beginning to peter out some. Willow slid her hands behind her and leaned back. Was she all right? She only felt weak and light-headed – the way she usually felt after a really good cry.

She turned her head toward Brand and saw him staring at her, his face drawn with worry. He thought he'd caused her to freak out. Willow smiled at him. "I'm okay," she said. "I think I just needed a good laugh."

Instantly, the expression on Brand's face changed. He stood up, looking totally insulted. "Will you come with me or not?"

Willow considered his question. It was either him or Sir Baldemar and since it seemed likely that she was going to be in Mistolear for a while, she figured one secret trip to Keldoran was probably as good as another. Plus, they would have more time if her pawn traveled with his knight, and if Brand was telling the truth about the losing team turning into chess pieces forever, they would need that extra time. And if she succeeded in doing what they wanted her to do, then she could make them do what *she* wanted – create another linking crystal and send her back home.

"Okay, I'll do it. I'll go with you."

CHAPTER 5

Willow leaned forward in her saddle and strained her tired eyes. "I can't believe you'd forget to bring a lantern. It's totally dark in here. We're lost, aren't we? How do you know we're not lost?" The moon had been close to full when they'd sneaked through the old postern gate. Definitely a bright enough night to see clay paths and cobblestone roads. But no, Brand, *Mr-Know-It-All-Boy-Scout*, insisted on traveling through a pitch-black forest. Even though for the twenty minutes they'd been packing up their horses, they had seen neither hide nor hair of any enemy sentry guards.

Brand was riding ahead of her, a stiff shadow making clicking sounds to urge his horse forward. He didn't bother to dignify her questions with an answer.

"Princess, I assure you that you can trust Brand," said an eager voice from behind her. "He knows Ashburn Wood as well as any forester."

Willow turned around in her saddle and smiled at the narrow outline of Malvin Weddellwynd, the mage apprentice, a tall, skinny boy Brand had chosen to teach her magic. He wasn't part of the Game but he was so white-skinned that he still appeared to glow. Willow could see him squinting at her, his pale wispy hair illuminating his egg-shaped head.

"Thank you, Malvin. I guess if *you* trust him, then I'll have to too."

A disgusted snort erupted up ahead.

Willow chuckled. Maybe this was going to be more fun than she'd thought. She wriggled her numb bottom around, trying to get her circulation flowing. But then again, maybe it wasn't any fun. Nothing was worth five straight hours in a hard leather saddle.

"Are you planning on stopping any time soon?" She stood in her stirrups and bounced up and down a few times. "My butt feels like a slab of meat. I need a break."

"We'll stop outside the forest."

Willow scowled. "And when will that be? Before or after my butt falls off?"

"See here, Princess," said Brand, gritting his teeth and spinning to confront her. He had put some special powders on their skin to counteract the glowing, but even so, his face had a fiery sheen to it. "I am trying to get your *butt*, as you call it, to Keldoran in one piece. And to do that, we need to put at least a day's ride between us and Carrus. Now, *please* stop talking! Ashburn is full of wolves." As if on cue, a chorus of mournful howls suddenly pulsed around them.

Brand grinned as Willow nervously scanned the forest.

He turned away and heel-kicked his horse to a trot.

Pompous pig! she wanted to spit out, but Malvin's broad white forehead bobbled into view, effectively leashing her tongue. "Princess," he said softly, "I know it's a long way. If you need rest, give over the reins and lean upon your horse. I shall guide you."

Willow smiled gratefully. At least *someone* knew how to be nice. "Thanks, but I think I'm okay." She didn't mention that she'd rather walk barefoot through live coals than conk out before Brand did.

He still hadn't forgiven her for laughing at him, that much was obvious, and a couple of cracks he made about how slow and picky girls were had made it so she couldn't forgive him either.

She pulled her cloak edges tighter, snuggling the reins and her cold hands against the warmth of her swan pendant. It was still giving off heat, but it hadn't done the energy jolt thing since she'd last touched it. She peeled off damp leather gloves, alternating her grip between the swan and the reins. She'd formed a crude theory about it: 1 faerie-made gift + 1 faerie godmother = 1 princess with a magic necklace. Willow sighed. She wondered just how much help, if any, Queen Cyrraena and her necklace were going to be to them.

Malvin rode up beside her again, holding out a dark object. "A drink, Your Highness? I have mutton pasties too, if you're hungry."

A ravenous gurgle bubbled up from Willow's empty stomach. She glanced to see if Brand was watching – he wasn't – then took the water skin and two mutton pasties, biting gustily into the greasy little pies. They were cold, but she didn't care. She hadn't eaten meat pie in ages.

Warm, flour-dusted memories and spicy meat smells suddenly flooded her thoughts. Nana had been a marvelous cook before her dementia kicked in. She'd made everything from scratch with no cookbooks or recipe cards and with lots of secret ingredients. Willow's mouth watered at memories of sugary tarts and crusty pies. And sauces. Nana's to-die-for sauces.

She bit deeply into the second pasty, blinking rapidly. It was weird how one minute she could be fine and then the next filled with so much grief. She drank from the water skin, trying to push thoughts of Nana to the back of her mind. She didn't want to start bawling. Brand would just tell her she was making too much noise.

The food helped to make her feel better. She handed the skin back to Malvin. "Thanks. You're a real lifesaver."

Even in the dark, Willow could see Malvin's red face. She smiled to herself. At least she wasn't the only one with a blushing problem.

They rode for a few more hours, until the darkness started to thin into a gloomy gray light. Brand announced the stop and Willow slid from her horse, saddle-stiff and bone-weary, without even the strength to walk the pins and needles out of her sore rump. She barely noticed Brand helping with her horse or Malvin setting up her blankets – she just sank into dreamless oblivion.

Willow woke up the next morning to the sound of sneezes blasting out one after the other like gun shots. She peered over her blankets and saw Malvin sleeve-wiping his dripping nose. "Sorry, Princess. It's my allergies. I didn't mean to wake you up."

"Doesn't matter. She has to wake up now – if she wants something to eat." Even half-asleep, Willow recognized Brand's derisive tone.

Willow pushed back her covers and leaned on an elbow. A few feet away, Brand was smothering a dwindling fire with dirt and Malvin was seated on a fallen log, rubbing his hand over a glass ball. Bare-limbed trees formed a dark semicircle around them. The thick forest stood to one side and clear open land stood on the other. The horses milled nearby, munching on long field grasses.

Brand tossed her a chunk of bread and some cheese. "Here. We are breaking camp soon, so eat up."

Willow grimaced at him. "Thanks a lot," she muttered, sitting up and picking dirt specks from the bread. She broke it in half, eating the soft middle part and leaving the crust. Brand rolled his eyes at her and strapped on his huge sword.

"Well, it appears that we have not yet been discovered to be missing," Malvin said. "I checked the king, Sir Baldemar, Lady Merritt, and the servants. Not a soul knows we've left."

"Check the Black knights, then," said Brand, "and the rest of Tarrant's forces."

"No need to worry, Brand. There is no movement on the board – yet. Probably won't start until after we pass through Graffyn."

Willow stared at the round glimmering object in Malvin's hand. "What are you guys talking about? What is that thing?"

Malvin held the ball toward her. "It's an image globe. It brings up any image you wish to see. Would you like to try?"

Willow nodded and Malvin sprang from the log to sit beside her. He reminded her of the overeager boys in her chess club team. "You see, Princess, it works quite simply. Merely hold it in your hands like so." He cupped the ball between her two palms. "And imagine what it is you wish to see."

Willow stared into the glass, rubbing her thumbs over it. *My room at the castle*, she thought. Colors began to swirl inside the globe, quickly solidifying into the purples and golds of her bed and the orangey-yellows of firelight flickering over stone.

"Wow! This is really cool! It's just like watching TV." She held the ball closer, peering through a slit in the heavy bed curtains at the girl-shaped lump that she and Brand had placed under the covers. Didn't look as if anyone had noticed it wasn't her. Her gold circlet and an untouched food tray were still sitting on the bedside table.

Willow frowned. The colors were beginning to fade, leaving the glass clear again. "But this is magic," she said confused. "I thought there wasn't any left."

Malvin nodded and reached for the image globe, cradling it between his fingers. "Yes, it's true. When the Finder Shadow came, it spell-sucked all magic from our world."

"The Finder Shadow?"

"It's the spell Nezeral used to steal everyone's magic. When it first came across the land, it was like a big black shadow and every person and thing it passed over were sucked dry of magic."

"But what about this globe – and the crystal that brought me here? And that medallion thing Sir Baldemar used when I first got here."

"Ah, the crystal," said Malvin. "It's a shame you left that in Earthworld."

Willow ignored the soft-pedaled criticism. "Well? How did they keep their magic? Like, how come castle windows disappeared but the linking crystal and your image globe didn't?"

"Simple," said Malvin. "There are two types of magic. *Intrinsic* and *extrinsic*. This globe is intrinsic." He cupped the ball. "Magic has become a part of it. Something separate from the mage. Do you see?"

He didn't wait for an answer but stood and began pacing,

while waving the globe around for emphasis. "Now windows, on the other hand –" he paused to look at her "– actually, not all windows, but some, are extrinsic. You are doubtless thinking of the castle windows back in Carrus. Sir Baldemar wrought them cunningly so that they draw heat in the winter and coolness in the summer. Most windows are just ordinary mage glass, but Sir Baldemar's were made with an extrinsic spell that he had to monitor continually. You see, in this type of magic, there is always a connection between the mage and the object. Anything happens to the mage, like an untimely death or a loss of power – *poof* – whatever was conjured disappears. Have I explained properly?"

Willow gave him a vague, math-class "uh huh." She understood now why Brand had brought him along. If someone was supposed to teach her magic, she supposed a guy who sounded like a textbook was the perfect candidate. But still he hadn't answered her question. "You said the Finder Shadow sucked out magic from people *and* things." She pointed at the image globe. "So why didn't it suck magic out of that?"

"Oh, I see what you mean. When our most important player, Queen Aleria, was captured, the faerie queen realized that we were in grave danger of losing the Game altogether. She smuggled these few magic items to us so that we might survive until you returned. They are, I believe, the only magical mechanisms in either Gallandra or Keldoran."

"Enough, Mal. End the magic lesson." Brand strode over and handed Malvin a padded sack. "We must reach Graffyn by nightfall."

Malvin nodded and carefully slid the image globe into the sack. "We can talk more about this at lunch time, Princess," he said, adding a shy, "if you like." Then he bowed and turned away, carrying his globe over to the horses.

Willow wolfed down the rest of her bread, pocketing the cheese for later. When she was done, she stretched her stiff leg muscles and pulled up the edges of her new leather boots. She'd convinced Brand to get her boys' clothing. Camping and horseback riding in long dresses was definitely not her idea of a fun time. She stood up, brushing crumbs from her tunic. And no way was she even going to *attempt* to ride sidesaddle.

"Would Her Highness mind quickening up the pace a little?" Brand glowered at her from atop his horse. "It would be best to leave before winter sets in."

Willow stuck her tongue out. *Big jerk!* Why had she ever thought he was cute?

She walked toward him, nose held high, smugly aware of how long and trim her legs looked in the dark hose and leather boots. She tossed back her ponytail and pretended not to notice Brand's dark stare.

Ruby, her horse, was already packed and saddled. She neighed softly as Willow scratched her under the noseband of her bridle. "That-a-girl," crooned Willow. "Good girl." She patted the sleek chestnut neck and moved around to Ruby's side, digging in the roomy saddlebag for her gloves. She found them wedged between her laptop and an extra tunic. Impulsively, she lifted out her computer and turned to Malvin.

"Hey, wait a minute," she called out. "Don't put that globe thing away yet. I have an idea."

Brand glared impatiently.

"Oh, c'mon," she said, refusing to let him intimidate her. "It'll just take a sec."

Malvin pulled the image globe from its padded sack and trailed Willow over to the fallen log. She sat down, opening up her computer and setting it on top of her lap. Of course, there was no place to plug it in, but she had a fully charged battery that would last six hours. Unless something had happened to the laptop in the portal, she would be fine.

Willow pressed the "ON" button and crossed her fingers. *Yes!* Her programs started loading up. Now came the exciting part. If her idea worked, she might be able to find a way for them to win the Game. She ignored Malvin's shocked gasp when her screen flickered and brightened to a blue-green.

"Make the globe show you King Ulor's chess set. And then tell me what position each piece is in." She opened her chess program and brought up its chessboard editor. She would make an exact duplicate of the chess game being played between King Ulor and King Tarrant. When Malvin finished dictating the positions to her, Willow adjusted the game on her computer so that both opponents were played by the computer. She made them both average players and then pressed START.

The three-dimensional pieces moved with amazing speed, making it hard to keep track of who moved where. But within thirty seconds the game was over, with Black winning easily. She restarted the game, this time making White a pro and Black a beginner. The game took a little longer, about a minute, but the result was still the same – Black won by a landslide.

Willow sighed. "It's no use. No matter what we do, Black will slaughter us."

"Is the mechanism moving the pieces?" asked Brand, who'd dismounted from his horse and was now peering over Willow's shoulder. "Or are you?"

"The computer's doing it right now." Willow adjusted the skill level again, making White a grandmaster and keeping Black a beginner. This time the game lagged on and on because White took forever to make each move.

Malvin's finger reached out hesitantly and brushed the top of her liquid crystal display screen, making it ripple like silver water. "Magic," he said in awe. "But Earthworld is a material realm. How is this possible?"

"It's not magic. Just a computer. A machine. Batteries are making it work."

"Bat-trees," repeated Malvin slowly. "Are bat-trees magic?"

Willow exited her chess program. There was no point in waiting to find out who would win – she already knew. "No," she said, shutting down the computer. "Batteries aren't magic either. They just generate electricity, but only for a short time. So I don't want to waste them."

"Can this mechanism help us navigate the Game?" asked Brand. He had a spark of excitement in his eyes that hadn't been there before.

"Don't know," said Willow, shrugging. She couldn't stand his eagerness. Now they expected some kind of techno-magic from her. She closed the lid of her laptop and stood up. "It can play the game and show moves. Maybe if I keep fooling with the skill levels, it can come up with some new strategies. Ones that nobody's thought of yet."

The light in Brand's eyes faded. "No," he said, "you were right before. Black is poised to slaughter us. Getting you to Keldoran and trying to stop the war is our only hope." He spun around and mounted his horse. "Hurry. We've lost enough time this morning."

Willow packed up her computer. One minute she was some sort of hero and the next he was yelling at her. She ignored her screaming muscles and mounted her horse, feeling thankful for all those butt-breaking riding lessons she'd had to take every summer.

"Well, come on, then," she whispered, spurring Ruby forward. "Wouldn't want to keep *Sir* Brand waiting, now, would we?" She nudged aside the loneliness that engulfed her, and pushed her body into the wind.

CHAPTER 6

*B*right sunshine. Crystal blue skies. No clouds. No rain. This day had almost been fun, thought Willow as she pulled her gloves back on. She took deep, earthy breaths. She loved late fall, especially those damp days that were indistinguishable from spring.

Behind her, Malvin was finishing a twittering flute song that sounded like happy little sparrows singing. Willow turned to smile. His flute songs had made for some really great wandering minstrel daydreams. Malvin blushed and smiled back. "I'm not very good yet," he mumbled. "Still learning." He leaned down, slipping his flute into the saddlebag, and then checked for the round bulge at the bottom.

Willow sighed. She hoped he wasn't going to start with the image globe again. Every time they stopped for a break, both boys ignored her to check the globe.

The first few globe-checks hadn't been boring at all. Lady Merritt finding the empty bed, and the armored knights squeezing through the postern gate had been pretty entertaining. And Brand's goofy relief dance when Baldemar decided to stay in Carrus was worth a few laughs. But the last twenty times they'd checked, nothing had happened. Absolutely nothing. The globe had focused only on King Ulor and his sad weary face, which, if Willow was honest with herself, was giving her a guilt complex.

Malvin straightened and pulled on his cloak hood. *Oh, thank you!* she mouthed, rolling her eyes. He'd left the globe in the bag. She copied him and pulled her own cloak hood low over her face. It was early evening now and they were at the outskirts of Graffyn. Brand was covering up too. He'd explained to Willow the dire situation around the areas that had been affected by Nezeral's game spell. Neighboring cities like Graffyn that were stuck between the two kingdoms had had *their* magic taken away too. And even though King Tarrant had only started warring with Gallandra four months ago, a year had passed since the cities and villages that comprised Gallandra and Keldoran had had any magic.

A prickle of foreboding shot through Willow. Mistolearians used magic for everything from cooking and cleaning to running machinery, just like she used electricity back home. She could imagine the chaos on Earth after a whole year without electricity. And from Brand's stories of sickness, pollution, poor harvests, and roving gangs of thieves, she could see that the Mistolearians weren't in any better shape.

She huddled under her cloak hood. According to Brand, castle nobles, especially Game players, weren't a popular sight.

They rode past black fields and a brown, sluggish waterway to Graffyn's main city gate. Willow reined in her horse and stared. Enormous sand-colored walls loomed ahead of her, spreading out as far as she could see, with roofs and chimneys and pointy spires rising above them.

"Whoa! They go *all* around the city like that?" Willow's hood fell back as she stretched out her arms.

Malvin nodded.

"It intimidates the thieves," explained Brand. "Graffyn and Carrus are now the main fair cities on the trade routes."

Malvin lifted his head, peeking at Willow from beneath his hood. "They are both very old cities. Their walls were built centuries ago. Most of the newer cities use magic ones. But, of course, since there is no magic, now ..." he swept his hand toward Graffyn, "walled cities are superior."

"Ssh! Enough talk," ordered Brand. "There's the gatehouse." He turned to Willow and lifted his hood up to his forehead. "How is my glow? Is it dull enough?"

Willow peered at him. The thick sticky powder that he'd plastered over his face had toned down his red shine, but it made him look like a stage actor with a bad makeup job. She fingered her own cheek, wondering if she looked as waxy. "As long as no one gets too close, you might pass for normal."

Brand frowned and pulled his cowled hood over his eyes.

"Keep your head low and covered. And don't say anything."
Then he rode slowly toward the gatehouse.

"State your business," said a gruff voice from high above
them. Willow risked an upward glance. A ruddy, broad-faced
man wearing an eye-covering helmet stuck out his head, along
with a spear, from the gatehouse opening.

"We're Kernish wool buyers," answered Brand. "Come
for the start of the winter fairs." He looked up so the guard
could see a small portion of his face. "Hear Graffyn's got the
finest wool markets in the kingdom."

"Aye, it's true," said the guard. He leaned farther out of
the opening, taking in the fine cut of their cloaks and the value
of their horses. "You're a bit early for the fairs, though, ain't
cha? They don't start till the end of the month."

Brand's stiff posture relaxed, a friendly smile crossing his
face. "Ever been to Kern? Snow starts in early fall and is up to
the gods' armpits by winter."

The guard laughed, then turned to the inside of the
guardhouse and roared, "Up with the gate, Rolf! We've got
some cold Kerns down below."

The iron-barred gate creaked as it rose. Brand pranced
Dusk, his black war charger, over the dry moat drawbridge
and through the wide passageway that opened onto the
cobbled streets of Graffyn. Willow and Malvin followed
slowly, with a little less showiness.

Willow gasped when she saw the crowded buildings.

The upper stories leaned together like bookends while the lower levels shouldered the streets like cliff sides. The long narrow streets and squeezed-together houses choked out warmth and daylight.

They rode single file, with Brand leading, Willow in the middle, and Malvin bringing up the rear. She glanced nervously from side to side. Garbage lined the streets and the stench made Willow gag. She removed one of her gloves and inhaled from it discreetly, fighting back a queasy knot in her stomach.

The narrow street weaved and twisted, then opened onto a local market square. Willow sniffed the air. Pleasant odors from cook shops and houses mingled with the putrid stench. She took the glove away, breathing in shallow spurts.

Market merchants were just beginning to pack up their stalls for the night. Willow pulled back her hood to look at their painted banners and bright circus colors. It was like being at a Renaissance fair! She wanted to stop and wander around, but Brand pressed through the crowds, weaving a path through the fruit and pie sellers. He turned a sharp left and headed toward a wide, cleaner street at the edge of the market. This was clearly the richer part of the city and everyone well-dressed was headed in that direction.

Willow watched as one by one the townspeople, heads straight, passed a crowd of destitute-looking peasants, paying no attention to the outstretched arms and wretched cries of, "Alms! Alms for the poor!" The sight of the thin, ragged children clutching at their mothers' skirts wrenched her heart. Brand was riding by without looking, just like the rest of the townspeople. Willow dug in her pockets and found the cheese hunk that she'd stored as a snack. She tossed it to a spidery little girl with enormous eyes.

Immediately, three rough-looking men swarmed her, demanding their share. They startled Ruby, who reared back, and Willow screamed as she tried to hold on to the reins.

Brand and Malvin were at her side in a second, kicking and yelling and pushing the men back. One of the men caught hold of Willow's cloak, almost pulling her from the saddle, but Brand shoved him aside and grabbed at her reins, yanking Ruby's front legs back to the ground.

Then total chaos broke loose.

Guards carrying short clubs and spears appeared and began beating the beggars. Shouts and screams filled the narrow street, and Ruby reared again. She jerked away from Brand and bolted forward. Willow clung to the saddle with one hand, trying desperately to reach the dragging reins with the other. Ruby veered right and Willow lurched to the left. She barely managed to hold on to the horse with her thigh muscles as her fingers latched on to Ruby's mane. She hauled herself upright, seizing the saddle pommel like a vise, while Ruby shot like a cannonball down the street.

By the time the horse calmed down enough for Willow to retrieve the reins, they were in a dark deserted alleyway, far from the ruckus of the market square.

Willow took deep breaths and waited for her body to unclench. "Oh man," she croaked as she collapsed against Ruby's neck. Sweat trickled down her forehead. Her legs felt weak and slipped limply from the stirrups.

She looked around and saw stained walls and black windows covered with thin jagged bars. Debris cluttered the street. A plump mouse skittered by, hugging the wall's foundation. Willow popped back up again. Oh God, where the heck was she? No, never mind that! Where the heck were Brand and Malvin? It was going to be dark soon. She didn't want to be lost *here* at nighttime!

A moan escaped her lips. *No! Hold on. You're not going to lose it.* She turned Ruby around and backtracked to the end of the alleyway, peering determinedly at the maze of dreary streets.

They all looked the same. She didn't recognize a single thing. She was either going to have to stay put or ask someone for help. Neither plan was very appealing.

Three rough-looking men started walking in her direction. She shivered when they leered and pointed at her. She chose the road that led away from them.

"Please," she wished, "let this be the right way." She pulled out her swan pendant and repeated the wish, hoping whatever magical powers it had might help her. Nothing happened. There had to be a trick to it. She tried making the wish again, this time closing her eyes. She didn't know what she expected, shimmering lights maybe or a voice or something, but when she opened her eyes, nothing was different.

Ruby snorted impatiently. She was tired and hungry and it was clear she didn't like this dark street any more than Willow did. Willow stroked her warm neck. "Sorry, girl. I'm tired too. Don't worry, though. We'll find our way outta here."

Ruby's ears flattened. A shadowy figure came rushing around the corner, scurrying and hugging the walls like the mouse had. Willow urged Ruby forward. Whoever it was looked more scared than her, and that gave her the confidence to ask for help. "Wait," she called out. "Can you help me? I need to find the market square."

The figure began to run. "No, come back!" cried Willow. She raced Ruby down the street after whoever it was – a girl by the looks of her long skirt. "Please, wait!"

A screech tore through the darkness. "Keep back, you filthy vermin!" the girl yelled. "I've a sharp blade here and the wits to use it!"

CHAPTER 7

A stout, wild-eyed girl jumped out of the shadows and waved a knife at Willow. "Stay back, I tell you! Stay back!"

"Hey, take it easy," Willow said, reigning in her horse. "I'm not going to hurt you. I'm lost. I just need directions."

The girl took some deep breaths and looked Willow over from head to toe. Then she lowered her knife and tucked it into her waistband. "All right," she said finally, "where're you heading?"

"The market square. I got separated from my friends there."

"Well, I'm going that way myself. I'll guide you, if you like." The girl reached her hand up to Willow.

Willow stared at it – at the thin, almost delicate wrist and the plump, meaty palm – then at the two hundred odd pounds that went along with it. "I – I ..." she stammered. Did the girl think Willow could pull her onto Ruby?

The girl's hand dropped away, embarrassment staining her cheeks. "The reins," she said softly. "Loosen them, and I'll lead you."

Willow reddened and picked nervously at a speck in

Ruby's mane. She lowered the reins, wanting to apologize, but a meek "Oh" was all she could say.

The girl chuckled good-naturedly and reached for the reins. "Thought I wanted you to haul me up, didn't you?"

Still red-faced, Willow nodded.

"Well, now, don't be feeling bad about it. I know you didn't mean nothing by it. You don't look strong enough to lift a goose, let alone the likes of me." The girl gave Willow another smile and started leading Ruby down the street.

"The name's Gemma," the girl said. "I'm maidservant to Mistress Swinton, the wife of Pastry Cook Swinton. Are you new to Graffyn, then?"

"Ah, not exactly. My friends and I are just passing through."

"What's your name? You don't sound like you're from around here."

Willow hesitated. Was she supposed to say her real name? Brand and Malvin hadn't said anything about disguising it. She decided to stick with the truth. "Willow," she answered.

Gemma threw a skeptical glance over her shoulder. "Willow, is it? And next you'll be telling me you're a princess or a faerie lass."

"What? How do ... What do you mean?"

Gemma rolled her eyes. "Come now, you're not trying to tell me you don't know the fey names, are you? A babe in a cradle knows that much."

"The fey names ..."

"Aye, you know – the twelve names." Gemma sang them off like a nursery rhyme. "Zinna and Caltha the lovely flowers, Vinna and Ivy the choking vines. Xylia and Felda are wood and field, Ulva and Fawna the creatures' delight. Willow and Laurel the trees of wisdom, Cynara and Acacia the thorns of pride."

Willow stared. Nana had never told her about any fey names. Or that Willow's name was one of them.

"Our own wee princess was a netherchild," continued Gemma. "Named Willow, like yourself."

"*Was?* What do you mean was?"

Gemma threw Willow another disbelieving look. "Where you been living, girl? Are you telling me you've not heard the rumors?"

"I – I don't know," said Willow. "I just thought she was still alive, that's all."

"Well, that's what King Ulor would have us believe," Gemma said with a sniff. She turned down another narrow street. "But she hasn't been seen in over two months now and the Graffyn mages say she's dead. That the little mite wouldn't eat." She bowed her head. "Goddess quiet her sweet spirit," she whispered, touching a fingertip to her lips and kissing it.

"Well, what does the king say?" Willow hadn't counted on people thinking she was dead. Would her grandparents in Keldoran even believe she was their infant granddaughter?

"Oh, he's not made any proclamation. Keeping real quiet about it, he is. There's another rumor, though. That's she's been sent to a different realm. That King Ulor had dealings with the faerie queen, Cyrraena."

Willow wanted to ask more about the rumors, but she was worried about making Gemma suspicious. Another dumb question and Gemma just might decide Willow was a spy or something. "Why do you think the king would hide the princess's death?" she asked instead.

"Wouldn't you, if your kingdom were crumbling?" Gemma stopped for a second and reached up to pat Ruby's nose. "He's losing the Game real bad. Lost his wife and son. If the people knew he lost his little granddaughter as well, there'd be riots. His only heir then would be his brother, Prince Varian. And believe you me, nobody wants to see that strutting peacock on the throne."

"But if people think she's dead, why aren't they rebelling then, like you said?"

Gemma snorted and started walking again. "They do," she laughed. "Just stay another few days and you're likely to see an uprise. We have one most every other fortnight. Last one was over flour shortages. The one before that, over leather prices. And now with the war, it's only a matter of time before they decide to have one over the king's heir."

"*There she is!*" roared a familiar voice.

Willow looked up to see Brand and Malvin racing toward her, their drawn faces pale masks in the dark.

"What were you thinking?" Brand thundered. A vein

popped in his forehead and he smacked the top of his thigh with a fist. "Giving food to a beggar and right in the market square!" His horse edged forward, nearly trampling Gemma.

"You there!" Gemma exclaimed. "Watch your mount!"

"And who is *this*?" he asked. "You know we can't afford to be trusting strangers. We must ..."

"Brand."

"We must ..."

"Calm. Down." Jeez! He was acting like she'd ridden off on purpose or something. "You know, it's not my fault the horse took off," she yelled back at him. "I couldn't reach the reins after you pulled them out of my hands."

Brand looked ready to explode. "And if you hadn't caused the riot in the first place, I wouldn't have had to."

"Umm ... pardon me," cut in Gemma. She was still standing between their skittish horses. "I'm not one to meddle in another's affairs, so if you don't mind, I'll be on my way." She handed the reins back to Willow. "It's been nice meeting you, lass. Take good care of yourself."

"No, wait," said Willow. "Can't we at least give you a ride?" She ignored Brand's glare. Gemma was the first person to help her who didn't want something in return. And besides, it served Brand right for trying to blame all their problems on her.

"It's a bit of a ways. And I don't want to trouble you any," said Gemma.

This time Willow glared at Brand and he frowned and

clamped his teeth together, finally rolling his eyes in mock defeat. "Very well," he sighed. "How far?"

"Do you know Pastry Cook Swinton's shop? Over by the west market?"

Brand nodded and reached out his hand, easily hoisting Gemma onto Dusk. "Come on, then. It's on our road."

They rode their horses to the pastry shop's closed doors and shuttered display windows. The building was three stories high and in the part above the shop, Willow could see a cloudy yellow light flickering behind the windows. Pie smells still clung to the air.

Gemma slid from Brand's horse and thumped to the ground. "Well, thank you kindly," she said, brushing out her skirts and smiling cheerfully. "Didn't much fancy that walk, I tell you. Streets aren't safe anymore."

Willow dismounted too and held out her hand to Gemma.

Gemma gave it a hearty shake and stared up at her. "Good goddess. You're as tall as a tree. Are you part giant, girl?"

People said stuff about Willow's height all the time, but they weren't usually that direct. But Gemma's words didn't bother her. She laughed and clapped Gemma's shoulder. "Listen, thanks for helping me. I'd probably still be lost if you hadn't."

"You're welcome indeed, and thank you for the ride, lass." She pulled away from Willow. "But I'd best be getting in, now. Mistress Swinton's waiting."

Willow hopped back up on Ruby's saddle and waved goodbye.

Gemma waved back. She stood beneath a sign with a pie painted on it. "Now, if you have time tomorrow, stop by for some pastry. I'll be minding the shop myself and maybe can spare a pie or two." She winked and waved, making the pie sign rattle as she disappeared into the dark shop.

CHAPTER 8

The Staff and Dagger was a large inn located a block from the pastry shop. Four stories high and built with its own stables and courtyard, it sprawled along the wide, well-kept avenue bordering the west market and was, according to Brand, the best inn in the city.

Willow had her doubts. From where she stood, just inside the doorway, the place looked like a dive. She curled her nose at beer fumes and sweat stink, and she peered into the dim, smoky barroom. It was just a thug hangout with booze, loud voices, and lots of leather. "What is this?" she whispered to Brand. "A medieval biker bar?"

He didn't answer. He looked as mortified as she looked skeptical. "I don't ..." he began, but before he could finish, a towering man wearing an eye patch and red silk suddenly swooped over him, giving Brand a hearty clap on the shoulder that rattled his chain mail.

Willow stared at the big man. With the eye patch and gaudy clothing, he looked like a pirate rock star.

"Squire Brand! It's good to see you, lad. I've not seen a

castle swordsman for six months now." He pumped Brand's hand as if it were a tire iron and gave him a gap-toothed grin.

"And how goes it with the king, lad? Does he still stand a chance against Tarrant? The rumors are not good, you know. Not good at all. *Ah*, but where are my manners! We need a drink first. You look near parched." He pulled Brand into the murky barroom.

Willow followed close behind Brand and Malvin, blinking when the pungent lamp smoke stung her eyes. She slipped her hood back to see better.

"How goes it, lass!" someone yelled out. "Come by me and take a wee drink." A big hairy guy just to the right of her lifted his mug and made a gross smacking sound, puckering his lips like a fish.

She glared at him. *As if*, she thought and flipped him her finger.

His arm shot out and knocked her back. Immediately, Brand was in front of her, sword in hand, and Malvin guarded her from behind, keeping her from falling. Pirate-Eye blocked Brand, trying to prevent a brawl.

"Don't worry, lad," he said. "We are well prepared here. Your lady friend has nothing to fear." A finger snap and another hand signal produced three heavily armed men who hustled hairy-smacking-guy out the door.

Pirate-Eye smiled another gap-toothed grin and then held back a doorway curtain for them. He led them down a hall and into a small private room decorated with furs and different types of wooden crossbows. A table and four chairs sat in a corner, and a warm fire burned in the hearth.

Not exactly the Ritz, but definitely a step up from the boozepit next door. Willow pulled off her cloak and took a seat close to the fire, crossing her arms and stretching out her stiff legs. Brand and Malvin did the same, collapsing in their chairs with thuds and tired groans.

"Looks as though you've had quite a journey there, Squire," said Pirate-Eye, smiling. "Nothing, of course, that a cold ale tankard and my Marta's quail stew wouldn't fix up. Rest yourselves then, and I'll be back in a wink."

Willow waited until he closed the door, then turned to Brand. "What's this squire business? I thought you said you were a knight."

Brand reddened slightly. "It's in the Game that I am a knight. And I would be a knight at court as well, except for ..." He paused, undoing the clasp of his cloak. He let it fall against the chair back.

"Except for ...?"

"Except for nothing – just stay out of trouble, will you? Everywhere we go, you keep starting a fight."

Willow glared at him. In the last hour she'd been mobbed, stranded, and sexually harassed. She'd definitely reached her crap limit for the day. "What's *your* problem? You've been nothing but a big stupid pain since we left the castle. And I'm sick of it! And I'm sick of you! In fact –" Willow shoved back her chair and stood up "– I think I'd rather just return to Carrus!" She stepped toward the door. But the moment she tried, she found her whole body had become as stiff as a statue.

Brand and Malvin watched her curiously, both waiting for her to do or say something.

"Can't ... *move*," Willow finally managed to croak. "Something's wrong." Her eyes circled wildly around the room. "Help me!"

Brand jumped to his feet. "Calm yourself, Your Highness. I think I know what the problem is."

Willow took deep breaths until she could do so without hyperventilating. "What is it?"

"Repeat after me," said Brand, "*I am going to Keldoran.*"

"*What?*" Willow stared at him in disbelief. "I'm *paralyzed* and you want me to change my mind about Carrus? What's *wrong* with you?"

Brand shook his head and clutched her shoulders. "Listen to me. You're a pawn in the Game. Pawns can't move backwards. So if you wish to unfreeze your body, say *I am going to Keldoran.*"

"I am going to Keldoran," said Willow through gritted teeth. Instantly, she felt her muscles and joints loosen and she fell forward. Brand steadied her, but Willow pushed him away and stomped to the fireplace.

"You knew this all along, didn't you?" She swore beneath

her breath, kicking at the flagstone hearth. *Damn. Damn. Damn.* She glanced over at Brand and Malvin and their sheepish faces. Unbelievable. Those two rats planned this, and now she was stuck here whether she wanted to be or not.

Willow kicked another hearthstone, ready to give the two boys a furious tongue-lashing. But just then Pirate-Eye burst through the door, carrying a huge platter of food. "All right, my friends! Feast first and we'll chew the fat later."

"But first of all," said Brand, leaning back in his chair and avoiding Willow's scathing gaze, "explain to us this new make of customer, that rabble out there."

"Ah Brand, my lad," sighed Pirate-Eye. He smoothed out his grizzled beard. "Things have changed since your last visit, I fear. All my fine mage-brewed ale is gone. The only stuff that I have now is what I can brew myself, and as you know, it's not fit for human consumption. Only that lot out there," he poked his thumb behind him, "will drink it. And rabble or not, I still need gold, or copper at least, to fill my purse." He noticed Willow lurking by the hearth. "Now lad," he boomed, "shall you introduce me to your friends, here, or must I do so?"

A moment later, Pirate-eye pulled her back to the table with an over-exuberant shoulder hug. Brand made the round of introductions and despite her foul mood, Willow listened with interest to their host's colorful history.

Pirate-Eye, whose actual name was Trumble Quillondale,

had been an arms master in King Ulor's army, a captain of the king's guards, and even, at one point, the king's own personal protector. He'd also been Brand's first sword and lance teacher and had been proclaimed one of the best horse trainers by three kingdoms. The inn, which he now ran with his wife and four daughters, had been his retirement gift from the king.

Trumble raised a mug to Willow. Brand had just told him the truth about her identity, and to his credit, his good eye widened only slightly in response. "Well then, Princess," he said, bowing his head. "I would like to drink to your good health. And may the gods be with you on your quest." He took a deep swallow from his cup and slammed it on the table, urging them all to drink up. Brand and Malvin smiled weakly. They clicked their mugs, then let them drift back to the table.

"You don't think I'd give you the grog that's out there, now, do you? This is the real stuff, lads. I've still a small cache hidden away. Just enough for a treat now and then. So drink up! You're not likely to find mage-brewed ale till you reach Keldoran."

Willow sniffed at the white foam in her mug. Didn't they have a drinking age here? This was the second time in two days an adult had given her liquor. She watched Brand and Malvin quaff back theirs and took a small sip. Cold bitterness filled her mouth. She grimaced and swallowed it down, not wanting Trumble to notice her distaste.

The quail stew, however, was different. It went down fast and easy, like a hamburger and a side of fries. She shoveled it in, savoring juicy bits of meat and soft chunky vegetables, amazed at what being outdoors could do to the appetite.

An hour and a half later, after a tasty dessert and a hot bath, Willow found herself tucked into a cozy, clean bed, playing a game of chess on her laptop. She stared at the computer screen, shocked by the Black queen's death shriek. Crimson silk billowed all around her as she fell to a chess square. The fair-haired White queen, holding a laser beam scepter high in the air, stood over her a moment, then lowered her arms. The Black queen vanished from the board.

Sickened, Willow quit the game, not bothering to save it. Her grandmother was the Black queen. She'd just killed her grandmother.

Willow snapped shut the lid of her computer. She'd brought the laptop out to fiddle with the strategy again, only this time she'd let herself play both sides, making sure that Black made stupid moves until she and Brand reached the back rank. As soon as her pawn was queened, though, she started using her new queen like a mob hit man. But the scream had stopped her, reminding her of something she was trying to avoid thinking about. *King Ulor thought capturing someone killed them.* A cold chill ran up her spine. She shoved the laptop under the bed, hoping she'd never have to test that particular theory.

Yawning, Willow snuggled beneath the covers, burrowing her head into the soft, feathery pillows. She smelled the fresh spot where her damp hair had just been. Well, there was one thing to be glad about. At least she was clean again. It'd taken over an hour of toting and heating, but Trumble's wife and two of his daughters had managed to ready a bath for her. She stretched her toes down into the coolness of the sheets then huddled them back up beneath her shift. She hadn't realized how much dirt and stink could accumulate in two days of horseback riding. Or how much she had taken her morning showers for granted.

She turned over on her back again, then to her other side. She still couldn't fall asleep. Her Game glow didn't help. Her bath had washed away the sticky powder stuff Brand had plastered over her and now her skin was as bright as a nightlight. Every time she closed her eyes, she felt as if the morning sun were shining in her face.

Finally, she sat up and looked at the simple wooden furniture and bare, stone walls of the inn room. The other part of the problem was *this* – this whole storybook place, with all its knights and princesses and faerie tale inhabitants. Could she keep pretending that it was make-believe? Today had felt too real. Willow clutched the woolen blankets to her chest. The starving people in the market, the vicious guards, the rough men in the alley, the thugs in the barroom – they were all too brutally real.

Fear crept over Willow. What if joining Brand had been a mistake? He was just a teenager like her. Could he really protect her from the Game? And whatever other dangers waited out there? She heard the Black queen's death shriek again. Her chin quivered. How could Nana have wanted her to come here? Have wanted her to risk her life in this way?

Her shoulders slumped as she stared into the glowing fireplace. Nana had always been overconfident of her abilities. It'd been hard to contend with sometimes, having to live up to all that expectation. She'd never wanted to disappoint her.

Fat, slow tears began to trickle down her cheek. Willow clenched her body at the sudden pain, struggling to control it. But a sob escaped, and then another, until she finally gave in, crying out all her rage and pent-up grief.

A little while later, a light tap sounded on the door. "Princess? Are you well?" She recognized Brand's voice. For a second, she wondered if he'd spied on her using the image globe, but then remembered that he and Malvin were right next door. He'd probably heard her.

"Yeah, I'm fine."

There was a long pause and then he said, "May I speak to you?"

Willow sniffed and wiped at her eyes. "Look, I'm kind of tired right now. And –"

"It will only take a moment." A second later, the door opened and Brand entered her room. Sighing, Willow pulled the covers up around her neck.

Brand walked to the side of her bed, keeping his eyes on the floor. Willow almost felt sorry for him. "Listen, if it's about the backwards thing ..."

"What you said downstairs is true," Brand blurted out. "Malvin and I both knew pawns couldn't move backwards. And we deliberately hid it from you. But we weren't trying to deceive you." He clasped his hands together and looked up at her. "We planned to tell you tomorrow. After we left Graffyn."

Willow swallowed. She knew why they hadn't told her – to protect the king.

Brand lowered his eyes again. "Will you still come to Keldoran with us?"

A fireplace log suddenly shifted, crackling and shooting off sparks. Willow watched a flickering spark trail, surprised at his question. *There was a choice?* Of course, she thought, staring into the fire. She could stay *here* if she wanted to. Trumble would look after her. She looked around the room again, at the rustic stone walls and the comfortable feather-stuffed bed. The lemony scent of Mrs. Quillondale's freshly scrubbed floors and linens filled her nostrils.

"Princess ..." Brand was looking at her, waiting for an answer. Willow didn't know what to tell him. Her gaze took in his leather-corded shirt, his long dark hair, and wide knightly shoulders. She could barely accept he was real.

"If you don't come with us," he pressed, "it will be but a

matter of time before King Ulor's men find you, and when they do, Baldemar will leave the king unprotected and force you to go with him."

Willow fell back against her pillows, remembering King Ulor's weary face. Accepting Brand was real meant accepting the king was real too. *Her grandfather*. It meant accepting she truly was a princess of a mythical realm. A netherworld champion. She shuddered at such fantastic thoughts and to her horror started to cry again.

The bed sank as Brand sat on it, pinning her silver-lit hand beneath his red one. "Forgive me," he said. "I didn't mean to distress you. If you wish to stay, we shall find a way to hide you. We could –"

"No. It's not that." Willow pushed her face into the pillow. "It's ..." What could she say? That she'd only just now realized he truly existed? "My nana died. And I just – I just *left* her there. I didn't know the crystal was real. I didn't know any of this was real. Honest," she peered up at Brand from the pillow, "this whole time I thought I was dreaming. That *you* were a dream."

Brand hung his head. "I am greatly sorry for the loss of Nurse Beryl. She was always kind to me. Kind to all the children who fostered at the castle. If she did not explain our world to you, she must have had good reason."

"She did explain it," admitted Willow. "But she made it seem like stories, like it was all just make-believe." She sat back up and wiped at her eyes. Knowing Nana had cared for

Brand made her feel a little better. It struck Willow then that if not for the Game spell, she'd only be a four-month-old and Brand a sixteen-year-old. *As if things could get any weirder.*

Brand let go of her hand, but stayed on the bed. Between the firelight and Game glow, his sharp-angled face looked golden soft. "I remember her stories," he murmured. "She could weave them as if from air. You know, before she left here, she told me I would play a hero's part. I didn't understand her meaning then. But now I believe I do." He smiled, flashing his dimples. "She must have meant a hero's part in her stories."

Willow nodded, then her mouth fell open as she realized who Brand was. *The white knight story.* Nana had always said, *The princess looked to the white knight for protection.* Brand was a White knight in the game. Was *he* the white knight Nana had meant? The white knight Willow had built her dreams around?

"Oh my God!" she cried. "She did! You *were* part of the stories. In chess Nana always used her knights to guard her pawns. *Always!* And she told me this story about a white knight – a knight who always protected the princess." Willow leaned forward and clasped Brand's arms. Nana hadn't left her without help. She'd shown her exactly who to use for defense!

Her eyes locked with Brand's. He gazed at her with such intensity, Willow swayed forward. Her stomach fluttered and her heartbeat picked up.

Then, suddenly, Brand was looking away – he fixed his eyes on a spot to her right and said in a tense voice, "Well ... Your Highness we should, um ..."

Mortified, Willow let go of him and sprang back. "Sorry," she said, clinging to her blankets again. "I should –"

"No." Brand leapt from the bed. "It is I that must apologize." He bowed low. "Excuse my forwardness. I should not be in your bedchamber." He started backing away.

A riotous shout and a heavy thud from downstairs shook Willow's bedroom floor. She shot Brand a frightened look, reminded again of the violent mob-rule feel of this world. *Don't go*, she wanted to say. He must have grasped her fear because he pitched from the room and returned moments later, dragging rucksacks, cloaks, weapons, pillows, blankets, and a yawning, owlishly blinking Malvin.

"I am sure Trumble will have any brawls well in hand," said Brand, frowning as roars boomed up and the floor once again shook beneath him. "But for your safety, Your Highness, Malvin and I will stand guard in your room."

Malvin grunted his agreement. He dropped to a spot at the foot of Willow's bed and promptly started snoring. Brand barred the door with one chair and pulled up another beside Willow's bed. "I'll take first watch," he said, huddling into his cloak and tipping the chair back against the wall. "Best try and sleep. We've a long day ahead tomorrow."

Willow nodded and nestled her head deeper into the feather

pillows. She peeked at Brand in the dim light. She couldn't help it – her heartbeat sped up a little again. Maybe Brand wasn't so bad after all ... she felt safer knowing he was here.

As she fell asleep, a dream began to form. She saw Brand, dressed in gold armor, sitting on a white horse. He held a gauntleted hand out to her and smiled with teeth that glowed white. She reached out to him, but the moment she did, he vanished.

A pair of turquoise eyes took his place. They stared at her mockingly before winking shut, and suddenly, darkness engulfed her. After that, she only dreamt of skittering mice and hungry, wild hands grasping at her.

CHAPTER 9

Willow ate her eggs carefully. She was wearing the thick, sticky make-up powder again, and didn't want to rub it off. Somewhere between dreaming about the eyes and watching Brand propped up in a chair beside her, she'd decided to make the best of things. So as soon as she woke up, she told Brand she would go to Keldoran. This is what Nana had wanted, and what Nana had prepared her for. And Willow was determined not to let her down.

She shoveled in a last bite of egg. Next thing on their to-do list was to get supplies.

Willow, Brand, and Malvin, along with two of Trumble's henchmen and a packhorse, strolled over to the west market, where they purchased vegetables, dried fruits, meats, nuts, flour, oatmeal, and packets of spice. Brand also selected small blades for Willow and Malvin that could be concealed in their boot tops, and slim ivory-handled daggers for their belts.

Willow rested her hand on the hilt of her new dagger, surprised she liked its cool feel against her palm. She hadn't wanted the knife. The thought of stabbing someone sickened her. Yet knowing it was there, close to her fingertips, was reassuring.

Her eyes roamed over the people milling about the market square. A sparse crowd today, due, no doubt, to the overabundance of guards positioned along the streets and between the merchant booths. She bit into a pear that Brand had handed her, wondering what had happened to all those poor, hungry people that had swarmed her yesterday. She'd asked Brand about them, but had only gotten a shrug and a disinterested, "Not my business."

Willow chewed her pear thoughtfully. Maybe she could get Brand to buy some extra food and donate it to a shelter or something. Her gaze fell to the purse of dwindling gold coins buckled to the side of Brand's belt. *Not likely*. They rounded a corner leading away from the market. All the extra guards must have made Brand less cautious. He was actually leading them somewhere fun – to Busker Alley, where gamers and street buskers entertained.

Lively music and the smell of fried pastry in the air jogged Willow's memory. She was reminded of her one and only trip to the Home County Fair and Exhibition with Nana. There'd been crowds, rides, bright kaleidoscopic colors, and lots of wares to buy.

Their first busker stop was an emaciated contortionist. Willow stared at him in horrified fascination. She blocked her eyes slightly, aghast but curious, as the man hand-walked with his legs wrapped impossibly around his neck.

Brand laughed and steered her in the direction of a shrill, chittering sound. "Take your hands away. You'll like this one."

Willow peeked between her fingers and squealed in delight as a tiny monkey dressed in a silver vest danced across a little red stage. His owner was decked out in a matching outfit and played reedy music from a bulbous flute. Brand and Malvin tossed copper coins onto the stage and laughed as the monkey ran around, scooping them up in his little pillbox hat.

They moved on to the fire-eaters, the jugglers, and a red-footed coal-walker. Willow noticed a huge crowd gathering at a wooden platform at the edge of the market. "Oh, let's go see!" she begged. "I bet it's dancing bears or something!"

Brand signaled Trumble's men to guide the packhorse over to the stage. Willow smiled and her cheeks flared when Brand placed an arm protectively around her waist.

She glanced at him as surreptitiously as she could. His long dark hair was tied in a tight ponytail. She could see the brightness in his black eyes and the curve of his smile. She marveled at the change in him. Since their talk last night, he'd been downright nice to her.

"The king cares not!" someone roared, startling Willow. "Our children starve. We have blighted crops and no guild work. And what does the king?"

Willow blinked and looked around in confusion, wondering where the voice had come from. Brand pointed at the stage. She could see the speaker now. A short, heavyset man, dressed in rich, fur-lined clothing. Not exactly the destitute beggar she'd been expecting. "I shall tell you," he yelled. "He wars with the Keldorians to ruin us!" A skeptical murmur went through the crowd. "You believe not?" The man shook his gloved fist at them. "Who captured the Keldorian princess? Who conspires with that fey witch, wagering his own granddaughter?" More murmurs. "It's King Ulor, I tell you, that we must blame for our troubles! King Ulor and his band of Game players." This time a few cries of approval came from the crowd.

The man continued on, railing against King Ulor like a fiery evangelist raging against the devil. Brand touched Willow's arm. "We must leave here at once. I know that man."

Suddenly Willow noticed the silence around them. She looked at the platform. The man was pointing accusingly – *at them*. "See there! *See there!* It's the White knight! One of the Game players! Arrest him! He will be our persuasion for the king. Our opening gambit!"

A group of men in the crowd sprang forward.

Brand grabbed Willow's hand. He didn't say a word. He didn't look around. He didn't hesitate. He just ran for everything he was worth.

CHAPTER 10

Willow struggled to catch her breath as she and Brand rounded a street corner. "Wait! I need – I need to stop." She tried to pull away from his grasp, but he only held on tighter, dragging her along after him.

"I have a plan." He glanced back to make sure Malvin was keeping up, then pulled her even harder.

Willow brushed sweat from her eyes and struggled to keep up. For the last five blocks, they'd managed to outdistance their pursuers by weaving in and out of dark alleys, but in the process had lost Trumble's men and the packhorse.

"Catch the White knight!" someone cried.

"They're just up ahead!" yelled another.

Willow staggered and pressed a hand on the knot in her side. The voices sounded alarmingly close.

"We're almost there. Come now, you can do it." Brand slowed down a bit and Willow sucked in gasps of air. Then, as they moved farther down the street, he yanked her and Malvin through a side door, closing and barring it from the inside.

Willow, aware of nothing but the pleasant, musty smell of flour, sank to the floor, gasping and wheezing. Malvin keeled over beside her.

"Good goddess!" cried a familiar voice. "You look as if the seven beasts of hell are chasing you!"

Willow looked up to see Gemma come bustling around a floury countertop. Gemma squatted down beside her, trying to help her up. "I can't." Willow pulled away and flopped bonelessly against the closed door.

Brand, who'd somehow managed to stay on his feet, assisted Gemma in hauling Willow and then Malvin to standing positions. "We need a place to hide. And quickly!"

"You check that side!" a voice yelled. It sounded as if it had come from right outside the door. "We'll check this one."

Gemma peered out the window, then turned back with a determined look on her face. "Come on. We can use the smuggling bins." She led them to the rear of the pastry shop where six large wooden barrels lined a side wall.

"Hunker down real low. And I'll put the flour pans overtop you." She pulled a lid from one of the bins and lifted out a round, basket-shaped pan full of flour, explaining that Master Swinton used the barrels for hiding black market mage ale.

Willow climbed into the first barrel. Gemma replaced the flour pan, plunging Willow into darkness.

"You see," explained Gemma in a muffled voice, "the pan makes it appear as if the barrel's full to the brim with flour."

Willow heard thunking noises as Gemma helped Brand and Malvin into their barrels and replaced the lids.

"Now, just keep quiet in there." Floorboards creaked as Gemma moved across the room. Willow heard the door bar lift and the sound of spry steps behind the counter. She shifted in the narrow barrel, her knees and arms pressed against her chest. She wrinkled her nose at the sour smell of old mage ale, and swore she could feel some of it seeping through the seat of her pants. Small bits of flour sprinkled down from the flour pan, resting like white dust against her shirtsleeve. She peered at the bright specks and realized something other than her Game glow was casting a light inside the barrel. There were tiny cracks along the barrel's upper portion where the damp leather lining didn't quite reach.

Willow moved herself up to a squatting position, pressing her eye to one of the narrow openings. She could see the door and part of Gemma's display window.

Two men – one tall, the other short – and a pimply teenage boy burst into the shop. "Have you seen the White knight, girl?" said the shorter man, breathless from running. "He's dressed in black like the knave he is, and running with a red-haired witch and a tall, thin-legged lad."

"The White knight?" echoed Gemma, true surprise in her voice.

The pimply-faced boy pushed forward, his eyes bright with excitement. "Aye, Lord Radnor's calling for his arrest."

Willow thought she heard a doubting snort come from Gemma.

"Well, did you see him or not, girl?" growled one of the men, the tall one this time. "We've no time for your prattle."

"Nay," said Gemma. "I been here the whole morning and haven't seen a soul run by but a messenger lad or two."

The tall man grinned dangerously. "You won't mind us taking a little look-see then, will you?" His eyes settled on the barrels in the back room. He strode across the shop, not waiting for Gemma's permission.

Willow ducked away from the crack. They'd called her a witch. Did that mean they really thought she was one, or were they just calling her something mean? Either way, she doubted they would treat her any better than they would Brand if she were caught.

Wood thunked and scraped as the men lifted the lids. "Nothing but flour," spat the man. "C'mon, lads. Let's check the shop next door." The floor trembled as he and the other men stomped out of the pastry shop.

A few seconds later, the lid from Willow's bin lifted. "It's safe to come out now," Gemma whispered.

Willow squinted at the sudden brightness and stood up, stretching out her cramped legs. Gemma hurried to the barrel next to hers and freed Malvin, who came up sneezing in short, rapid bursts.

"Gods! It's lucky ... *achoo* ... I can hold my ... *achoo* ...

breath for so long."

Brand came up next. He was covered head-to-toe in white flour and every time he blinked, white flakes fell from his lashes. "Mine had a leak," he said dryly, brushing away flour.

Willow hid her chuckle behind a fist.

"C'mon, c'mon," Gemma said. "The master'll skin me if the shop's closed for more than a minute. You can hide upstairs till the ruckus dies down."

"Is there a rear door?" asked Brand. "We could try circling back to Trumble's."

Gemma shook her head. "Nay. They've left men behind to watch the shops, and no doubt they're watching the alleyways as well. Your best bet is to hide out here till it's safe." She grabbed a pie off the countertop and headed toward some stairs.

Brand hesitated a moment, then followed, shaking a huge flour cloud from his head as he went. Willow and Malvin, both trying to contain their laughter, straggled behind him.

Gemma led them to a small and dingy room. Willow wrinkled her nose at the filthy straw-stuffed rags sitting in a corner. *A bed?* Malvin started to sneeze again and he almost tripped over the loose boards.

"You'll be all right here," said Gemma. She pushed a basin off a rickety chair and set down the pie. "The master'll be home soon, so you mustn't make any noise." She backed toward the doorway. "Help yourselves to the pie. And I'll tell you when it's safe."

She closed the door and her footsteps thumped down the stairs. Brand went to the only window in the room and opened a closed shutter.

"She's right," he said. "There are two men searching the alleyway." He closed the shutter, leaning his head against the wall. "I am sorry. This is all my fault. I swore an oath to protect you, but I've just led you into danger." His chin fell to his chest. "You may wish, Princess, to wait for the king's men after all. Maybe it's better that you have a contingent of knights to escort you."

Willow stared at Brand in surprise. "But you said we couldn't leave King Ulor unprotected," she argued. "He needs those knights. He's under siege, remember?"

"She's right, Brand," added Malvin. "We can't turn back. We are past the area of battle now, and once we are past Graffyn, there's but Thorburn Wood. Then the worst will be behind us. And besides, what happened at Thorburn –"

Brand whipped around, grabbing Malvin's tunic front. "Don't!" he said, gritting his teeth. The fabric tore and Brand returned to his senses. He quickly let go of Malvin's shirt. "Mal, I am ..."

"It's all right," said Malvin. When he turned away from Brand, Willow saw the hurt in his eyes.

She managed to hold back her questions about Thorburn. Clearly it was a sore subject. She went for the pie instead.

"Hey, I don't know about you guys, but I'm starving."

Her new ivory-handled knife cut deeply into the pie's flaky crust. "Mmm, cherry. My favorite." She scooped up a big piece with her hand and bit into it. "This is too good! You guys have to try it."

Willow slid her finger along the knife blade and licked off the cherry goo. Brand and Malvin joined her. She cut off more pieces of pie and the three of them ate until there was nothing left but crumbs.

"Now that was good pie," she said, turning the knife over and using her finger to clean off the other side.

"Indeed," agreed Brand. He groaned and rubbed his stomach, falling back against the straw bed. Malvin copied him, groaning even louder.

Willow rolled her eyes at them and tucked her knife back into her belt. Well, at least they weren't fighting. She plopped down next to them, pushing them both and laughing at their moans. "C'mon, you big pigs. Get up. I want to ask you something."

Malvin sat up and straightened out his tunic. He seemed a bit embarrassed. "Umm, you have a question, Your Highness?"

"You know," said Willow, "you probably shouldn't keep calling me that. I mean, if someone heard you, they might get suspicious."

Brand leaned on his elbow and nodded. "Aye, I was going to mention that the other day. It's best, I agree, not to use our titles." He sat up and studied her a moment. "The name

Willow is fey, though. People might get suspicious over that as well."

"What about just Will? That was my nickname back home."

"Could be short for Willa or Wilda," Malvin added.

Brand nodded. "All right then, we shall call you Will." He stood up and moved over to the window again. "Blast, there's still someone down there. It will probably be nightfall before we are able to leave here."

Willow pulled out the swan necklace hidden beneath her shirt. "Well, let me ask a question then," she said. "Can you tell me more about this?" Brand and Malvin stared at the necklace. "What?" she said. "What's wrong?"

"Queen Cyrraena's gift!" breathed Malvin. "I thought you had left it in Earthworld."

Brand moved in for a closer look. "Oh, but this is truly good fortune. It's the proof we need for King Tarrant." He reached out to touch the pendant. "With this, he will never doubt that Willow – Will – is his granddaughter."

Malvin dropped the pendant and Willow tucked it back down her shirtfront. "Make sure you keep it hidden," Malvin warned. "You saw what happened when they saw the White knight. If they knew we had the princess pawn with us as well, we would have the whole countryside after us."

The princess pawn. That seemed an apt name for her role in all this. Willow touched her pendant again. "Is it magic? When I put it on the last time in Carrus, I'm sure I felt something. It was hot and made me feel real focused."

"Oh yes," said Malvin, "it's magic all right. It's your nethergift. The emblem of Queen Cyrraena's protection. This means," he pointed at the pendant, "that the faerie queen is watching over us. She is lending us her support and protection, which is indeed remarkable, since she has hidden herself from humans since your trip to Earthworld. She isn't permitted to intervene, but she has risked much to help us."

Willow glanced at Brand. She decided to take her own risk. "Who was that Lord Radnor guy who got the people in the marketplace to chase us?" Brand looked at Malvin in warning.

A shout prevented Willow from finding out what that look meant.

"*What's this?*" an unfamiliar voice roared. "You lazy sow! There's a half crown missing from the till and only five pies sitting on yonder table. Are you eating me profits again? I'll teach you to steal from me, you thieving wench!" A sharp slap cracked against the silence, followed by another and another.

Willow crawled across the floor over to a corner where she could peer down into a part of the pastry shop. "Oh my God," she whispered. "He's beating her."

CHAPTER 11

Willow had seen violence on TV, but not like this. Nothing was censored in reality. Each time the man struck, she could see the shock to Gemma's skin and the instant red blotches. She could see the man's bullish chest, his pasty skin and glistening sweat, the powerful arms that pounded back Gemma's efforts to shield herself.

And something else.

She peered closer at the man. At the evil smile stretched across his face. He enjoyed this.

Willow's stomach roiled. She couldn't bear it anymore. A shout gathered in her lungs, but Brand pulled her away from the crack before she could say a word.

"Don't look," Brand muttered. He sheltered Willow's face against his shoulder.

"Leave the girl be," ordered another gruff voice. Willow pulled away from Brand to look through the crack again. "There's a whole pile of dishes that needs washing and I don't need the little chit laid up for a week like last time." A woman stomped into view. "Come now." She tapped the man's arm with a wooden spoon. "There's paying customers out by the window."

The man shrugged his shoulders and stalked off. The woman bent over Gemma and said something. Willow couldn't hear her words, but she saw Gemma's bruised lips tighten. Gemma walked away without saying a word, head held high.

Willow marveled at her courage. Gemma hadn't cringed or cried or any of the things that Willow probably would've done. She just walked past that woman like nothing had happened. Her gutsiness reminded Willow of someone else. Someone else who never let anyone bring her down.

Abby.

"I think she's going to be all right," whispered Malvin.

Willow moved back to the straw bed. She felt numb. Brand and Malvin sat down beside her quietly.

They waited there, not saying a word, until it grew dark and the muffled sounds from below disappeared. Finally, Gemma climbed the stairs, her tread slow and tired. The door opened and closed silently behind her. "It's just me," she whispered. A cloak hooded her face and she was carrying a basket and flask.

"Thought you might be needing another meal," she said, handing Willow the provisions. "It's just a bit of bread and cheese and some cold well water."

Willow stared at the food and drink. After what had

happened to her, Gemma was still more worried about *them*. "Gemma, we saw that man hit you. Are you all right?"

"Oh that." Gemma chuckled. "It's nothing. Master Swinton, he just loses his temper sometimes. He doesn't hit that hard." The blue hood trembled as she spoke. Willow reached over and pulled it back gently.

"Oh, Gemma." Gemma's face was red and swollen. One eye was shut entirely and a nasty bruise had formed on her forehead. Her bottom lip was cut and protruded painfully.

Gemma let her look, and then drew the hood back up. "There isn't time to worry about me. Something's going on down at the main gate, so the streets are mostly clear now. Where is it that you need to go?"

Brand joined Willow. He untied his money pouch and set it in Gemma's hands. "This isn't very much. But I hope it's enough to thank you for all your help."

"That's not necessary, Master Brand." Gemma handed the pouch right back to him. "If you're the White knight like they say, then I figure it's my duty to help you."

She pulled a woolen scarf out from under her cloak. "Here," she said, tossing it to Willow. "To cover your hair. If anyone does happen to be out and about, they'll be looking for three people, not four. And I know the city well. If you tell me where you're heading, I can likely find you a shortcut."

Brand held the money pouch in his hand, clearly debating whether he should argue or not. Finally, he tied the pouch back to his belt. "We're heading for the Staff and Dagger. Along the west-end market."

Gemma's hooded head bobbed up and down. "Aye, I know it well. Mistress Quillondale's a good customer."

Gemma's shortcut took them through a refuse-clogged canal that flowed behind the tanner district. Between the stretched-out animal skins and stinking vats of liquid, Willow felt as if she'd stumbled into a small section of hell. The section, she was sure, reserved for smelly polluters and public farters.

They reached the Staff and Dagger just as a servant was lighting the oil lamps that hung on either side of the inn's large entrance door. Trumble was waiting for them inside.

"Where've you been, lad? I've had me men scouring the city looking for you all afternoon! The whole town's in an uproar about the White knight!"

Brand quickly told their story and introduced Gemma to Trumble. "This end of the city, at any rate, seems deserted. Would be best if we pack the horses now, and try to leave by the south gate."

"Aye," agreed Trumble, "I've had your horses and supplies ready for near twenty minutes now. Seems as though King Ulor has sent some knights after you. A whole herd of them just rode in through the main city gates. Of course they weren't expecting to be greeted by the mob that's searching for you too."

"Are they okay?" asked Willow, suddenly anxious. She didn't want anyone getting hurt because of her.

Trumble patted her shoulder. "Now, don't worry, lass. The people here in Graffyn are always looking for someone to blame for their troubles. They switch scapegoats like me Marta changes bedsheets. And once they see they're no match for mounted knights, they'll hightail it outta there. C'mon, now, let's get you and the lads back on your way, because crumbcakes to crowns those knights'll be coming here first to search for you."

Brand retrieved the image globe and Willow's laptop from Mistress Quillondale's strongbox while Willow said her goodbyes. She was about to say them to Gemma when Gemma sidestepped her and went over to Trumble. "You know the guards aren't going to let you through, don't you?"

Trumble nodded. "Aye. Lord Radnor's got the city closed tighter than a drum. It'll take, no doubt, a pouch of gold to change their minds." He jingled a heavy money pouch tied to his belt.

"My father was captain of the guards for the south gate," Gemma told him. "If you take me with you, I can make sure you get through."

Trumble stared at Gemma, trying, it seemed, to see under

her hood. "Well, you might save me my bribe money. Can you ride?"

Gemma's hood bobbed up and down in the form of a nod.

"Good enough, then. You there, lad, give her your horse." Trumble stalked out the backdoor into the stable yard where ten saddled horses milled over the cobblestones. Trumble and five of his men mounted up. "We shall be your escorts as far as the gate," he told Brand. "Then we'll circle back to the inn and see what can be done to stall them knights." He winked at Willow with his good eye and then grinned wickedly.

Trumble and three of his men led them at a fast pace toward the south gate. The streets were dark and deserted except for some indifferent citizens. Willow heard a skirmish at the north end, and turned to see dim lights peppering the darkness. Ruby's ears pricked nervously, and Willow slid a calming hand along her smooth neck. She hoped the knights weren't actually hurting anybody, just scaring them away.

The riding party approached the narrow edifice of the south gate. Brand's horse brushed up against hers as they slowed to a stop beneath the gatehouse window. Two guards stuck their heads out and looked them over. Finally, one of them growled, "State your business," while the other one moved his spear into view.

Gemma drew back her hood so the guards could see her mouth, though not her whole face. "Tully?" she called out. "Tully Tupper? Is that you?"

The guard that had spoken to them tipped farther out the window. A ferocious-looking moustache hung below his chin and twitched when he talked. "Who's that, calling me name?"

"It's me, Tully. Gemma Fletcher."

The man peered down at Gemma. "Aldwin's daughter? From the pastry shop?"

"Aye." Gemma cupped her hand around her mouth. "How's your little boy doing? He like the pie I brought him?"

A bushy blond smile lit the guard's face. "Oh, aye," he yelled back. "The lad lit into it like a priest off a fast day. And the swelling's down to nothing now. Lad's as good as new." Tully paused. "Where're you off to, lass? You're not leaving Graffyn, now, are you?"

"Aye," said Gemma. "These are my mother's people. They've come to take me south with them. To Trahern, where my aunt lives."

"Well, we'll be sorry to see you leave, lass." He gestured to the other guard to open the gate, but the other guard was pulling on his arm. Willow could hear snatches of their conversation. "We can't ... but Lord Radnor said ... all right, all right ..." The heavy iron gate started to rise.

Trumble sidled his horse up to Brand's. "I'll be leaving you now, lad," he said in a low voice. He clapped his huge hand on Brand's shoulder and turned to Willow. "You've a fine knight here, Your Highness. If anyone can get you to Keldoran, it's Brand here." He turned back to Brand and shook his hand. "I envy you, lad. What I wouldn't give to be off on an adventure. Ah well. The missus made me promise." He smiled and tipped his head to both Willow and Malvin, then reined his horse around. "C'mon men! We've some knights to befuddle."

Willow smiled and waved at him. "Thanks," she called out. The gate was all the way up now, and Brand took the lead through the narrow passage. Once they were clear of the gate and drawbridge, Brand steered his horse around and trotted back to Gemma.

"We must now take our leave," he said. A tiny stream along the road trickled quietly, echoing Brand's solemnity. He took Gemma's hand and kissed her fingertips. "You have risked much for us, Milady. And for that, the entire kingdom of Gallandra will be eternally in your debt."

Gemma pulled her hand away gently. "I think there's been a bit of a misunderstanding," she said, smiling broadly. "I'm not going back to Graffyn. I'm coming with you!"

CHAPTER 12

*B*rand's warm smile disappeared and his mouth dropped. When he returned to his senses, he said, "Now look here. We are grateful for your help, but we can't take you with us. It's too dangerous. We –"

"No, you look," interrupted Gemma. "The princess needs someone to tend her, and I've made up my mind it's to be me."

Willow glanced from Malvin's surprised face to Brand's accusing one. "Don't look at me," she said. "I didn't tell her anything."

Gemma laughed. "Nobody needed to tell me. A halfwit could've figured it out. You said your name was Willow, right? Captain Quillondale just called you Your Highness, and you're gallivanting around the countryside with the White knight. And so, I just figured the rumors must be true. You're Princess Willow, aged by realm traveling." She folded her arms with stubborn determination.

Brand pursed his lips. "We've three days of hard riding still ahead. There are knights chasing us, knights hoping to turn us into chess pieces, and a faerie prince who may or may not kill us, depending on the mood he's in."

Ruby tossed her head and stamped the ground. "Ssh," soothed Willow, stroking the horse's mane and frowning at Brand, whose dismal scenarios were even starting to scare the animals.

Gemma, though, remained undeterred. She drew back her hood, exposing her bruised and scabbed face. "I've nothing to go back to," she said quietly. "So, if you don't mind, I'd rather be taking my chances with you. Besides, I know how to cook, I'm handy in a knife fight, I can use herbs for healing. And –" she smiled at Brand, "I can dab your powders on, so you don't look so much like a corpse."

The wind whipped up the leaves, swirling them into a wild dance. The horses snorted and milled nervously. Willow stared at Gemma's round, hopeful face. The other girl was waiting for her to say something. Willow opened her mouth to speak up, but Brand spoke before she could. "Keep up," he said, "and you can come." He whipped Dusk around and the horse galloped down the roadway.

Willow urged Ruby forward. An image of Gemma's awful beating flitted into her mind. She'd helped them escape and asked nothing in return – except friendship. Willow owed her some gratitude.

Tugging on Ruby's reins, Willow sidled close to Gemma. "Just wanted to let you know," she began, "that I'm ... I'm glad you came with us."

White teeth flashed in the dim light. "I'm happy to be with you as well. Been a long time, Your Highness, since I've been where I wanted to be."

A new thought struck Willow. "But what about your mom and dad? Aren't they going to be worried about you?"

Gemma seemed surprised. "Why, I'm an orphan, Your Highness. My ma died back when I was ten, and Da a few years ago, when a horse trampled him in the marketplace."

"Oh. I'm sorry." Willow felt a pang. Now that Nana was gone, she was like an orphan herself.

"Da died a hero, though. He saved two little boys from being run down on the street, and being a soldier and a guard, it's how he would've wanted it. The whole town came out to pay their respects. Even the mayor."

"Why did you stay with them? That baker and his wife? Couldn't you have found someone better?"

Gemma remained quiet for a moment. She poked gently at the bruises on her face. "I wish it'd been as easy as that," she finally said. "You see, after they died, I had nothing. Not a penny to my name. Da owed money to a local lender, and seeing as I was the last surviving member of my family, his debt fell to me. Mistress Swinton helped me out. She was kin to my ma, and said I could come and live with her and work off the debt till it was paid for." Gemma fell silent, her hands holding tightly to the reins. "He started beating me," she rasped, "soon as I moved in."

Willow's stomach clenched. "What about the police? Was there no one to help you?"

Gemma lifted her head and stared at Willow. "Don't you understand? Mistress Swinton paid off my debt. She owned me – like a purse or a new dress. It didn't matter what she or her husband did to me, I was their bought and paid for property. They could do with me what they liked. I did run away, though, once. Sheriff Tilford brought me back." She reined in her horse, opened her cloak, and pulled down the shoulder of her dress. An ugly black circle puckered the whiteness of her skin. "They branded me. And if they catch me this time – I lose a foot."

Willow flinched. It was unspeakably cruel. How could they treat people like that? And how was it that Gemma was so brave? She grabbed the end of Gemma's saddle horn. "No one will *ever* hurt you like that again. I can guarantee you that."

Gemma pressed her hand over Willow's, squeezing it and smiling her big, beaming smile. "Thank you, Highness. I'll be a good servant to you. Loyal and honest."

Servant! Willow shook her head. "No, you're my friend. I want you to be my friend."

Gemma stared at her. "Forgive me, Your Highness, but you're a princess, and I'm nothing but a peasant lass. It wouldn't be quite fitting now, would it?"

"Well, I'll make you a lady then." Why not? If a king could dub a knight, why couldn't a princess dub a lady? Willow placed a hand on Gemma's shoulder. "Gemma Fletcher of Graffyn, for bravery and daring beyond the call of duty, I now dub thee Lady Gemma." She dropped her arm back to her side. "There, now we can be friends."

"I – I," stammered Gemma, "I don't know what I should say."

"Say yes."

"Yes, please do," said a mocking voice.

Willow and Gemma spun around to see Brand eyeing them skeptically. "If you two *ladies* are finished with your heart-to-heart, we'll be on our way." He flicked Dusk around and trotted away from them. Willow stuck her tongue out at him and Gemma snorted in response. *Yup*, Willow said to herself. *She and Gemma would get along just fine.*

After riding for two hours through thick pine trees and near blackness, Willow found herself huddled under a fur blanket, staring at star patterns in the inky sky. According to Malvin's last globe check, the Black rook, Lord Garnock of Grisselwait, was patroling this area with a company of twenty knights. He was the one who had captured both her father and grandmother. Willow's heart fluttered, imagining the Black rook skewering her like a juicy shish kebab.

Brand coughed into a gloved fist, his chain mail clinking

as he repositioned himself against the wide tree trunk. He was keeping watch as usual. Willow crawled toward him.

He tilted his head, squinting at her in the dark. "You should be asleep."

"I know." Willow wrapped her blanket tight around her. "But I can't stop thinking about the Game."

Brand nodded and settled against the tree trunk. Willow took a deep breath, gathering her courage. "Have you ever captured anyone? Do you actually have to *kill* them to do it?"

Brand didn't answer for a full minute. He fingered the blade of his sword, and the light of his red glow flickered eerily across the metal. Finally, he heaved a tired sigh. "I was there when your father and grandmother were captured."

"You mean ... you mean, you saw it happen?"

"Yes." A pained look came into Brand's eyes. "We were on our way to Keldoran with news of Princess Diantha's capture. Lord Garnock found us – in Thorburn Wood. He pretended to be our ally at first, then he ambushed us when we were not expecting it." Brand's jaw tightened. "He captured the prince first. Told him that King Tarrant wanted the queen to know what it felt like to lose a child."

Bile rose in Willow's throat. King Tarrant was her grandfather. How would she face him now, knowing how cruel he had been?

"They dragged Prince Alaric from his horse," Brand continued, "and tied him to a tree. With his sword, Lord

Garnock drew a thin cut on the prince's neck. That was all it took, a tiny cut, little more than a pinprick, and Prince Alaric was changed into a chess piece. Your grandmother he cut on the cheek."

"So, he didn't actually kill them?"

Brand shook his head. "No. He only drew first blood."

Willow exhaled slowly. "So what if someone who *isn't* part of the game cuts me? What happens?"

"Well, from what we have learned, drawing first blood only works if it's done by a player on the other team. If another does it, Malvin or Gemma for instance, nothing happens. You would still be in the Game."

"And if the cut's more than just a cut? What then?"

"Well, you *can* die. The Game doesn't make us invincible. But if you are killed, and it's not by another player, then the Game will find a replacement."

"A replacement?"

"Yes. A player who has been killed by chance has his place taken by another who isn't part of the Game. Nurse Beryl was a pawn before she died. And after her death, one of the blacksmith's sons woke up with the pawn glow."

Willow considered this new twist on the rules. It meant that she might have to defend herself. Might even have to hurt someone. Her hand strayed down to the knife hidden in her boot. Reality washed over her. This *wasn't* a game. It was deadly real.

Brand must have seen the anxiety in her eyes. He set aside his sword and pulled her under the heavy wool of his furred cloak. His arms encircled her protectively, and she lay there, warm and comforted, until another thought began to niggle at her.

"Brand," she whispered, "you're part of the Game. Why didn't Lord Garnock capture you too?" But Brand didn't answer. He was fast asleep.

CHAPTER 13

Willow gasped awake. She'd had the same nightmare about the eyes – except this time she'd seen a reflection in them. Not her own, but someone else's. Someone with ivory skin and long, silvery hair.

Chilled by the thought, Willow snuggled against a warm, bumpy lump that suddenly groaned and shifted beneath her. She froze. Brand's red-glowing face grinned sleepily down at her. "Sleep well?" he asked, shaking out the chain-mailed arm that had pillowed her head.

Willow jerked away from him, cheeks flaming. "Um," she faltered, searching for something that would relieve the awkwardness, "your um ... your powder's all off."

"Aye," he said, pointing at her own bright face, "yours is off too. We had best get Gemma to redo us." Unlike last time, he seemed at ease with their cozy contact. Maybe fully clothed and not in a bed together made it a little less shocking for him. He jumped to his feet and strode over to the horses, searching his saddlebag for the powder.

Willow stood up too and began folding her blanket. She

cast a furtive glance around their small clearing to see if anyone had noticed her and Brand sleeping together. Malvin was studying the image globe and Gemma was setting out bread and cheese for breakfast. Neither seemed the least bit interested in how she'd spent the night. Willow brushed twigs and dirt off her cloak, the burning sensation in her cheeks starting to subside.

A cry from Malvin made her twist in his direction. The young mage was hurriedly returning the image globe to its leather bag. "Mount up! Mount up! Garnock is upon us!"

Before anyone could respond, the sound of a horn blasted through the woods. Seconds later, armored men burst from the forest and into the clearing, surrounding them.

One of the men rode forward. Willow quailed. Beneath his plumed helmet, the man blazed blue.

"Well, well," he growled, "what do we have here? Not the White knight again?" His fierce eyes raked over the clearing, noting the pearly glow of Willow's skin. "And a young pawn to boot." Gravelly laughter rumbled up from his throat. "Thinking of sneaking your pawn to the back ranks, were you, boy?"

Brand didn't answer. He scanned the circle of knights, looking, Willow thought, for a way to escape.

A second man rode forward – he looked like a medieval Liberace, all curled hair and fancy beribboned clothing. "*Varian!*" Brand snarled at the flamboyantly dressed man. He looked from one man to the other, putting two and two together. "So, you're the traitor!"

"Squire Lackwulf, you would find it best to address me as *Prince* Varian," the man retorted. "And, yes, Lord Garnock and I do have a suitable arrangement in place." He laughed and cocked his head toward the blue-glowing man. "The boy doesn't learn his lessons very well, eh, Garnock? Looks as if you'll have to teach him again."

Willow squinted at Prince Varian, the name suddenly ringing a bell. Wasn't her great-uncle named Prince Varian? The one she was supposed to have met up with in Thorburn Wood?

A metallic hiss answered Varian's veiled threat. Willow turned to see Brand pull out his sword. Her heart began to hammer. But then something else caught her eye. Something that made fear rise in her throat. Varian was gazing at her, his eyes as cold as winter. And that's when she saw the signal, the almost imperceptible nod of his head.

A savage cry cut the air, and a young man plowed forward, aiming a crossbow at Willow. "For Wren and Keldoran," he shouted, firing the arrow.

All Willow saw was the Black player's face. The clear white of his pawn glow. The anguish in his eyes.

"*No!*" Brand roared. Something pushed into her, knocking her to the ground. Horse hooves stomped dangerously close to her head. "Shoot the girl! Shoot the girl!" Varian kept shouting, while Malvin yelled, "No, it's Princess Willow!

It's Princess Willow!"

Finally, she raised her head. Brand was beside her, a crossbow bolt sticking out of his shoulder. "My fault," he said weakly. "Should've told you the truth. I'm sorry." He began gasping for breath. Willow, terrified, grabbed at his flailing hands, trying to calm him. Trying to keep him from striking at the crossbow bolt. But his hands had turned to stone and began to shrink.

Willow rubbed her eyes. But he was still there, his tiny bewildered head poking up through the grass. She reached out for him, her heart beating painfully in her chest. He was dressed in armor, holding a shield in one hand and a sword in the other, sitting on top of a horse. The crossbow bolt had disappeared, leaving him tiny and perfect.

Gemma squeezed her shoulders. "You're not past harm yet," she whispered, pulling Willow to her feet. "Look." She pointed to where Varian and Malvin were standing with Lord Garnock, arguing over her identity.

"I swear it's true!" cried Malvin. "That girl is Princess Willow."

Varian shook his head. "The boy is addled, Garnock. The infant princess is dead. I saw her body with my own eyes. *This girl*," he sent a mocking look Willow's way, "is but a stray peasant that the Game chose in her place."

Willow raised her chin and fanned her dusty cape over her sleep-rumpled tunic front. Gemma grabbed on to her arm.

"Don't do anything," she advised, brandishing her knife. "They'll have to come through me first, before they can get to you."

Willow held Brand out to her. "He saved me," she said brokenly. She kept her gaze on the creamy chess piece, avoiding Gemma's sad eyes.

"Arrest him!" Varian ordered suddenly. Two men moved in and grabbed Malvin.

"No!" yelled Malvin. "I speak the truth!"

Varian snorted. "The boy's making sport of us. Come now and let's finish this business." He gave Lord Garnock's shoulder a friendly clap and attempted to turn him away from Malvin.

"No, wait," Malvin insisted. "I have proof!"

"That's enough," Varian hissed. "Speak another word and it will be your last." Ten crossbows were instantly at the ready, pointing at Malvin's heart.

"Here, now!" bellowed Lord Garnock, brushing off Varian's arm. "I'm in charge here." He clanked over to Malvin and glared down at him. "Well, boy, this proof of yours had best be good."

Malvin swallowed hard. "Sh-show him the gift."

As Willow pulled out the pendant, heat tingled against her fingers, then seared her skin. She jerked her hand away, staring down at her now brightly lit swan.

"By thunder," cried Lord Garnock. He strode over to Willow and cupped her chin. "Is it truly you, then? The princess?"

"Great gods, Garnock!" burst out Varian. "The girl is near full grown! How could she be Princess Willow?"

"Begging your pardon, Milords." Gemma squeezed in beside Willow and did a quick curtsy for Garnock. "But I think I can answer your question. Her Highness was realm-aged and has only just returned to Mistolear a few days ago."

Willow collected her wits, giving Gemma a grateful smile. "I'm trying to stop the war, because, as you can see, I'm not dead."

"She lies!" Varian pushed Garnock aside and grabbed for Willow's pendant. "See, I ... *ahhh!*" He pulled his hand away, clutching it as if it'd been burned.

"Oh, someone's been lying." Garnock drew his sword from its scabbard and pointed it at Varian. "And I'd say I've got the knave right here." He pressed his sword tip to Varian's throat. "Thought we'd do all your dirty work, eh? Start a war. Eliminate the heirs. Checkmate the king. You had the scheme planned from the beginning!"

Varian's men rattled their weapons, but they were out-bladed by at least three swords to one. A small line of blood bloomed at Varian's throat.

"Come now, Garnock." Varian tried to back away from him. "There's no reason for this. Our plans have not changed."

Garnock followed him, keeping the sword tip firm against his jugular. "How so? To me it would appear that everything has changed." Another line of blood sprouted on Varian's neck.

"Don't you understand? Tarrant won't forget about Diantha's capture – whether *that girl* is the princess or not." Varian dabbed a leather glove to his throat and smiled. "So you see, my services are still very much required."

Garnock snorted, shaking his head. "By the gods, man, you've more shameless, boldfaced gall in you than a swaggering peacock!" The sword tip fell away from Varian's smug face and plunged back into its well-oiled scabbard. "I'll not kill you today. But if our paths meet again ..." His voice trailed off meaningfully.

"Release the boy," Garnock ordered, turning to Malvin. "I think he speaks true."

"Wh-what are you doing!" sputtered Varian. "You cannot mean to disavow me now! After all that I have done for you. After *all* that I have done for Keldoran!"

Garnock stroked the ends of his grizzled beard and scowled at Varian. "Enough talk. Take your men *now*, Varian, and leave – before I change my mind."

Varian's murderous gaze raked over Willow, and his fingers hovered restlessly above the pommel of his sword. Willow stepped closer to Lord Garnock.

Varian smiled at her, his hateful look changing back to a pleasant one. Then he bowed in elegant defeat, his long curls cascading over his shoulders. "You win, Milord. I will withdraw." He signaled to his men and began to move out of the clearing.

Halfway across, he stopped. "That is, till our paths meet again." Willow couldn't tell whether his words were meant for her or Garnock, but the hairs on the nape of her neck stood up anyway.

Gemma asked the question that Willow had been thinking. "Why are you letting him leave? If it were up to me, I'd be arresting him."

Lord Garnock gave her a wry glance. "Arresting a prince is not a simple matter. He has lords and knights aplenty to go to war for him. Better, I say, to let the Gallandrians deal with their traitors. Besides, he has not harmed us Keldorians. King Tarrant wanted him to deliver players and ... well, that is exactly what he was doing."

"What do you mean?" asked Willow, a bit bewildered by what had just happened. "You mean King Ulor's own brother has been helping him lose the game?"

"Aye. And helping himself as well," said Lord Garnock, frowning. "He wants King Ulor's crown and figured to gain it by using the Game against him. You see, when your mother, the princess Diantha, was captured, it was Varian that sent us word that King Ulor had given the order for it."

Malvin choked at this information. "It's not true. King Ulor would *never* do that!"

"Aye, I believe you, lad," said Lord Garnock. "I always had my doubts about Prince Varian. He gave us no good reason for

Princess Diantha's capture and was too quick in offering up the whereabouts of Prince Alaric and Queen Aleria."

"Then why capture them?" asked Willow, feeling even more confused. "Why not talk to them first?"

"I had my orders."

Willow couldn't help but remember what Brand had said – King Tarrant wanted Queen Aleria to suffer as he and Queen Morwenna had.

"You must understand," said Garnock, seeing the aversion on her face, "Princess Diantha was the sun and moon to King Tarrant. When Queen Morwenna told him their daughter's chess piece held no life force, he was filled with more grief then I've yet seen in a man. He could not see Varian's deception. He could only see his own pain."

Lord Garnock placed a hand on Willow's shoulder. "I tell you all this, Your Highness, so that you shall not judge your grandfather too harshly. He did what he did out of love for your mother, and for what he thought was a wrong done to her. When he hears the truth, though, he shall listen to reason. I can give you my word on that."

Willow still wasn't sure what the truth was. "Do you think then that it was Varian who captured my mother?"

"He isn't a part of the Game," said Lord Garnock, "so he couldn't have done it directly. My guess, though, is that he did have a hand in it. Which reminds me ..." he glanced to where his men were holding the young player who'd shot Brand, "I wonder what young Terrill Longbottom has to say about all this?" He marched over to the boy, ordering him to stand up straight. "Well, Squire Longbottom, I assume you have a reason for disobeying my orders. I should like to hear what it is."

The boy hung his head. "Yes, Milord," he whispered.

"What's that?" Lord Garnock barked. "Speak up, boy. I can't hear you."

"I said *yes, Milord*!"

"Good. Let's hear it, then."

Squire Longbottom raised his head and looked guiltily around him. "I – I talked to Prince Varian, Milord. And he said ... he said that girl there was the player that captured my brother, Wren. He said it was my duty as a brother, Milord, to capture her back."

Willow squinted at Squire Longbottom, surprised at his accusation. She'd forgotten that two pawns on the Black side had been captured by White. This boy's brother must have been one of them.

"So what you are saying, then," said Lord Garnock, "is that for your own personal affairs, you jeopardized the life of Princess Willow and disregarded my orders."

The boy's head hung back down again. "Yes, Milord. I'm sorry, Milord."

Lord Garnock sighed and waved his hand at Squire Longbottom. "I shall deal with you later. Now, mount up! We must get the princess to Keldoran and put a stop to this blasted war!"

Willow squeezed Brand's chess piece. She couldn't bring herself to look at him. The last time she had looked, his face still had that horrible, bewildered expression. She couldn't bear to see it again. She set him gently in her pocket.

"Just call me Alice," she mumbled, "for it's off I go to Wonderland."

CHAPTER 14

"Tell me the truth," ordered Willow, settling down beside Malvin. "What really happened between Brand and Prince Varian?"

She'd been thinking about that question all day. Even as the first winter snow came swirling down and the bitter wind made her eyes water and her lips chap, she'd clung to Brand's marble figure, wondering what he had meant by his last words.

Malvin blinked at her, surprised. He'd been staring into the fire and hadn't noticed her approach. It was late at night and all around them rugged Keldorian men slept beside their swords, their blanketed bodies looking like dozens of small, snow-fuzzed hills.

Willow waited as the cold air around her and Malvin filled with the silence of the falling snow. Malvin looked down at Brand's chess piece, clutched in her gloved hands.

"Brand revered your father," he whispered. "Listened to his every word."

Willow nodded, trying hard to imagine her father. Nana had always painted him as tall and handsome, the hero in a story. Hero-action Dad! That's how she'd thought of him. A half smile twitched across her lips. He and Brand had probably been a lot alike.

Malvin studied the chess piece. "When Queen Aleria decided to take the sad news of your mother's capture to Keldoran," he began, "King Ulor was against it. He knew King Tarrant's temper and didn't trust him to act with reason. The queen refused to listen. A message was too cold, she told him. It had to be done by a family member. She convinced Prince Alaric of this as well, and together with two regiments of King Ulor's knights they set off for Keldoran."

Willow tucked her legs close to her chest and rested chin to knees. The half smile twitched across her lips again. Her grandmother sounded an awful lot like Nana. Both big sticklers for doing the right thing.

"Brand, of course," continued Malvin, "was also required to go. As squire to the prince, he rode at his side." Malvin turned away. "If you could've seen him that day, you wouldn't have believed he could betray Prince Alaric. He would have died for him!"

Betray? Willow looked down at the chess figure. "What do you mean?" She said in a sharp voice. "How did Brand betray Prince Alaric – my father?"

Malvin stared back into the fire. "Brand was the only player who returned to Carrus that day. People didn't know what to think. A rumor spread that it was Brand who had captured Princess Diantha and who set up the capture of the queen and prince."

"*What?* Why would anyone think that?"

"It's a long story, but to begin it, I must tell you that Brand and your mother were scarcely speaking at the time. Brand believed the best strategy for the Game would be to queen each and every pawn, both Black and White. We could then use their combined powers against Nezeral."

"But that's a great idea!" burst out Willow. So great, in fact, she was surprised she hadn't thought of it herself. She did the math. Sixteen pawns plus two queens. Eighteen players with magical powers, instead of just two.

Malvin nodded. "I know. I thought it was a good strategy as well. But Princess Diantha didn't. She opposed Brand, saying that his plan held far too great a risk."

"Why?"

"All the pawns, except for the princess herself, were either ordinary folk like the blacksmith's son or older people like your nurse. They might have been hurt. And they would not have known how to use the power. Like your other grand-mother, Queen Morwenna, they might have caused more harm than good."

"Queen Morwenna caused harm?" No one had mentioned that to Willow before.

"Aye. Your Keldorian grandmother was not a mage before the Game and could not properly harness the magic of the queen." A grin inched across his face. "She caused a fair bit of havoc for near six months. She has improved much since then, however. Doesn't make her court ladies bald or turn them green anymore and doesn't cause hail storms in the summer. But still, to think of all those pawns unaccustomed to magic and all that power ..." Malvin shrugged. "Well, you see the dilemma."

"But what about my mother? You said all the pawns except her had no experience of magic." Then she thought of something else. Something she'd never even considered before. "And what about me? Do I have magical powers?"

Malvin stared down at his booted feet, clearly uncomfortable with the question. Finally he cleared his throat and spoke. "To answer your first question, yes, your mother was a mage before the Game spell. But when the Game first started, she married Prince Alaric and very soon was pregnant with you. She didn't want to be queened because she didn't know for certain what would happen to either her or to you, her unborn child." His eyes fastened back to his boots. "No one has yet attempted the queening move," he admitted. "We are learning the intricacies of the Game as we go along."

Willow took a moment to digest this new information. They wanted to queen *her*, didn't they? Did that mean she would be used as their guinea pig?

"And as to your second question," added Malvin, "I don't know. Your mother and paternal grandmother have power. So you might have inherited it as well. But then again, you might not have. It's hard to say."

Willow shook her head. "Okay, so let's get back to Brand. Who started the rumor about Brand's betrayal?" As soon as the words left her mouth, though, she knew the answer. *Varian.*

Malvin flung a stick into the fire, scowling as flames ate at its curling bark. "I was never certain until this very day," he spat out. "But now it all makes sense."

Varian's cold eyes surfaced in Willow's thoughts, right alongside Brand's earnest glare and deep dimples. How could anyone distrust Brand with someone like Varian around?

"At least we know the truth now," said Malvin. "Varian must have bribed one of our White players to capture Princess Diantha. He told King Tarrant that White captured the princess, and then told the king where he could capture Prince Alaric and Queen Aleria. Then he started the rumors about Brand – all in a bid to win himself the crown." Malvin paused, a new idea dawning on his face. "And that man we saw – Lord Radnor – creating unrest in the marketplace yesterday. He's one of Prince Varian's men and must be part of his scheme."

Something clicked in Willow's head. The "truth" that Brand had wanted her to know was that he had never betrayed her father. In fact this whole get-her-to-Keldoran mission was not just a way to protect the king, but also a way for Brand to prove to everyone that he wasn't a traitor. "Brand was helping me, wasn't he, so people would see that those rumors weren't true?"

Malvin nodded in agreement. "He did it for your father too, because he thought he owed him something."

Willow stared down at Brand's glowing white face. She understood him now. Understood why he'd been so touchy in the beginning. He had seen her hesitate to believe in him – like everyone else.

"I'm sorry," she said over the lump in her throat. "You know, about not believing in him." She glanced shyly at Malvin. "Did he ... say anything about it? About me?"

Malvin didn't answer. The thick quiet of the snowy night crept into his silence, prompting Willow to look up. She found him smiling at her, a glint in his eye.

"You are fond of him, aren't you?"

A hot blush raced over Willow's cheeks. "No, I ..." The words hung in the air. She didn't finish them, because she knew they weren't true. She'd been thinking about Brand all day – and *not* just about what truth he'd wanted her to know. She'd been grieving for him. Worrying if they'd ever find a way to set him free.

"It's nothing to be embarrassed at." Malvin looked down at his feet, sparing her the huge grin on his face. "I asked him the same question about you."

The hood around Willow's head suddenly felt suffocating. She brushed at the fur, making an effort to appear cool and calm.

"He said that you were the bravest, most bad-tempered,

and stubborn girl he had ever met, but that when you smiled, you made his knees go weak."

Willow laughed nervously. "That's a *good* thing, right?" She snuggled closer to Malvin and held Brand up between them. "Brand told me that when Lord Garnock captured my father and grandmother, he only pricked them with a knife. And Brand was only wounded in the arm. None of them were actually killed. So you know what I think? I think he's alive in there. And that he can hear us."

Malvin studied Brand's small figure. "It's possible. Perhaps there's some other reason why the queen saw no life force in your mother's pawn piece." He pitched a few twigs into the fire and nodded at Willow. "Maybe they can be rescued. It will be something to ask Queen Morwenna and something to hope for."

Willow rested her cheek on her knee, close to Brand. She tried sending him telepathic messages. *You are alive in there, I know you are. Just hold on a little while longer, and I promise I'll get you out.* She felt Malvin's arm slip around her shoulders and her eyes began to drift shut.

Brand stirred. Someone was talking to him. Willow's soft voice whispered in his ear. *I'll get you out*, the voice promised. *Just hold on a little while longer.* Then the voice was gone and a terrifying blackness surrounded him.

He tried to feel for walls or a floor, but all he felt was empty air. Was he hanging from a rope? How could there be no floor? There had to be a floor!

Suddenly he remembered. The crossbow bolt. The boy who'd tried to kill Willow. He tried to find his shoulder, but there was nothing there. No bolt. No pain. *No shoulder!*

Brand twisted and turned, trying to feel something. *Anything* that would prove he was still alive. A terrible realization set in. He'd been captured. He was inside a chess piece. That was why he had no body. That was why he couldn't see anything.

He strained to hear Willow's voice again, but the silence around him was just as profound as the darkness.

"Willow!" he called out. *"Willow!"* The name echoed around him. How, he didn't know. He called her name again, hoping that if he had heard her, that she in turn would be able to hear him.

But there was no answer.

CHAPTER 15

Willow blinked rapidly, still adjusting to the brightness now that they were out of the forest. After their second day of riding, the snow had finally stopped and now both the sky and landscape sparkled white. She watched the setting sun as it dipped behind a range of snow-capped mountains. Pink and gold deepened to brilliant scarlet, painting the jagged peaks into a toothy red smile. Weird, but kind of beautiful at the same time.

A storybook castle stood at the foot of the mountains, but above the city. Willow stared in awe. Even in the shadow of the great mountains, she could see that the Keldorian castle, with its hulking walls and towers that rose a hundred feet, was immense.

"Crumbcakes! What a view!" Gemma whistled under her breath. "Who would've thought a city could look so grand?"

Willow agreed, smiling. She noticed that Gemma's bruises were beginning to heal. They were only a dull yellowy brown now.

Brand's warhorse, Dusk, whinnied and head-butted

Malvin impatiently. Since Brand's abrupt change into marble, his big charger had become mule-stubborn and as skittish as a colt, calming down only when Malvin's little brown mare was near. Which meant poor Malvin was stuck leading him.

"Dusk! Stop it!" Malvin gave Dusk a firm stare, then moved in closer. "Aye, it's a grand city. Almost as big as Carrus."

"Ah, Your Highness, look," said Lord Garnock, pointing down at the castle. "The banners are flying. His Majesty must have received my dispatches."

Willow stared at the blue and gold pennants that whipped and waved from each tall tower. She'd been in shock when she'd met her first grandfather. Nothing had seemed real to her then. But now it was different. Excitement tingled through her like a live current. This was real. Very real!

A gloved hand patted Willow's arm. "Come then," said a smiling Lord Garnock, "your family awaits you."

A procession of guards carrying bright banners met them at the city gates and led them through the main thoroughfare. Willow barely noticed the crowded buildings and gawking crowds. All she could think about was meeting her grandparents.

"Are you nervous?" asked Gemma, excitement trembling in her voice. "Because I swear if you're not, I'm nervous enough for both of us." Her blue eyes widened. "To think, *me*, Gemma Fletcher, is going to see the inside of a castle. Why, it's enough to make me pinch myself to see if I'm really awake!"

Willow laughed. She'd gone way past pinching. It was the reality/acceptance stage that was the real kicker. She leaned over to Gemma. "That's nothing. Try meeting a family you never knew existed. Now *that's* what I call nerve-wracking!"

Gemma's eyes goggled in mock horror. "Cripes! Your Highness, you must be near to fainting!" She leaned over and reached into her saddlebag. "Here." She handed. Willow a leather flask. "Drink this. It'll give you courage."

A spicy apple smell wafted from the small container. Willow tipped it up and took a sip. It tasted kind of good. Like a cross between cider and Trumble's mage-brewed ale. She took a bigger drink. "Hey, this isn't bad. Where did you get it?"

"A soldier gave it to me. He said it came right from your grandmother's apple orchard and that she mage-brewed it herself."

Willow took another big swallow and handed the flask back to Gemma. *Her grandmother.* The words sounded strange and familiar at the same time. They stabbed her with pain, making her eyes burn. "You know, I had another grandmother ..." Willow looked straight ahead. She hadn't meant to tell Gemma about Nana.

Gemma waited for her to go on.

"I just miss her is all."

After a minute of silence, Gemma asked, "Was she the one who looked after you in Earthworld?"

Willow nodded and lowered her chin.

"I'm sorry. I know what it's like to lose someone. Me da and I were pretty close. I thought I would never get over the missing of him." She paused for a moment then leaned over and added in a whisper, "You know, I talk to him sometimes. When I'm feeling lonely, I pretend he's watching over me. Helps me not to miss him so much."

"Really? That helps?"

"Oh aye. And next thing you do is pretend they answer back."

A hesitant smile came over Willow's face. "Thanks. Maybe I'll give it a try." She turned from Gemma and stared at the high gray walls of the Keldorian castle that were coming into view at the end of the street.

Well, Nana, she said inside her head, *we're here. We finally made it, and I'm going to meet the rest of my family.* Willow blinked. As soon as she thought the words, Nana appeared next to her, riding a sturdy white mare.

I'm proud of you, dear, Nana said. *To find your courage is no small feat.*

Willow eyes prickled. *But I haven't really,* she told her grandmother. *I'm scared all the time.*

Nana smiled and touched Willow's cheek. *But you go on anyway, right? And isn't that what courage is about?*

A trumpet blast echoed over the street. Startled, Willow looked up and saw six long horns draped with blue and gold ribbons overhanging the castle gatehouse. The wooden drawbridge was lowered and as their horses clattered across, the trumpeters released another deafening blast.

She stared into the murky moat water, trying to collect herself. What had happened there? That was more than just a fantasy. She'd *seen* Nana. Felt her touch!

The water moved at a sluggish pace and its fungus smell permeated the air. Willow looked away, peering at the sharp tips of the gatehouse portcullis. She was in Black's back rank now. Maybe that had somehow affected her.

The gatehouse tunnel ended and Willow entered an empty snow-covered courtyard that faced the four front towers of the castle. She pulled on her reins, stopping to consider Nana's words. Her fate waited for her on the other side of the narrow opening. Did she truly have the courage to go through there?

Malvin sidled up next to her. "I wish Brand were here. It would have eased him greatly to know you've arrived safe and sound."

"Yeah." A hard-squeezing lump made it impossible to say more. Willow slid her hand into her pocket and hugged Brand with her fingers.

Nana was right. Courage was about being afraid, but going on anyway. She flicked her reins, moving her horse toward the inner portcullis.

Retainers of the royal family separated Willow from Gemma, Malvin, and Lord Garnock's men. They led her horse behind an honor guard of six men. In the middle of the courtyard, the guard split into two lines, forming a path through which she could ride. More trumpets blared and Lord Garnock appeared at her side. He led her toward a line of spectators, bundled in rich fur clocks, straining against one another to catch a glimpse of her.

Willow's heart thumped against her chest as she rode, painfully aware of how she must look. She'd tried to do something with her hair. But without a brush, could only manage a bushy ponytail. She pulled her cloak forward, trying to hide her torn pants.

Lord Garnock stopped and dismounted, bowing to the crowd. Willow scanned their faces. No, she thought. He wasn't bowing to the crowd, but bowing to *them*, the two people wearing gold crowns.

A hand touched Willow's wrist. Lord Garnock was waiting to help her dismount. She slid her leg over, letting herself fall into his arms and onto the ground. He took her hand and held it high, as if he were going to walk her down a wedding aisle.

"Your Majesties," he proclaimed, "I present to you your granddaughter, the princess Willow." He bowed again and moved aside, leaving Willow to face the King and Queen all by herself.

No one budged or tried to speak. They were all staring at her, entranced. Finally, a small regal woman glowing as golden as the sun – her grandmother, Willow reminded herself – broke away from the others and ran forward. She flung her arms around Willow and squeezed her tight.

Willow stared down at the sparkling blue sapphires and blood-red rubies that decorated the crown on her grandmother's head. Oh God, she was like a giant next to her.

The queen broke the embrace first and looked up at Willow, grasping her arms firmly. "Welcome, my dear. Welcome home."

"Th-thank you." Willow couldn't get any more words out.

Another arm wrapped around her, and this time her face was pressed into a broad shoulder. "You are safe now. And home, where you belong."

The proprietary way the king said that – *where you belong* – made Willow a bit uneasy. King Tarrant stepped back and gripped her arms as the queen had done. "Look at her. It's plain to see the Somerell blood."

Willow didn't know what he meant at first, but as she stared past his purple Game glow, it soon became clear. Brown eyes, pale skin, and thick hair a deep shade of auburn – she and her grandfather had the exact same coloring.

"Well, now that we have done with the introductions," he said, folding her into a shoulder hug, "let's get you out of this cold. It would seem, from what Garnock has written, that a warm hearth and a hearty meal would do you some good."

"Now my lord," interrupted the queen, claiming Willow's

left arm, "she needs a bit of time to herself first." They began leading her toward one of the towers. The crowds followed in their wake, a long train of quietly swishing cloaks and dresses. "There are new clothes and a nice hot bath awaiting you. Then ..." the queen smiled brightly and squeezed Willow's hand, "we've planned a lovely feast, all in your honor."

"Aye," agreed King Tarrant. "Cook tells me he's even managed to snare a peacock or two. A rare delicacy in these parts."

Willow smiled, basking in their warm, excited chatter. It felt good to have someone else in control again. She ignored the twinge of anxiety she felt. Tonight, she was going to be happy. Forget the Game for one night and just enjoy being part of a family.

Inside the castle, Willow's newfound grandfather gave her another quick hug and set off, saying he needed to take care of some matters with Lord Garnock. Queen Morwenna shooed away the courtiers and led Willow to the room she would be staying in.

A wooden tub filled to the brim with hot, sweet-smelling water sat in front of a blazing fire. Willow flushed with embarrassment when her grandmother and three servants began to strip off her clothes. But then she gave in and relaxed, letting the older ladies natter and fuss over her. They soaped and washed and oiled her, until she came out gleaming like a seal. They slipped her into a royal blue dress with gold silk edging the neckline and sleeves.

"You're a vision," sighed the queen. "Like seeing my Diantha again."

Willow stared down at herself, aware of a breeze. The dress was pretty, but it fell well above her ankles. She stretched out her arms, noticing the sleeves and waist were also too short and the bust had more space to fill then she could manage.

One of the ladies tried to fit some blue slippers on her feet, but only got as far as the toes before giving up.

"I could wear my boots, maybe," offered Willow.

Her grandmother laughed, a high tinkly sound that made her seem like a young girl. Willow looked at her, wondering for the first time how old she was. Beneath her golden queen-glow, she had long honey blond hair, smile-lined eyes, and an impish dimple in the corner of her mouth. Maybe mid-thirties or early forties. Definitely a weird age to be calling someone Grandma.

"Oh, no, no," said the queen. "I knew the dress would not fit. I was planning to alter it." She placed her hands on Willow's waist. "This won't take but a minute."

Willow's jaw dropped as Queen Morwenna's dainty hands slid down to her hips, the too-short fabric sliding and stretching under her fingers.

"Now, lift here," she said, raising Willow's arms. She touched her sides, and the fabric around Willow's chest magically shrunk to the proper proportions. Her sleeves were next, and then the hem length.

"Wow, that was amazing!" Willow patted her hips where the fabric now fit snugly. No tears. No loose threads. It was as if the dress had been made that way.

"Yes, it's quite startling the first time one sees true magic." Queen Morwenna brought the blue slippers back to Willow's feet. "Also quite startling," she added, her hands magically stretching them to fit, "the first time one performs it."

"What else can you do? Disappear? Turn me into a bird? Can you *fly*?"

"No, yes, and sort of," said Queen Morwenna, laughing. "I'm still just a beginner, you know. It takes years and years to really excel at it."

Willow picked up her swan pendant from the table where she'd set it before her bath. "My gift," she said, "you know about this, right?" Maybe the queen would understand how to use its magic.

Queen Morwenna's mouth tightened. "I never attended your christening. Never saw you as a babe. But yes, I did hear about the gift."

Willow flushed. She'd been so busy dealing with her own feelings about having a new family that she hadn't considered what *they* were dealing with. This poor woman had missed out on her only granddaughter's whole childhood. Had never seen her first steps or heard her first words. Everyone in her family had missed that.

Queen Morwenna pulled back Willow's hair and helped her fasten the necklace. "You know, your mother's hair was this red too, even as an infant."

After a few moments, she added, "I know what the pendant means."

Willow waited for her to continue, feeling bad that she'd ever brought it up. It obviously upset her grandmother.

"It means that you are the faerie queen's netherchild and will have to be queened. And that you will have to leave us to go into battle against Nezeral." She sighed and pulled Willow into her arms. "I don't want to think about that tonight. Let's pretend it doesn't exist. Just for this one evening."

She's so tiny, thought Willow as she hugged Queen Morwenna's small frame. She pushed away the many questions she still wanted to ask, determined to grant her grandmother's wish.

Willow looked down at Queen Morwenna. "Grandmother, there's something that I really have to know."

"What's that, dear?"

She didn't seem offended at being called an old-lady name, so Willow took her hand and began to walk toward the door. "What exactly does a roasted peacock taste like? And what do they do with all those feathers?"

Queen Morwenna's laughter pealed all the way down the hallway.

CHAPTER 16

Willow paused outside the doors to the feast hall. Her stomach was spiraling already. *Oh great, that's all I need – to be sick, clammy, and breathless in front of a bunch of strangers.* She smoothed her sweaty palms against her dress, trying to relax.

Queen Morwenna glanced at her, taking in her white face and nervous gestures. "Are you all right, my dear? You look a little shaky. Perhaps it's too soon for a party. Would you prefer to do this another night?"

"No, no. I'm always nervous when I meet new people. Don't worry. I'll be fine."

A round of merry laughter burst from the feast hall. Queen Morwenna poked her head through the open doorway. "No need to fear tonight, my dear. Come and see." She waved at Willow to look inside.

Willow hesitated, then peered around her grandmother into the feast hall.

"See," said Queen Morwenna. "They're festive and well into their cups. A good combination. It's only when they're quiet that you need fret."

Festive wasn't the word for them. Willow gaped in wonderment. *Magical*, maybe. Or *fantastical*. The explosive colors took her breath away. Blues and greens and the brightest scarlets, yellows and purples and browns, all in their truest, deepest shades. Her eyes raced over the crowd, taking in their silks and furs, their jewels and their elaborate hats.

Too much, she thought. *This is too much.*

The room was alive with her fantasies.

"Just imagine them all in their smallclothes. A trick your grandfather taught me."

Willow blinked down at Queen Morwenna. She wasn't sure, but she thought her grandmother had just told her to imagine the feast crowd in their underwear.

Queen Morwenna signaled to a man across the hallway and he blasted his trumpet. All eyes turned to the doorway. Willow felt her legs go wobbly.

"Her Majesty, Queen Morwenna," the man bellowed, "and the princess Willow."

Queen Morwenna waited in the entrance long enough for her husband to walk to the front of their table, then she hooked her arm through Willow's. She marched, dignified and confident, into the great feast hall.

Willow concentrated on her grandmother's slow, steady steps. When they reached the other side of the room, King Tarrant nodded to his wife and claimed Willow's hand. He led her up the steps of the dais where their table was placed and turned her around to face the crowd.

"Lords and Ladies of Keldoran," he said in his big, booming voice, "your king and queen welcome you." Cheers and clapping erupted from the assembled guests. "This eve," he continued, after they settled again, "brings us much to celebrate. Diantha's daughter, *my* granddaughter, is returned home to us. Thus our quarrel against Gallandra has been settled, as we now have reason to believe that King Ulor may *not* be responsible for our dear Diantha's capture." He paused as more cheers echoed throughout the room. "And now, I present to you the princess Willow!"

This time the applause was thunderous. People climbed to their feet, clapping and cheering. *The Gifted One!* some cried out. *Death to Nezeral!* others shouted.

Willow blanched at their enthusiasm. She'd forgotten that it wasn't just Brand she had to help. Two whole kingdoms were counting on her.

King Tarrant's hands swept up and instantly the audience quieted. "And now, let the feast begin!" Another cheer rose and people dropped back into their seats, resuming their gossip and merriment.

"You did well," said King Tarrant, patting Willow's shoulder. He steered her around the table to their seats. "Don't you think so, Morwenna? Did you see those courtiers? They haven't been this energetic since the last tourney."

"Yes, dear," agreed Queen Morwenna. They were seated in comfortable gold-cushioned chairs, with Willow nestled between them.

Willow looked around the room again, her eyes drawn to the dazzling décor. Bright blues, golds, and reds were everywhere – in tapestries and banners, tablecloths and carpets, all of which depicted in some way the boar's head and crossbow, the symbols used in her grandfather's coat of arms.

The other guests were seated at tables that spread out from the king's table in an enormous U-shape. She could see Malvin to her far left, but couldn't see Gemma anywhere. She scanned the room, wondering if Gemma had been too tired to come.

"It's quite a sight, isn't it?" King Tarrant leaned in close, engulfing Willow in beer-scented breath.

Willow leaned away as far as she could without being rude. "Incredible. Absolutely incredible." She looked up at the ceiling. It was covered with enormous vaulted beams that resembled the rib cage of some great beast. Iron chandeliers hung from them, dangling from long, thick chains and flickering with hundreds of dancing, smoking candles.

"What was your feast hall in Earthworld like?" boomed King Tarrant. He tipped back in his chair to look up too. "Was it as big as ours?"

Willow smirked. "Not quite. We just had a small dining room." She omitted the fact that by small, she meant the size-of-the-king's-closet small. "There were just the two of us. My nana and me."

King Tarrant's laughter echoed around the room. "You jest with me, Granddaughter!" He clapped her back so hard she spilled wine on her gown. "What about your servants and guards and cook?"

Willow didn't answer. She patted at the wet spot on her lap. Her grandfather, she realized, was a bit drunk and wasn't too likely to understand her frugal life on Earth.

An army of white-aproned servants marched into the room, carrying platters of food. First came the meat dishes. Roasted venison, grilled rabbit, chickens glazed in orange sauce, swans and peacocks resplendent in their redressed feathers, and even a boar's head made to look as if it breathed fire. Each sumptuous tray was paraded around the room and then brought to the king's table for inspection and the first cut.

Older servants placed soups, puddings, vegetables, breads, and sauces on every table. Servant boys posted along the walls poured wine and ale, while musicians, seated inconspicuously in a far corner, played slow, relaxing dinner ballads.

Willow had never seen anything like it, except maybe in a movie. Her grandmother said the cooks had learned how to prepare food without magic after they'd discovered a cache of ancient cookbooks.

But Willow's grandfather was making it difficult for her to enjoy the evening. She picked at her food, trying to ignore his increasingly intoxicated condition. Difficult to do, though, when he spilled salt on her meat and spit pieces of carrot at her. She gazed at Malvin, wishing she could sit with *him* instead.

Finally, after what seemed like an eternity, a troop of servants started to clear off their table. King Tarrant reached over to squeeze Willow's shoulder. "The nobles wish to meet you, my dear. We're setting up a receiving line."

For two hours, Willow stood uncomfortably between her grandparents, putting up with King Tarrant's loud voice and tight shoulder grasps, greeting so many Lords of This and Ladies of That that by the end of the receiving line she just smiled, thanked the person for coming, and didn't try to remember anyone's name. Finally, after the last guests had bowed and introduced themselves, King Tarrant ordered the dancing to begin.

Willow sank into her seat, wondering if, as the guest of honor, she would be allowed to leave. She looked around for her grandmother, but saw that she was busy talking to a group of ladies. King Tarrant caught Willow's eye. She glanced away. But it was too late. The king started toward her, dragging a young man behind him.

"This is my granddaughter," he bellowed, pushing the boy at her. "Dance with her!"

A blond head bowed over her hand. "Your Highness, may I have this dance?"

Wanting to get as far away from her grandfather as possible, Willow allowed the young man to lead her on to the dance floor. Once there, she pulled her hand away. "I'm sorry, but I don't know how to dance. Could you please just take me to the queen?"

The boy nodded. Instead of looking perturbed, he seemed to understand. "The king," he whispered, "doesn't usually drink this much. I think it's meeting you that has him in such a state."

Willow gave him a wan smile. It was good to know that her grandfather wasn't a drunkard, but that still didn't abate her present embarrassment. She let the boy guide her to the queen's table.

"Your Majesty," he said, bowing to Queen Morwenna and backing away.

The queen, her golden Game glow brilliant in the candle-light, acted the proud grandmother as she drew Willow into her circle of friends. "You see, ladies, it's as I told you: my granddaughter has my nose and chin."

"I'll wager she has your smile too," added a short woman in a feather hat.

Another woman, one with thin lips and narrow eyes, gave Willow's swan pendant a hard stare. "And when has Your Majesty planned the queening ceremony?"

Queen Morwenna's soft voice turned frosty. "Well, Countess, a decision hasn't yet been made. The princess, as you know, has only been in our world for a few days. She needs some time to recover her strength. I am sure you understand."

"Of course, Your Majesty," said the thin-lipped woman. She lowered her head in a deferential bow, eyes sparking with anger. "And I'm sure that *you* understand that my son, Wren, has been a captured pawn for over a week. And now Lord Garnock has put my other son, Terrill, in jail for trying to avenge him. The queening, I believe, should be sooner rather than later."

Some of the ladies in the circle gasped. Queen Morwenna's small stature seemed to increase as she lifted her chin. "I, too, have a captured pawn for a child. So I will forgive your impertinence." She turned to a green-gowned woman. "Lady Lyris, please escort Countess Longbottom to her chambers. I believe she requires a rest."

Countess Longbottom's lips thinned into an even finer line, but Willow didn't miss the tremble about her mouth. The woman was holding back tears. Lady Lyris and the Countess bowed and left the circle.

Willow stared after the two women. She realized Countess Longbottom must be the mother of Terrill Longbottom – the boy who'd captured Brand. Her sympathy for the woman flared into anger then simmered down again. It wasn't Countess Longbottom's fault – nor her son's fault – that Brand was now a chess piece. It was the stupid Game's fault. And the fault of the one who'd started the game in the first place – Nezeral.

The queen placed a hand on Willow's arm. "What is it, dear? Are you upset?"

Before Willow could answer, the music stopped and a voice thundered over the great hall. "Lords and ladies," King Tarrant bellowed, "I have another announcement to make." He searched the room until he found Willow. "Granddaughter, come up here."

Willow glanced at Queen Morwenna, who shrugged her shoulders uncertainly. "I don't know. He's had much too much to drink tonight, though."

"Come, come," said King Tarrant, waving Willow to the stage.

Queen Morwenna patted her arm. "Go on, it's probably nothing more than another speech to welcome you."

Willow had a bad feeling, but she began moving toward the platform. She *should* just ignore him. Turn around and walk right out the door. But Lord Garnock's words niggled at her. He'd said not to judge King Tarrant too harshly. That his grief had made him distraught.

A seed of pity began growing inside her. She thought of poor Countess Longbottom and her two sons, of King Tarrant and his daughter, of King Ulor and his son. Only four months had passed for them and they were still in the midst of their grieving. The least she could do is forgive King Tarrant a few too many drinks.

When she came up the dais stairs, the king took her hand. "I have come to a decision," he announced. "From this day forth there shall be no more Game playing!"

Willow stared. What did he mean by that? No more Game playing. A frightened whisper rose around the room and people crowded in closer to the dais to listen.

"That's right. No more Game playing. I have decreed that war with Gallandra is at an end. My granddaughter is returned to our arms. We must now move ahead and let go of our grief. That is what my dear daughter Diantha would have wanted. *Her* daughter won't be sacrificed on the same altar. We must accept what is. We shall learn to love our lives, such as they are, without magic." He motioned to a man who was holding a covered tray. The man stepped forward and pulled off the linen cloth, revealing a beautiful jeweled crown. Willow heard gasps as the crown was set on her head.

"As her mother, the princess Diantha, was before her, I now proclaim the princess Willow heir to the throne of Keldoran. And as such, she shall never be queened in this cursed Game. Never shall she be forced to do battle with the faerie prince, Nezeral."

"No!" Countess Longbottom, restrained by Lady Lyris, thrashed around like a wild animal. "You can't do this! You can't allow my son to perish like this!" She broke away from Lady Lyris and flew across the hall to Willow. Kneeling, she clutched Willow's gown. "I beg you, Your Highness, *you must save my son!*" Two burly guards appeared. Holding an elbow each, they hustled her out of the room.

On the platform, Willow stood frozen as the crowd began

to mutter more and more loudly. King Tarrant loomed beside her, silent, his face growing redder each second. Finally Queen Morwenna came to the stage and raised her arms. Something crackled from her fingertips and then there was silence. People's mouths still moved but no sound could be heard.

Willow felt in her pocket for Brand's chess piece. Fear trembled through her. How could she defeat Nezeral all by herself, anyway? She couldn't plan attacks or use a sword. She couldn't even survive by herself in the woods.

Fear leaped into panic. Still clutching Brand's chess piece, Willow raced down the stairway and through the now silent crowd. She knew the answer to her question. She had always known the answer.

She couldn't do it. She could never defeat Nezeral.

CHAPTER 17

*D*aylight streamed through the windows. Real windows this time, Willow noted. She lay pillow-propped on her canopied bed, considering her options.

Option number one: do what her grandfather wanted. Stay the way she was and spend the rest of her life in the castle.

She imagined the king and queen as doting grandparents. She'd get to wear pretty dresses, go to balls. Maybe learn to dance and sing and whatever else princesses did. And maybe Nezeral would just get bored and go back to wherever he came from.

It seemed like a sweet set-up and even a big relief.

Relief. That's exactly what she'd felt when King Tarrant had declared the Game over and made her his heir – once the shock had worn off, that is. And oh, how she wanted to let it happen. Just let her grandfather look after her and protect her.

"But I can't let him, can I?" she said to Brand. She held his valiant knight figure to the light, tracing over him with a finger. She knew she couldn't live with herself if she didn't at least *try* to save him. Him and who knew how many others?

Maybe even her own parents, her grandmother, *if* they were still alive inside those chunks of marble.

She'd spent the night arguing with herself. She didn't know how to use magic, she was scared to death of Nezeral, she had no idea how to find him, and most importantly, she didn't have a clue as to how she would defeat him. But she'd imagined Brand giving her encouragement, telling her she could do it, she *could* stop the Game spell and defeat Nezeral. She saw Brand's dark looks, his dimpled smiles. She saw him step, without hesitation, in front of the arrow meant for her. And she knew she had no choice. She had to save him. And the others. She just couldn't let them down.

"So, I guess that leaves option number two," she sighed, "make them queen me, and go find Nezeral."

Brand recognized Willow's voice. It sounded as if she were speaking right into his ear. He'd been calling out to her over and over again, but she didn't seem to hear him. She was promising to save him by queening herself and confronting Nezeral on her own.

Dread took hold of Brand. He'd never told Willow his true plan. Of how her powers, once she had them, were meant to aid *him*, not her, in getting past the barriers of the Game. She was supposed to be safe in Tulaan, while he defeated Nezeral and rescued *her*. At least, that's how he'd always pictured it.

He let himself drift into his hero fantasy, to the part where he returned to Gallandra after having defeated Nezeral and ended the Game spell. It always started with a parade through the city, with teeming crowds cheering him and Dusk all the way to the castle. The king and his father and all the great Gallandrian lords would be there in the courtyard to greet him, with smiles and honors, all rumors of treason banished from their eyes. And Willow ... she would be there also.

He saw her the way she'd looked that first day in Carrus, tall and fragile, hair unbound like a child's, her wide tawny eyes sparkling with fiery pride. Only, in the scene he had imagined, her eyes weren't angry. They were soft and filled with admiration.

Brand shook the images away. His foolish dreams of heroism had endangered her. Because of him, she would try to fight Nezeral on her own. He flinched inwardly at the thought. Nezeral, he knew, would destroy her. Would, in the end, destroy them all.

A light tap sounded on the door. "Willow? It's me, your grandmother. May I come in?"

Willow pushed back her coverlets and hid Brand's chess piece beneath her plump feather pillows. "Yeah, sure. C'mon in."

Queen Morwenna swished into the room. Instead of her crown, she wore a black hat studded with pearls. "Did you sleep well, dear?"

Willow shrugged. She swung her legs out of bed and sank her bare feet into a furry rug.

Queen Morwenna sat beside her, wringing the ruby necklace she was wearing. "I'm – I'm truly sorry for what happened last night. Tarrant is ... well, he is only doing what he thinks is best."

Willow nodded.

The queen grabbed her hand in a sudden death grip. "I want to show you something." She rose from the bed and pulled Willow up with her. "Would you please come with me?"

Queen Morwenna led Willow into the chilly hallway. The cold bit into Willow's bare feet, but they didn't go far, only to the room next door. Willow looked around the empty bedroom, wondering what her grandmother was so keen to show her. Then she saw it. Over the blazing fireplace hung the portrait of a woman who looked so much like Willow that they could have been sisters. The woman in the portrait wore the same blue dress that she had worn at the feast.

"Your grandfather loved Diantha very much." The queen put an arm around Willow's slack shoulders. "I think the sight of you in that dress last night was more than he could bear. He simply couldn't risk losing you too."

Willow moved to the fireplace to get a closer look. Her

mother had finer, more delicate features. But her eyes ...

Willow stared at the portrait. She knew those eyes. Those were her eyes.

"How old was she? When that portrait was made?"

"She was nineteen. It was just before her marriage to your father."

Yes, thought Willow. That made sense. She looked happy. Like a woman in love.

"Tarrant will have to change his decree eventually."

Willow faced her grandmother. "What do you mean?"

"Tarrant *must* change his mind about queening you sooner or later. He's being stubborn about it now, but I am sure he'll come to his senses soon."

A thin stab of disappointment went through Willow. Somehow, she liked having option number one to fall back on, in case she couldn't handle option number two.

"Well, come on, dear," said Queen Morwenna, slipping her arm around Willow again. "I have another dress for you to wear. And then after you have had a good breakfast, I'll show you around the castle."

Breakfast, due to the king's "ale-head," was a private, uncomfortable affair in the king and queen's chambers. The king avoided eye contact or any mention of the feast, and he was churlish the entire time. He barked at a servant for spilling water and frowned at his plate with distaste. Willow picked at her food and awkwardly answered his brusque inquiries concerning her sleep. After the servants cleared away the dishes, Queen Morwenna rushed Willow into the hallway.

"I fear a night of ale drinking turns him into a bear," she confided. "But once he has had a nap, he'll be right as rain. Till then we better stay clear of him."

Queen Morwenna took Willow on a tour of the castle. They walked down carpeted hallways, up twisting staircases, and into large sumptuous rooms. She showed her dark, somber paintings of her ancestors, rich tapestries embroidered with Keldorian history, and a library filled with shelf upon shelf of Mistolearian literature.

Willow held one of the heavy leather-bound books, staring at a map of Mistolear. In Nana's stories, she had heard only of the two countries of Keldoran and Gallandra. But there was more to Mistolear than that. There were continents and islands and mountains with exotic names such as Issander, Tuumagia, and Doomriel. There were oceans, lakes, rivers, deserts, forests – it was a world, Willow realized with surprise, much like Earth.

She carefully placed the book back on its shelf and gazed out a window at a distant line of snow-covered trees, vivid and stark against the blue horizon, wondering how far the Game spell spread.

Queen Morwenna followed her gaze, guessing at her thoughts. "That row of trees," she said, pointing eastward, "is one of the borders of the Game spell."

"Borders?"

"Yes, in the beginning, when we were still in the midst of trying to make sense of the Game, your grandfather and his knights set off for the east to see how far the spell extended. They could go no further than that tree line. There is a magical barrier, you see, that keeps us enclosed in the spell. It encompasses both Keldoran and Gallandra, but nothing beyond." The queen turned away from the window and sighed. "We have heard no news from the outside world for over a year now, so we must assume that the barrier, as well as keeping us in, keeps them out."

Willow knew the Game spell stretched over Keldoran and Gallandra, but she'd never heard anyone mention a barrier before. "Where *is* Nezeral? Is he inside the spell or outside it? And if he's outside it, how am I supposed to find him?" Brand's plan had only gone as far as her being queened. He'd never talked about what would happen next.

Queen Morwenna looked back to the window again, staring out at the distant horizon. "There is a castle, a hunting stop for Tarrant, that lies ten leagues beyond those trees. Nezeral, we believe, is there."

"But then that means he's on the other side of the spell. So what can I, or anyone else, do to stop him? Is there a way through the barrier or something?"

The queen looked uncomfortable. "No. We could find no way, magical or physical, to go beyond the barrier."

"Then how am I supposed to get through?" Willow threw her arms up in exasperation. The more she learned about this crazy Game, the less sense it made.

"Well, we don't really know. But you are the faerie queen's champion. So perhaps that will make a difference. Or –" Queen Morwenna's lips pursed shut.

"Or?"

"Or Nezeral will come for you as he threatened to do when you were born."

Willow froze, shocked at this terrifying new twist.

Queen Morwenna moved away from the window and ran shaky fingers over a chair back. "He swore the very moment you were queened he would ... he would destroy you."

Air caught in Willow's lungs. No wonder the plans never went beyond her queening. There *was* no beyond! "Does – does everyone know about this?"

Queen Morwenna nodded. "Cyrraena, the faerie queen, will protect you. She swore she wouldn't let him take you before you were ready." Her arm stole around Willow's shoulders. "I am sorry. I would do anything to take this burden from you. But ..."

"Why me?" Willow shrugged away from the queen's embrace. "Why did she pick me for the champion? I'm just a kid. I don't know anything about magic or faeries or *anything!*" Anger crashed through her like a tidal wave. *Who were these faerie people anyway, playing with her life as if she were a toy?!*

"I am sorry. I don't know the answer to your question. The ways of the fey are a mystery to us. You are her choice. That's all I know."

"Well, where is she? I mean, I know how Nezeral got here, but how did this Queen Cyrraena get here? How is she protecting me?"

"The faerie queen is Mistolear's guardian. She lives in her own realm of Timorell, which is a part of Mistolear and yet not a part. I have been told that there are faerie stories of Earthworld, where humans could enter the fey realms only through the will of the faerie folk. The same is true here. We can't see Timorell or Queen Cyrraena unless she wishes it."

"What is she then – like *God* or something?"

"No, not a god, but a being like us. I'm sorry," she said, her chin trembling, "that I can't be of more help to you. But as I just said, their ways are a mystery to us. She may help, or she may not. We can only wait and see. For now, though," she took Willow's hand, "my ladies await us in the solarium. It will do us both good, I think, to let these matters lie for a bit. It isn't every day, after all, I get to spend a whole morning with my granddaughter."

Willow wanted to throttle someone. Preferably a couple of mysterious faerie beings. But she let her grandmother lead her from the library and down another hallway. None of this was the queen's fault and Willow couldn't deny the poor woman one day with her granddaughter.

They passed by a table draped in black velvet and covered in white roses. Willow stopped to touch the soft petals. Their beauty helped dispel some of her anger. She bent over to smell them.

"They are for Diantha," Queen Morwenna said. "Tarrant would not allow any funeral ceremonies. He still hoped ... well, they are my reminder of her. I've kept them blooming since her capture."

Funeral ceremonies. Willow's hand fell from the rose, guilt stealing over her. The woman in the painting, her mother, had been captured and maybe killed only a few months ago. She imagined growing up with Diantha as her mother, feeling a daughter's grief. Her eyes grew hot. She couldn't imagine it. The woman in the painting was a stranger.

"I'm sorry," she whispered. "I shouldn't have ..."

Queen Morwenna shook her head. "Please don't be sorry. I should have sent them back to the greenhouse before your arrival. At any rate," she tried to brighten her smile, "my solarium is just around the corner. Come, we can listen to harp music and chat some more."

Listening to harp music was about the last thing Willow felt like doing, but the queen insisted, imprisoning her arm and leading her down the hallway to a large cheery room crowded with girls and ladies working on embroidery and practicing a slow, twirling dance. A musician sat among them with a golden harp, providing a steady flow of music.

The queen's entrance with her new granddaughter caused a flurry of curtsies. "Ladies, ladies," she said, "please carry on with your sewing and dancing." She signaled to the harpist to continue playing and led Willow over to two comfortable chairs by a sunny window.

Willow studied the fluid movements of the dancers. She'd watched them for a bit last night and had admired their gracefulness. With sunbeams catching their colorful gowns, the young women looked like bright jewels swirling around the room.

"Why don't you join them?" said Queen Morwenna, nodding at the dancers. "I shall call Lady Tavia over to give you a lesson."

"No, no. I'm afraid that when it comes to dancing, I'm too tall and I've got two left feet. Two *big* left feet."

"Nonsense! Your grandmother Aleria was at least an inch taller than you, had feet longer than a candlestick, and she danced beautifully. It just takes time, is all. And lots of practice."

Time and practice. Willow sighed. Two things she might never have. She looked down at her own gold-slippered size nines, wishing they were an un-clod-like size six.

"You know, dear," said Queen Morwenna, speaking low so that only Willow could hear her. "I could cast a dancing spell on you so that you would know the steps."

"Really? You can make me dance like that?" Willow looked at the laughing girls holding hands and dancing in a loose ring. They reminded her of Melissa and her posse of girls, so carefree and happy.

"Yeah," she admitted, "it'd be nice to dance like them."

The queen's hand gripped Willow's and sent a startling jolt through her.

"Then it's done. Your wish is granted."

CHAPTER 18

Willow tingled all over. She looked down at her feet. Still the same klutzy size nines as always.

"Go on, give it a try." Queen Morwenna clapped her hands, telling the dancers to stop and allow her granddaughter to join them.

The girl who was playing at being a boy giggled and bowed before Willow, offering her a hand. "May I have this dance?"

Willow hesitated, not wanting to make a fool of herself in front of all these people, but with the queen prodding at her back and the brown-haired girl clasping her hand, she rose to her feet and let the girl lead her to the dance circle.

Queen Morwenna clapped again and a lively harp song filled the room.

At first Willow felt nothing. Her feet moved beneath her gown like their usual leaden selves. But then the spell ignited. A surge of energy rushed down her legs and crammed into her toes, making them move of their own volition. And suddenly she was doing it. She was dancing!

Faces and kaleidoscopic colors flew by as she stepped in

giddy wonder to the music. She remembered how much she'd hated dances in school. All those horrible afternoons when she'd either cowered at the refreshment table or stayed in class pretending to do homework. She crossed hands with the brown-haired girl. If only she'd known that it could be like this. That it could be such *fun*!

The dance slowed. She completed a graceful turn and a new partner grabbed her. "You are an excellent dancer, Your Highness," the girl said.

Willow grinned and pirouetted. For the first time since she'd arrived here she felt like herself again. Like a regular teenager who didn't have to fear faerie princes or Game spells. No worries about multitudes of people depending on her. She was just a girl, having fun like other girls. A normal-ordinary-everyday girl.

When the music stopped an hour and a half later, Willow collapsed with the other girls, and all of them giggled and laughed as if they were old friends. It hit her then that she was a *princess*. That these girls respected and admired her. She gave them all a brilliant smile. "*That*," she panted, "was the best fun I've had in a long, long time. Thank you so much."

The girls nodded and curtsied. Queen Morwenna came up behind Willow, hugging her shoulders. "Lovely dancing, ladies. Just lovely. Now, we shall refresh ourselves with lunch."

The feast hall was again filled with courtiers and their families, only this time no one looked excited or happy. A dark cloud of gloom rested over them. Willow entered the room with the queen and her ladies. People stared and whispered, obviously still upset over the king's no-queening policy. Willow let her eyes find King Tarrant's. He sat tall in his chair on the raised dais, shooting daggered glances at his unhappy courtiers. No change of heart there.

"Why don't you sit with the younger ladies this time," said Queen Morwenna, who must have noted King Tarrant's sour demeanor. "It would help you to get to know them better. Tavia, dear, escort the princess to your table, please."

Lady Tavia bowed and led the way to a table to the left of and just below the dais. Willow sank into a chair, relieved that she wouldn't have to sit up high with her grandparents, the focus of everyone's dirty looks.

Servants brought in roast chicken, apple tarts, and leftover peacock doused with raisin sauce. Willow began to eat as Tavia made a round of introductions. The girls seemed unaware of the tension in the room and vied for her attention with questions about Earth.

"Is it true," asked one girl, "that your Earthworld is a material realm with *no* magic?" She said the last part as though Willow had grown up in some primitive caveman place. Willow chuckled at her. "It's not like what you think. We have things there that are almost as good as magic."

"Oh, I know what you speak of, Princess," interrupted another girl. "My uncle is a seer who has seen Earthworld in his visions and tells tales of horseless carriages and mechanisms that produce pictures and voices."

"Oh, Desma!" snorted Tavia. "Don't pester the princess with your uncle's ridiculous notions of Earthworld." She turned to Willow, sighing. "Please forgive Lady Desma, Your Highness. Her uncle grows senile and is beginning to spout nonsense."

"No, wait, she's right." Willow had put it together. "Horseless carriages are called cars. And we have lots of mechanisms – mostly televisions – that produce pictures and voices."

The girl named Desma smirked at Tavia and said, "See! I *told* you." This brought on a whole new flurry of Earth questions. The girls wanted to know about everything from food and clothing to boys and courting. Willow answered their questions as best she could, surprised to discover that she enjoyed being the center of attention.

After they'd finished eating, servants began clearing away the dishes. "Tavia," Desma whispered, nudging the other girl. "Is the chamberlain hiring actors again? See the new clearing wench. She looks like Big Bess from last winter's pageant."

Willow frowned, not having a clue what they were talking about. She glanced at the other table. Gemma, wearing a clean white apron, was stacking dishes on a tray. *Her* Gemma. Not some clearing wench. Willow tried to stand up to go to Gemma, but found herself glued to her chair. Magic prickled at her skin.

"Nay," Tavia scoffed, "the chamberlain isn't the one who found her. Tell us, Your Highness – where did you find such a porkling?"

"Why, I found her in a pastry shop, of course." The words spilled from Willow's mouth involuntarily. "Where else?" Her hands flew to her shocked lips. Why had she said such a horrible thing?

The girls all smiled knowingly and then a few of them said, "Ssh! She's coming!"

Willow fought to move, but something continued to hold her fast to the seat. Her eyes widened. Queen Morwenna, she suddenly remembered, was known for magic spells that backfired. *Crap!* Willow wriggled frantically in her chair. The spell that had made her dance like the other girls must also be making her talk like them.

Gemma reached a hand between Willow and Tavia and scooped up an empty plate. "Your Highness," exclaimed Gemma, "I'm that glad to see you! How've you been? You're looking very fine in your fancy new duds."

"Thank you, Gemma." The words somehow squeezed through Willow's gritted teeth. "I see castle life agrees with you too. You're also looking well." She winced. *God!* She sounded like a condescending creep. A few girls snickered and Gemma stepped back, her mouth quavering into an uncertain smile.

I'm sorry! I'm sorry! her mind screamed. *Please forgive me!* But what she said was, "I hope my family found you a job that suits you."

Gemma looked crestfallen. "Aye," she answered stiffly. "I work in the kitchens now." This answer brought on another wave of snickers. Gemma blinked back tears and made a terse curtsy. "Excuse me, Ma'am. I need to finish clearing the tables."

Willow flushed with shame. "Nn ..." she began, then stopped. She'd almost said, *No, don't go*. But she wasn't able to finish the words. Instead, she smiled and nodded. She felt like a robot. Gemma backed away and hurried out a side door.

"She seemed weepy," said Tavia. "Do you think perhaps she'd prefer working in the laundry? I could speak to the chamberlain for you."

Willow wasn't listening. She was using all her strength and every bit of willpower to move her legs. And it was beginning to work. Her foot had twitched. *I can do this!* One whole leg moved. Then the other. She was starting to stand. Starting to walk, then run, toward Gemma.

"Your Highness, where are you going?" called out Tavia.

Willow didn't answer. She ran from the room and down the hall through which Gemma had left.

A lone figure disappeared around a corner. "Wait!" Willow cried. "Gemma, wait! I didn't mean it!" She rounded the corner at a run, nearly smacking into Gemma, who was leaning against the wall, breathing heavily.

"Oh Gemma, I'm so sorry. I didn't mean it, honest. It was a spell!"

Gemma palmed away tears and kept her hurt eyes glued to the floor.

"Really, I'm so sorry," Willow pleaded. "Nothing I said out there was me. It was this spell my grandmother made. I think it had side effects. But, I really meant what I said before, Gemma. You're my friend, not my servant."

Rustling skirts swished along the hallway toward them. Willow turned to the sound just as her grandmother came hurrying around the corner.

"Willow, dear!" she cried, stopping short. "Whatever –" Queen Morwenna's words were cut off as Malvin plowed into her backside, nearly barreling her over.

Willow leaped to steady her, but her grandmother weighed more then she'd thought, and the two of them went tumbling down in a big velvet heap.

"Oh Your Majesty!" gasped Gemma. She and Malvin reached down to help Queen Morwenna to her feet. "Are you all right? You're not hurt, now, are you?"

Queen Morwenna patted her golden hair and smoothed out her skirts. "No ... I – I don't believe so." She frowned at Willow, who was still lying flat on the floor. "Whatever were you thinking, running from the room like that?"

A moan escaped from Willow's throat. A hand or a sharp knee had rammed into her stomach, knocking the wind out of her.

The queen understood in a flash. "You there," she

ordered, looking to Malvin, "help me get her up. She's hurt."

Malvin reached beneath Willow's arms and hauled her to her feet, holding her until she stopped swaying.

"I'm okay. Just have to ... catch my breath ... is all."

Queen Morwenna started her questions again. "You must tell me what happened. Did someone at court do or say anything to upset you?"

"No. Nothing like that." Willow stared at the worried faces of her friends, suddenly feeling like a total and absolute jerk. She'd been here for a day now and hadn't even introduced them to her family yet.

"Grandmother, I want you to meet my friends." She linked an arm through Malvin's and pushed him forward. "This is Malvin Weddellwynd from Gallandra. And this," she took Gemma's hand and pulled her over beside Malvin, "this is my best friend, Lady Gemma Fletcher. Without her and Malvin, I'd never even have made it here."

Gemma stared at her in astonishment then pinkened and smiled nervously.

"Pleased t-to meet you, Your Majesty."

"Likewise," said Malvin, bowing his head so low, he nearly bumped the queen again.

Queen Morwenna nodded back and graciously acknowledged Gemma and Malvin's greetings. Then she stared at Gemma's kitchen apron, a horrible realization dawning on her face. "Oh my dear child, my chamberlain's made you a servant, hasn't he? I am so terribly sorry! In all the excitement, I never thought ... We never meant ..."

Gemma gave the queen one of her big, full-faced smiles. "Your Majesty, begging your pardon, but you've got nothing to be sorry for. I've been in much worse spots then in your clean and tidy kitchens. It was scarcely a trial."

"Well, be that as it may, I shall endeavor to make it up to you." The queen untied the apron. She grasped Gemma's shoulders and slid her hands down the entire length of Gemma's body, changing the plain wool of her dress to glossy velvet.

Gemma trembled as she touched the fabric. "Your Majesty, this is ..." She trailed off.

The queen reached under Gemma's chin and gently lifted her head. She stared at Gemma's cuts and bruises for a moment, a frown pinching her lips. Then she reached out, tracing over each injury with a steady fingertip, erasing the yellowing bruises and the peeling scabs until Gemma's face was smooth and whole again.

Willow stared. Gemma was beautiful. She wondered why she'd never noticed the crystal blue of her eyes. Or her translucent skin.

"Now," said Queen Morwenna. She led them back toward the feast hall. "Willow, I would like to hear more about the heroic deeds of your young friends here."

CHAPTER 19

Willow frowned as she held Brand up in front of her. He was warmer to the touch now and his expression had changed. He seemed calmer. Last evening, Willow had found the courage to ask her grandmother to check Brand's chess piece for a life force. To Willow's relief, the queen proclaimed that he seemed conscious on some level – that she could see his energy aura shining clearly around the chess piece. Now Willow wondered if Brand had heard her.

She stretched her toes closer to the hearth fire and leaned back on the plush carpeting, staring up at her mother's portrait.

Willow had insisted that Gemma take her old room, and she took Princess Diantha's. The painting had drawn her here. Made her feel like her mother really had existed and wasn't just a heroine in one of Nana's stories

Sparks crackled in the fireplace. Willow snuggled deeper into the blanket she'd wrapped around herself and contemplated Brand again. Even as a marble figurine he was pretty cute, but dull white really didn't do him justice. He should be in tan-bronzes and black-browns – earthy, *alive* colors. She wondered if he could feel her touch. She kissed him gently. "Wish you were here," she murmured. "Wish my kiss could turn you back."

Willow curled into a pillow on the floor. She had told Queen Morwenna what she had done today – broken the spell – and learned that it was a big deal. Apparently, this meant she had some kind of natural power or something and that maybe the faerie queen wasn't so mental after all.

She tried to imagine a life here without the Game spell. Her breath puffed out at the thought. Wow. Could she really live here? Be a princess in another realm? Yeah sure, they didn't have Internet or MP3 players or televisions here, but what they did have – family, friends, castles, magic, Brand – was maybe even better. She missed Abby, but with Nana gone, there was nothing left to go back to on Earth.

Willow sighed. Maybe, she *would* get to see Abby again ... if she survived her battle against Nezeral. She scooped up Brand and climbed to her feet. The portrait of Princess Diantha – *Mom*, she reminded herself – smiled down from the mantle. Willow realized that her mother would be ... twenty-one years old right now. Willow snorted. How weird was that? She'd be more like an older sister than a mom.

"Goodnight," Willow said to her, then she held Brand up and whispered goodnight to him too. He didn't answer, of course, but an urgent knocking on the bedroom door almost made her drop him into the fireplace.

Queen Morwenna came striding in before Willow had even crossed the room. She was in her night robe and her face was chalky beneath her Game glow. "You must come with me at once."

Willow followed her wordlessly. She could see the panic in her grandmother's eyes. Panic and stark fear. Outside the bedroom door, a tall, blue-glowing man was waiting for them.

Queen Morwenna continued down the hallway without bothering to introduce them. She led them down two spiraling staircases and a passage lit only by the magical light-casting jewel her grandmother wore. The passage led to another spiraling staircase, and then at its bottom, a large metal-braced wooden door that had neither lock nor handle.

The queen paused and her shaky hand hovered over a gold disc built into the wood. "Oh, Lachlan. I fear I can't do it."

The tall man moved closer. He pressed the queen's hand to the gold disc. "You must," he said.

A single guttural word fell from the queen's mouth. Willow gasped as the huge door creaked and groaned in response, releasing a gray cloud of dust when it finally grated open. Silent, gloomy darkness lay beyond it. The queen lit candles with her fingertips.

The light revealed row upon row of thick leather-bound books that reached to the ceiling. Queen Morwenna lit an enormous brazier in the middle of the floor and stared somberly into its flames.

A firm hand ushered Willow into the room.

"My dear, a dreadful thing has happened." The queen turned her wide, frightened eyes to Willow. "You must be queened. Right now – tonight."

Willow swallowed, suddenly afraid. Why was Queen Morwenna acting this way?

Something was wrong. Horribly wrong.

"It's Terrill Longbottom. You remember the boy who was put in jail after he shot the crossbow at your young knight? Well, he's ... he's gone and hanged himself."

Willow blanched. *Hanged himself!* She remembered Terrill – he was *her* age. Why would he do such a thing?

"Now wait, Your Majesty." The tall man stepped forward. "That may not be entirely true. You did not give me a chance to finish earlier. The boy might not have done it himself. Apparently a rope was used that the guard captain swears was not in the boy's prison cell an hour ago."

The queen looked stunned. "What are you saying? That someone murdered him?"

"Aye, madam. There was no chess piece, just the body, so anyone who was not part of the Game could have done it. My guess would be that it was a spy for Prince Varian, as he is the only person who would have gained by it."

Willow heard their words, but nothing they said was making any sense. "Uh, would somebody please tell me what's going on?"

"Oh my dear, please forgive me." Queen Morwenna raked back her loose hair. "It has all happened so suddenly, I am afraid I am all a muddle." She took a deep breath and touched the tall man's arm. "Let me present my mage knight, Sir Lachlan Montrose."

"Your Highness, it's a great honor." He turned his fierce eyes to Willow and gave her a terse nod.

Willow nodded back. Sir Lachlan reminded her of Brand. He had that same trustworthy, honor-above-all-else kind of quality that made her feel safe.

"I summoned Sir Lachlan," said the queen, "because I felt poor Terrill's death. As a queen in the Game, I am able to sense when the players are captured or killed. And I know if they have been replaced or not. And in Terrill's case, there was a replacement." She paused, a frown lining her face. "You are in grave danger, my dear. Which is why we must act now."

"But why? What does his replacement have to do with me?"

Queen Morwenna stared at her, terrified. "It's Varian."

"Varian?" Willow still didn't understand. "But he can't hurt you, can he? He's miles away and ..."

"No, child," blurted the queen. "It's not me he can hurt. It's *you*."

Willow blinked at her. "Me? How can he hurt me?" Then she understood. Varian had replaced Terrill. He was a pawn now. A *Black* Pawn! All he had to do was prick her with a pin and she'd be toast.

Her grandmother grasped the edge of the blanket, which had slipped off Willow's shoulders. "It'll be all right," she reassured her. "I promise. Varian's not in Tulaan yet. He didn't kill Terrill. Not directly, anyway. When I felt his change, he was at his castle."

Sir Lachlan snorted. "This Game," he growled, "does nothing but confound me. The man's no Keldorian. Why would *he* have been chosen for Black? It makes no sense."

The queen shook her head. "I simply don't know. But it's well known he delivered White players to Tarrant. Perhaps the Game knows too." Her fingers dug into Willow's shoulders. "But we can't give up yet. This could be in our favor. Varian's castle is a full four-day ride to Carrus. It's not too late. If we train the child tonight and all day tomorrow, that will still leave her with three days to find Nezeral before Varian becomes a threat. Maybe even four or five, knowing Varian." She smiled grimly. "Setting the trap, after all, is half his fun. King Ulor may not be his only, nor his first, target."

Willow was just beginning to realize what the queen was saying. Varian didn't just want to hurt her. No, he was going for the big win. If he went to Carrus instead of Tulaan, all he had to do was capture King Ulor and there'd be no more brother, no more heir – no more problems. The Game would not only be over – Gallandra would be all his!

"But wait." A new thought occurred to her. "Won't King Ulor know? I mean, about Varian being a Black pawn? You knew and ..."

Queen Morwenna shook her head. "He won't know in the same way that I did. Only the queens feel the changes, and without Aleria ..."

"But he's got a really big chess set," insisted Willow. "Won't he notice the change himself? Varian's his brother. I think he'd notice his own brother's face!" Even as she said it, her heart sank. She remembered he hadn't noticed Nana's changed face. And now that the war was over, what reason did the king have to keep watching the chessboard? He'd been lulled into a false sense of security.

"Yes, it's possible," admitted the queen. "But we can't depend on it. I don't know how often he studies his board nor for how long. And who's to say, even if he does notice, that Varian will not find a way to checkmate him regardless. So you see my dilemma now, don't you, dear?" She turned away. "No matter how I look at it, I must queen you. It's the only chance we have."

Queen Morwenna started waving her hands in wide, flanking circles. A shiny ghostly image started wavering in and out of reality in front of them.

"Concentrate, madam. Aye, that's it! Just a little more." Sir Lachlan shook his fist in the air when an exact duplicate of King Ulor's chess set finally appeared – right down to the people-faced players and the white marble pedestal. "Well done, madam! Well done! Your focus is most definitely improving. You see," he said, turning to Willow, "we keep our set invisible as an extra security measure to ensure that no one attempts the queening move without our approval."

A small smile flickered across Queen Morwenna's face, but then disappeared as she strode to the pedestal. "There's no movement yet," she pointed out as she studied the board. "Varian's piece is still at mid rank. He'll probably wait till morning to set off. So we mustn't waste any time. Willow." She made a waving motion with her hand. "Come here and I'll show you what to do."

Willow's thoughts of Varian changed to thoughts of the magical power she would soon acquire. Was she *really* going to be able to make things appear and disappear? Stretch fabric, heal bruises and cuts – all with just the twitch of her hand? Tight with anticipation, she stepped toward her grandmother.

"Now, we believe all that's really required is for you to touch it like this." The queen placed a finger on the back rank square that would queen Willow's White pawn.

Willow gusted out a big breath. She closed her eyes and reached for the board.

CHAPTER 20

Adrenaline pumped through Willow's body. At first, the marble felt cold and smooth against her finger, but suddenly her whole hand was on fire. On fire and burning up her arm. She tried to pull away, but Lachlan's strong blue-tinged fingers crushed her hand against the hot marble. Searing heat exploded inside her. Something was loose and free. Something incredibly powerful. Willow clutched at the board, struggling with all her might to control it.

"That's it," said Lachlan. "Tether it, Princess. *Command it!*"

Willow shrieked, tearing her hand away from the scalding marble and Lachlan's heavy grasp. Her eyes flew open. She was shaking uncontrollably, her breath coming in great gasping heaves.

She felt hot and dizzy – something flowed through her like mage-brewed wine. *Magic.*

"Well done, Princess. Well done." Lachlan smiled broadly. Sweat glistened on his forehead. "Never before have I seen such a surge of power."

"Is she well?" The queen peered at Willow.

"For one who has just tethered in a surge of power the size of the Valandrean Mountains, Your Majesty, I would say she's doing just fine."

Queen Morwenna hugged Willow, a jubilant smile lighting her face. "Did you hear what he said? We have succeeded! Touching the board queened you!"

Willow stared at her grandmother. She could see her mouth moving. Even hear the words. But she was so absorbed by the new blue-white glow of Queen Morwenna's halo that nothing else registered. She reached out and passed her hand through it. Little tingly vibrations licked at her fingers.

The queen moved away. "It's the aura of my energy. It will soon fade."

Willow peered down at her own hand. A green light flared around her golden Game glow. She lifted her head to look at the room. The light – it was everywhere. It surrounded the books in the cramped shelves. The candles and their flames. Even the smooth stones of the floor and walls. She looked closely at the wall's niches and grooves. The wall didn't seem solid anymore. It was as if her hand could slip right through it.

She turned to Lachlan and Queen Morwenna. "Why is everything glowing?"

"You are seeing the auras of energy," answered Lachlan. "Every living and nonliving thing has one. They will fade, and then you won't see them again unless you wish it."

Lachlan's new crimson glow glimmered next to Queen

Morwenna's soft blue one. "You both have different colors. Does that mean something?"

The queen's face went slack and she stared at Willow vacantly. "Your green aura ..." she began but then stopped to blink her eyes back into focus. "Oh, I hate the way that feels. It's like being cross-eyed." She gave her head a shake before continuing. "Each color is a different soul gift. There are many colors: yellow, purple, orange, and hundreds of varying shades of each." She held out a hand to Willow. "Look closely and you will see that I glow yellow and green as well as blue."

Willow studied the bright pattern of Queen Morwenna's aura. She was right. Strands of yellow and green wavered inside the blue light she had seen earlier. It reminded her of the way the sun shimmered if you looked at it too long.

"We each have colors that define us." Morwenna flipped her hand over so that she was now holding Willow's. "In you, I saw traces of red and bits of my blue."

"But I see light from *all* of these things." Willow gestured at the wall and the bookshelves. "A white light with no color. How can something not alive have energy?"

"I have some knowledge of your Earthworld, Princess, and I believe that you would call that energy molecules." Lachlan stepped toward a bookshelf and pulled out a red leather book, bringing it to Willow to examine. "When you look at something with your inner vision, the structure of its life force, its energy, becomes quite evident. Here." He held the book close to her hand. "Try to pass your fingers through it. Because once you can see that inner structure, you should also be able to change it."

Goose bumps rose along Willow's arms and up the back of her neck. Her blanket had fallen to the floor, but she wasn't cold. Intense excitement overwhelmed her. She could actually see the tiny, clinging molecules that banded together to create the book.

She touched the red leather. It felt solid ... but not at the same time. Somehow she knew what she had to do. She closed her eyes and pictured those tightly packed molecules letting go of each other ...

"By the gods," said Lachlan, his eyes wide in disbelief. "She did it!"

"You didn't even tell her how."

Willow stared at the book that now lay on top of her hand, instead of below it. She'd passed her hand right through to the other side!

"It took me a month to learn that!" exclaimed the queen. "How could she ... It's not possible, Lachlan, is it?"

"Well, I would have thought not. But after today, I suppose I stand corrected." He knelt by Willow's bare feet. "Let's try something more difficult. Take the energy from the air and see if you can shape it into slippers."

Willow narrowed her gaze, trying to see the white aura of

the air. If she squinted just right, she could see nothing but light. It moved all around her, alive and pulsing. She let her eyelids drift shut and visualized her favorite frog slippers. Imagined them in every detail, right down to their plastic eyes and the red-stained nose of the left slipper.

"What manner of footwear is that!"

Willow blinked until she couldn't see the light anymore. Queen Morwenna was right. It *was* like being cross-eyed. She gave her head a shake and focused on her grandmother. Queen Morwenna was staring at her and pointing at something on the floor.

"Do they require feeding? One seems to have spit something up."

Willow glanced down at her Kermit the Frog feet. "I did it!" She squatted down, poking and probing at the bright green slippers to make sure they were real.

Lachlan gaped at her. "Never in all my years as a mage knight have I seen anyone arrange air energy on their very first attempt. It's unheard of." He reached out to touch a plastic Kermit eye. "How did you do it? How did you know what to do without being taught?"

Willow was puzzled herself. How *had* she known? She hadn't even thought about what she was doing. She'd just done it. "I don't know. I just imagined my slippers and then there they were right on my feet. I have no idea how I did it."

"Evidently," said the queen, "you are a magical genius.

And the faerie queen must have known it. Think of it, Lachlan. Why else would she have chosen an infant?"

Willow stood up, bewildered. *Magical genius.* How could she be a magical genius? She wasn't a genius at anything. All she had done was use her imagination.

Suddenly, an old memory popped into her head. Nana had loved to quote an Einstein saying – something about imagination being more important than knowledge. "What makes the magic work?" she asked. "I mean how did I do it, technically?"

"I don't know how you did it," said Sir Lachlan, frowning. "I've never seen anyone below a sixth level mage arrange air energy."

"But how is it done? What process has to happen before the molecules will do *this*?" She wiggled a Kermit-slippered foot.

"Well, it requires concentration. A great deal of it, in fact. More than people your age are capable of. Then – and this is the next most important thing – the imagining of the visual construct. You must be capable of visualizing whatever it is you are going to do in complete detail. Then –"

"I knew it!" Willow broke in. "I knew it had to do with imagination! That's why I can do it, isn't it?"

"What do you mean, child?" asked the queen.

"I mean, in my world, that's all I ever did – use my imagination. The toys I had ... my dolls, my books, chess, role-playing. Nana used them to teach me how to visualize.

Don't you see? She trained me with toys and games! That's why I'm so good at this magic stuff. I'm not some kind of genius – I just had a good teacher."

"Being able to see a thing clearly is only a part of the process," Lachlan said. "A most important part, yes, but still only a part. The focus, the visualization, and the degree of your talent all need to work together as a whole. And it's only when all three are in balance that the magic can work." He rubbed thoughtfully at his beard again. "Your abilities are a great mystery to me, Princess. A mystery I am sure I shall ponder further once the Game is over. But for now, our goal must be to prepare you.

"Here, have a look at the board. See what you make of it."

Willow gazed down at the large chess set. The lights and auras had finally faded. The marble figurines were now only lustrous from the orange glow of candlelight. Queen Morwenna picked up one of the pieces. "You have truly become a queen."

Willow was slightly weirded out when she saw the new, taller version of herself on the chessboard. Gingerly, she took the queen piece from her grandmother and held it nose-level. If she unfocused her eyes, the auras flared back into view.

The white figure only had a pale glow around it, the energy aura of the marble. Willow placed the piece back on its space in the back ranks of Black. The Game had changed somewhat. White had lost a knight but had gained a queen. There was some forward movement of the White king, rook, and bishop. She wondered if they were planning on coming to Keldoran. Hopefully, if they did, they would bypass Varian.

She picked up the Black pawn closest to her left. Varian's handsome face glared back at her. She knew he would destroy her if he could – destroy anyone and anything that got in the way of his plans to become king.

With a shudder, she placed him back on his square, squelching the wormy feeling that enveloped her.

And that was when she noticed that some of the White players had changed.

The captured pieces lined alongside the Game had auras too. *Colored* auras. She picked up the two White knights that glowed scarlet. "I have Brand's piece upstairs. How is he down here as well?"

"These are not the true pieces," Queen Morwenna explained. "The Game manufactures these ones for keeping track of things. King Ulor has them on his board as well." She slipped past Willow and opened a drawer, pulling out a small silver tray. "These are the real ones. The ones we captured. And this one," she pointed to a lone Black pawn, "is our dear Diantha."

Willow stared at the tray. On it lined up like toys were a blue-auraed queen and rook, a red-auraed knight, a few multi-colored pawns, a green-auraed bishop, and a sad Black pawn that had no color at all, just a white, lifeless glow.

She knew without looking who the red-auraed knight was. She picked him up along with the Black pawn.

Her parents. She was holding all that remained of her parents.

CHAPTER 21

Willow knew she should feel tired. She'd been up all night morphing into cats and mice and birds, making things appear and disappear, and memorizing the construct sequences for spellcasting. Construct sequences were, according to Sir Lachlan, the most important part of her training. They were a series of steps that – once remembered and understood – could be used in almost any spell, provided you had the corresponding magical talent to match it. And Willow apparently possessed every magical talent imaginable.

A yawn escaped her. Well, maybe she was a bit tired. She'd better get some sleep if she was going to face King Tarrant today. He didn't know about her queening yet, and Willow imagined he wouldn't be too happy about it.

She stretched her arms out. It was early dawn, and the feast hall where she'd been practicing her magic hadn't yet filled with the breakfast crowd. Broad shafts of light illumi-nated the empty room. Her eyelids began to grow heavy as she watched dust motes swirl.

She had tried to sleep earlier and even conjured warm

flannel pajamas and a fire, but that was about as far as she had gone. Being able to do magic was a bit like winning the lotto. She couldn't turn her excitement off. And so she had dressed and wandered back to the feast hall again, somehow finding its great tapestried walls and smooth-tiled floors comforting.

She settled against the cushioned back of her chair, draping an unladylike leg over its arm. Memories of the magical things she had done through the night came back to her. The crunch and grind of shrinking bones. Arms that changed into weightless feathers. A dizzying flight to the ceiling tops. Being a bird had been her favorite construct, the closest thing to being free from a body that she could imagine.

Footsteps and voices interrupted Willow's reverie. She lifted her head. Three servants had entered the feast hall and were snuffing out the candles on the wall and beginning to set the tables for breakfast. Willow slid back down in her chair. Could she fool these servants? Make them believe she was something else?

She ducked beneath a table and waited for a red-booted servant to pass by. A platter banged over her head, drifting odors of bacon and fresh bread.

Willow peeked through an opening in the tablecloth. The place was now swarming with servants. This was going to be fun. What should she be? A bird? A mouse? Nah, those constructs would just freak people out. Plus, birds were cool, but mice were just gross. They had this totally disgusting need to squeeze into tight spaces.

She heard hissing noises down by the doorway and squinted. A servant shooed a gray tomcat out of the room. Willow grinned. Now *that* was a transformation she could handle.

The aura lights winked around her like stars. She focused on them and began building the cat construct in her head. She could see its small triangular face, sleek body, and short-haired fur. The heat of magic washed over her, liquefying and reshaping her bones, molding her skin over a lithe new skeleton with fluid ease.

Willow blinked. The sharp smell of bacon made her small nostrils twitch. She arched her back, ready to spring onto the chair and investigate, but a boot poked at her and brought her back to herself. She was Willow Farrandale and not Grisard the Cat. It took a moment for her own brain to override the cat brain, and then she was off, padding across the feast hall and out through one of the doors that a servant held open for her. No one had noticed anything unusual.

The hallways, at her new ten-inch height, seemed unfamiliar. She started down one direction and then stopped. Map images of the correct route surfaced in the cat's mind. Willow loosened her control a little, allowing the cat's keen senses to guide her. She found the stairway and the corridor that went past Queen Morwenna's solarium and then the hallway that led to her own room.

Outside her doorway, she dissolved the construct and her own body shot up from the cat's. Weariness hit her like a punch. It was definitely time for bed. She entered her room sluggishly.

The drawn velvet curtains and the inviting glow of the fireplace cast cozy shadows across her bedchamber. Willow collapsed on the bed, not even bothering to cover herself.

She fell asleep instantly, but in what felt like only minutes, suddenly came awake again. Her whole body from head to foot was flopping and jiggling like a fish out of water.

Earthquake!

She tried to move, to warn everyone. But nothing happened. For a second she thought she had magicked away her legs, but she could see their outline under her dress. They just wouldn't budge. In fact, now that she could see clearly, nothing moved, not even the bed. But somehow she could still feel herself shaking and bouncing.

"You are not fully out of your body yet," said a soft voice. "Don't be afraid. I will help you." Willow's hand tingled. She felt herself being lifted away from the bed.

"There. Have the vibrations stopped?"

Willow stared at the ghostly woman who was holding her hands. The woman's cloudy outline was etched in gold, but her touch felt solid. Willow looked down at their clasped hands. Her green aura merged with the ghost's shimmering gold one.

"What have you done to me?" Willow spun and gasped.

Below, she could see herself, still asleep on her bed covers.

She lifted a see-through hand and watched as her shiny green fingertips glowed eerily. She moved it back and forth in a hypnotic sway.

"This is your spirit body," said the woman, "the one you dream with." She reached out to take Willow's other hand. "Come, you have much to learn and little time."

She felt as if she were being inhaled up a straw. Inky blackness surrounded her as she gasped for air, struggling to breathe.

Then, just as suddenly as it had started, it was over.

Bright sunlight dazzled her squinting eyes. Summery wood smells and sweet trilling birdsong drifted to her, and she relaxed her grip on the woman's slender hands. She could see the woman clearly now. Dark russet hair, green, tip-tilted eyes and a wide, sensuous mouth. She was amazingly, almost inhumanly beautiful, an ethereal angel being.

"Are you ... are you ..."

"I am Queen Cyrraena, your nethermother." The woman twisted her fingers into Willow's gold chain and pulled out the swan from beneath her bodice. "And you," she said, setting the pendant against Willow's dress front, "are the princess Willow, my own christened netherchild." She drew Willow into a stiff embrace. "I am sorry for all you have suffered. If there had been another way, I would have taken it."

Willow pulled back, still awed by the woman. "Is – is this

a dream?" Her hands and arms, she suddenly realized, had become flesh again, and she had lost her golden Game glow. She looked down at herself, at her slippered feet and bright blue gown. She *seemed* real enough, but somehow lighter, more airy, as if she could float away.

"No, not a dream," said Queen Cyrraena. "But an awakening. I have freed your energy from its physical bonds and have brought you to the fey realm of Timorell. It was the only way to bypass Nezeral's shields.

"Come." She stepped away from Willow and spread apart some lacy tree fronds. "We have much to speak of."

Willow peered past Queen Cyrraena and through the gap in the leaves. She could see blankets and cushions and an array of food spread beneath an enormous willow tree whose long slim branches formed a breezy wall around them. Willow edged her way through the branch curtain and sat opposite the enigmatic faerie, who leaned comfortably against the willow's vast trunk.

"Would you like some refreshment?" Cyrraena gestured to the hot buttered buns and a brimming silver goblet.

Willow shook her head no. She remembered old legends about eating faerie food. Something about how if you ate their food, you couldn't return to your own world.

The queen's lovely mouth swept into an amused smile, giving Willow the niggling feeling the faerie had read her thoughts. The food and wine disappeared with a graceful wave of hand. "Perhaps you are right," Cyrraena said in her soft, breezy voice. "We have much to discuss. I hardly know where to begin."

The question tumbled from Willow's mouth before she could stop herself. "Why me?"

The faerie queen regarded her for a long moment. "The wisdom name suits you," she finally said. "You ask the most difficult question first. There are many reasons why I picked you. Mostly, though, it was merely a matter of timing. I was not allowed to intervene unless Nezeral broke the laws. He broke the first one when he rigged the initial chess game so that King Tarrant could not possibly beat him. It was then I knew a netherchild must be chosen."

"But I was just a baby."

"I needed someone Nezeral would not anticipate." Willow laughed bitterly, but the queen continued speaking as if she hadn't heard her. "He expected me to choose a battle champion. He wanted a fight and in the beginning, no one agreed to play his game. So he waited, hoping I would select a worthy opponent. When I chose you, he was enraged. I thought he would go back to Clarion. But ... he didn't."

Despite her words, Queen Cyrraena sounded and looked indifferent. Willow shuddered. More than one Game was being played here. And she was obviously a pawn in both of them.

"You chose me, then, because you hoped Nezeral would get bored and go home?"

"Yes." She sounded so blasé, Willow didn't find her quite so lovely anymore. "But once the human war began," she continued. "I had no choice but to train you to be the champion he wanted. And I had to do it quickly. There was no other choice."

Anger clenched Willow's gut. She was being used – her whole childhood changed just to injure some faerie prince's pride. Well, she had her own pride too. And a family to protect.

"You got me into this," she accused. "Now get me out. What do I have to do?"

The queen shook her head. "The answer to that question will have to come from you. All I can do is tell you about Nezeral's weakness."

"Weakness?"

"Yes. He is from an upper realm dimension called Clarion, as am I. But I choose to live here in Timorell to serve as a guide to the humans. You do, of course, know the story of King Tarrant's lung fever and how his mage summoned a higher power? The mage should have summoned me, but he knew I wouldn't save the king. My role as guide does not include changing what must be. So the mage broke a great law by calling out to the upper realms."

Willow was amazed. Not because of what Cyrraena was saying, but because of how icy she sounded. "What does any of this have to do with Nezeral's weakness?" she asked, trying to match the faerie's nonchalance. "What's the big deal about the upper and lower realms? He was just asking for help."

"To explain that," said the queen, "you will need to understand our history. Eons before the laws of magic were created, the fey were free to journey through all realms – upper and lower. In those times, we lived side by side with you humans. We tried to help you advance. The problems started when some of us proclaimed that humans were not true beings but merely physical shells. They believed that because you had a short mortal lifespan, you were nothing but beasts."

Willow felt sick. That tale was an old one. Humans had been using it for centuries to rationalize slavery and genocide. Only they used skin color and different beliefs as an excuse, not lifespans.

"The fey who believed this committed atrocities," went on Cyrraena. "Pretending to be gods, they made slaves of the humans and convinced human leaders to make wars and to partake in other aggressions. Your own Earthworld's mythologies are rife with gods and goddesses. Deities who demanded worship and temples and wars. Some who even decreed human sacrifice." Cyrraena's eyes brightened with something – either anger or excitement. Willow wasn't sure.

"Nezeral's father, Jarlath, was one of the worst," she continued. "In one of his disguises he asked for the sacrifice of human blood and hearts in order that the sun might rise each morning. He was the cause of death for hundreds of thousands of people."

Willow reeled. *Gods and human sacrifice.* Just what had the faerie queen gotten her into?

The queen didn't seem to notice Willow's horror and continued to tell her story as if she were talking about the weather. "Jarlath was not the only one to believe such things. Many shared his views. But those of us who did not feel the same formed an alliance and called a council. A vote was held, that in the end, favored the humans.

"So, child." Queen Cyrraena peered down at Willow. "Can you guess how Earth was changed then?"

Willow gaped. Cyrraena's cool manner made it hard to tell if the queen was on her side or Nezeral's. "W-what?" she stammered. "What change?"

"After the vote your world was changed. Do you know how?"

Old legends and faerie tales ran through Willow's mind. Had there been one about change? She remembered Merlin from the King Arthur tales, how when his mistress Viviane tricked him into the faerie realms, all magic was said to have disappeared. Had something like that really happened at some time in the past? Had all the old legends and tales been based on actual events? "Was it the end of magic?"

Queen Cyrraena smiled a lovely smile that didn't reach her glittery eyes. "Yes. Exactly so. The council banished all magic and all magical beings from Earthworld. Furthermore, they cast a spell so that our magic would sicken if ever we were to come near iron. All material realms have iron cores. So now, were we to visit them, our magic would vanish and we would become powerless."

So the faeries were allergic to iron. Willow sat up straighter. *Finally*, something she could use against Nezeral.

Cyrraena nodded and an attendant materialized from among the willow fronds. He carried a long narrow wooden box that he kept as far from his body as possible.

Willow stared at him. She couldn't help it. Like Queen Cyrraena, he had an otherworldly beauty. His moss-green clothing and bright robin-orange hair made him seem part forest and part summer. As soon as he placed the wooden box between her and Queen Cyrraena, he disappeared back into the lacy tree fronds.

When Willow looked back at Queen Cyrraena, the faerie queen was edging away from the box.

"It contains a sword," she hissed. "An iron one. See if you can open the box."

Willow hesitated. The faerie boy hadn't looked happy about having to carry the box and now the queen herself was looking queasy. "Why is the sword in a box? Is there something wrong with it?"

"There are four elements. Earth, air, fire, and water." Cyrraena took a long deep breath, as though trying to gather strength. She moved even farther away. "These elements are the elements of protection. The elements of life. The wood of the box is an earthen element. It helps to shield me, absorbing some of the iron's power."

Queen Cyrraena really didn't look well at all. Willow peered at her. "Are you sick?"

"Don't concern yourself, child. I'll grow used to the iron's pull. Go now. Open the box."

Willow's hand drifted to the carved wooden lid. She felt nothing weird or powerful. She glanced at Queen Cyrraena again. Could she trust her? What if, after all this, she was only being manipulated into another scheme? A thought prickled at the back of her mind. Something didn't feel right. Something ...

Willow raised her head and looked past Queen Cyrraena to the swaying branches of the willow tree. It was too quiet. Where had all the singing birds gone? She saw bright glimpses of orange and green: the boy who had brought the box was still out there. Like Queen Cyrraena, he was waiting to see if she would open the box. Patches of crimson and gold appeared next to him. He wasn't alone.

Suddenly, she understood their fear. They weren't scared that she *would* open the box – they were scared that she *couldn't*.

CHAPTER 22

Willow rested both hands on the box's lid, narrowing her eyes until she could see the shining band of aura light. White and pure. Nothing indicated danger. A flick of her fingers, and the lid lay on the ground next to her. She peered into the box – it was filled to the brim with dirt.

Earth, air, fire, and water. The four elements of protection. Wood alone hadn't been enough. The faeries had needed a double dose to absorb the effects of iron.

Willow dug her hands into the cool soil until she felt something hard. She pulled the sword, rough-grained and heavy, from the box. Willow held it up so that she could see it in the sunlight. The sword wasn't shiny or decorative, like the one she'd seen Brand carry, nor was it razor-edged like Lord Garnock's. It was dark and ancient, pitted with battle scars and dull from lack of use. A sword for a museum – or a scrap heap.

"What ... what do you feel?" Queen Cyrraena's slack face had become a white mask. Alarmed, Willow reburied the sword. *She* had felt nothing. The queen, however, looked ready to keel over. Willow knelt beside her and helped prop her against the tree trunk. "Are you okay?"

Queen Cyrraena nodded, but her eyelids drooped. The orange-haired boy appeared again. Carefully, he replaced the box's lid and then carried it away. More faeries scurried into the open and fussed over the queen with fans and water goblets. A few moments later, Cyrraena's eyes reopened.

She shooed away the attendants and sat up. "It has been a long time since I was last exposed to pure iron. I didn't know I would be so vulnerable." She fastened her green eyes on Willow. "You held the sword. I *knew* you would be able to."

Willow didn't get what the big deal was. So she'd held some rusty old sword. Was she supposed to react the way the faerie queen had? What about everyone else on Mistolear? There was iron all over the place: weapons, armor, eating utensils, those brackets for holding candles – they were all made of iron. If everyone in Mistolear was allergic to it, how could people stand to have it so close to them?

"No one in Mistolear fainted from iron. Why did you?"

Cyrraena sipped from a goblet that one of the attendants had left her. "Well, not everyone in Mistolear has magical powers. It's inherited here, like blue eyes or curly hair. And few are blessed with it. Since you and Queen Morwenna are now the *only* two humans in either Gallandra or Keldoran with magic, you are now the only two who should be sensitive to it. If there is no magic, there is no sickness. And the more magic you have, the more the iron affects you. But even with your enhanced Game powers, your magic does not reach even a tenth of a faerie's. Our power is so great that even to be near iron sickens us. You would have to touch it and wear it upon your person to sicken as I do."

"But I did touch it. So how come *I'm* not sick?"

"You should be. Your magical powers mean that you should have the same sensitivity to iron that human mages do. You should not have been able to touch the sword."

Things started clicking into place. "It's because I grew up on Earth, isn't it?" said Willow. "I'm immune."

The faerie queen nodded. "I had hoped that you would become safe from the iron sickness – become immune, as you say."

Willow stared at Queen Cyrraena's hands – hands that still trembled from being so close to the iron. Was this what she'd meant by Nezeral's weakness, then? Willow's mind spun with the dark implications. Was the iron sword to be her weapon? Did she have to *kill* him with it?

"Am I supposed to kill Nezeral with that sword?" she blurted out. "Because if I am, I can tell you right now I won't do it."

Queen Cyrraena actually laughed. "Nezeral's powers are intensified in this realm. You wouldn't get within a league of him with a sword in your hand."

Relief flooded Willow, then frustration. How could the queen treat this so lightly? "Well, what exactly am I supposed to do then? Have a magical showdown with him?"

"I can't say."

"Can't or *won't*?"

Cyrraena rose to her feet. "See this tree?" She pointed at the thick willow trunk. "This is your name tree. It stands for the strength and wisdom that I have gifted you with." She drew Willow up to stand beside her. "See how firm and strong its trunk is? How steady?" She pressed their hands to the scratchy trunk bark. "And yet its branches are supple and easy to bend. Wisdom, your gift, works in the same way. You must be strong in your knowledge of who you are, but at the same time, open up to what is still possible."

Nice sentiments, thought Willow. But hardly something that was going to help her defeat Nezeral. She flopped back down. "This isn't helping. Couldn't you just gift me with a magical plan instead?"

Queen Cyrraena stared at her coldly. "Not one person in this whole realm, human or fey, would dare to gainsay one of my gifts. It wouldn't even enter their minds to *think* such a thing." An unpleasant smile curved her full lips. "And *that* is why you might yet best Nezeral. Because of your life on Earthworld, you see things very differently from us. You examine every situation in a manner completely foreign to a magical being. Nezeral won't expect that. Nor will he expect your immunity to iron. These things together are meaningful. But it's up to you to figure out how."

237

All this sounded like crazy talk to Willow. She rose back up from the blanket and scowled at the faerie queen. "I don't understand you *or* this Nezeral guy. I mean, I know King Tarrant's mage summoned the higher power and all that stuff, but why did Nezeral even answer? Why would he, if he's so above humans, even have bothered to come here in the first place?"

The queen took her time answering the question, as though she were gauging how much to say. "What I told you earlier regarding lower and upper realms isn't entirely correct. Lower realms that have magic, such as Mistolear, are more middle than lower. Middle realms that *could* become upper realms. Beings like Jarlath don't want this to happen. He sent his son here to create chaos. And that is what keeps humans from progressing. Chaos and war."

The grove had grown silent again. Willow studied Queen Cyrraena's luminous beauty. She looked mostly human, but a vague difference that Willow couldn't pinpoint hinted at her alien nature. Something feral, maybe.

Hopelessness and exhaustion suddenly overcame Willow. Everything that had happened to her – losing Nana and Brand, growing up without her family, being exiled to another realm – it had all happened because of something she had no control over – her humanness. She was nothing but a puppet, hated by faeries like Nezeral because she was human.

A hand slipped over Willow's shoulder. "I wish," said the

faerie queen, "that Nurse Beryl were here to see you. She would have been proud."

Willow blinked, surprised at Cyrraena's unexpected kindness. "You knew her? Because she sure never mentioned you. Or that you gave me this." Willow lifted the swan pendant, then let it drop back to her chest.

The faerie queen gazed at the necklace. "She knew what I had done. That I had gambled your life to rid Mistolear of Nezeral. She was quite angry with me." She glanced back at Willow. "She is a very strong spirit, your nurse. She visited you on the moat bridge in Tulaan. Did you see her?"

"You mean that really *was* Nana? I wasn't just seeing things?"

"She asked me for a favor. She asked that if you defeat Nezeral and come back unharmed, you have the chance, if you wish it, to return to infancy."

Willow's mouth dropped open. *Return to infancy!* Her nana wanted her to be a *baby* again? "You can't be serious. Why would I want to do that?"

"I assume she wants you to have a normal human life. To grow up with your own family. But the decision is yours. She only requested that I offer such a choice."

The decision is yours. All these decisions. It was just too much.

"It's late morning in the human realms," stated the queen, seemingly unconcerned with Willow's turmoil. "I must get you back to your body before someone tries to awaken you." She drew Willow closer to the tree and held her shoulders.

"There's one more thing I must tell you. Since you arrived in Mistolear, I have shielded you from Nezeral. But now that you have your powers, I can no longer do this. I can, however, grant you one last protection."

Her voice turned steely and her eyes closed. "Nezeral won't be allowed to enter your thoughts. Your mind will be closed to him." She touched the swan pendant and popped her eyes back open. "And, of course, I *will* be watching."

The same powerful sensation that had brought Willow to Timorell engulfed her again, and Queen Cyrraena's eerily beautiful face faded into blackness. Willow screamed, but then the tightness squeezed her breath away and sent her plummeting sickeningly downward.

CHAPTER 23

Willow's eyes sprang open, her panicked screams still echoing in her head. She scrambled to sit up. She was back in her body, and back in bed. The hearth fire was burning beside her and cast warm colors over the room.

Willow punched her pillow in frustration. Of course, Queen Cyrraena saved any mention of the protection barrier until the last minute, when Willow couldn't ask her anything about it.

So, what *did* she mean? Hesitantly, Willow scanned the dark walls and murky corners of her room. If Queen Cyrraena wasn't protecting her anymore, did it mean that Nezeral could see her? Could he take her away the same way Queen Cyrraena had? Another image filled her mind – her dream of the eyes. Maybe Nezeral had been watching her all along, sneaking into her dreams without Cyrraena knowing.

The thought propelled her out of bed. She went to the windows and threw open each shutter, letting pale light spill in. Fresh snow blanketed the ground outside and powdered bare tree branches. Willow pressed her face to the glass, feeling its chill against her skin. Fear gripped her. She sensed the Game spell now, could see its thin wiry aura weaving a net all around her – all around everything – making it terrifyingly clear just how powerful Nezeral really was.

She turned from the window, blinking away the aura light. Dread made her heart pound and mind race. What if she failed? What would Nezeral do to her? Kill her? Stick her in a chess piece? Make her a prisoner? What?

Willow hugged herself and sat back on the bed. Thinking about chess pieces had also reminded her of Prince Varian and the fact that he was poised to checkmate King Ulor. Her gaze fell to the pair of knights that sat on her night table. She didn't need Nezeral to destroy her. She knew what her fate would be if Varian succeeded.

Stay and be captured or fight and be captured. There were no other options.

The realization numbed her, blocking out her fear. She squinted until she could see the energy of the air. She visualized herself wearing her warm tunic and pants, a fur-lined cloak, and sleek leather boots. When she opened her eyes, she was ready.

She scooped up Brand and her parents' chess pieces from her night table and plopped them into her pocket. If by some miracle she actually did beat Nezeral, the first change she wanted to see was theirs. Her face clouded. *Damn it!* She'd forgotten to ask the faerie queen if defeating Nezeral *would* bring the captured players back. *Stupid!* She dug the heel of her palm into her forehead. What if she did all this, risked her life and defeated Nezeral, and Brand and her parents still remained chess pieces?

She sighed. The thought hurt, but it didn't change anything. She had no choice but to stay or to fight.

A metallic gleam drew Willow's eyes back to the night table. The pearl-handled knife that Brand had given her reflected the flames from the fireplace. She picked it up, running her finger over the sharp blade. Queen Cyrraena had said that Nezeral would know if she carried iron, that he would not let her near him if she did. No sword. Not even a little knife. So how could she defeat him without a weapon? She set the knife back on the night table, a new realization slowly dawning on her. Faeries were immortal. Maybe weapons couldn't even hurt them. *Crap.* If she kept this line of reasoning up, she'd end up hiding beneath the bed or something.

She walked over to the wash basin and splashed cold water onto her face. Every line of thought she pursued led her here, to this decision.

"Okay, Nezeral. I'm ready whenever you are."

"Well, now, Princess," said a voice ripe with laughter. "I'm glad to hear that."

Willow spun around, but no one was there. Her heart began to hammer and her breath shortened. She fell to the floor, striking her head hard on the stone tiles.

Willow woke up with a throbbing head, a tongue that felt like it was wearing a sock, and eyes that refused to open. She massaged her temple, where a golf-ball-sized lump exploded with pain. She winced and forced open an eyelid. She was definitely not in her room.

She closed her eye. So this was it, then. No chance to say goodbye to friends or family. Nezeral had come for her and that was that. She pried open her other eye, alternating between the two until they could both open at the same time.

She felt strangely calm. Relieved, almost. Whatever was going to happen, she told herself, was going to happen. She just wanted to get it over with.

Very slowly, she pulled herself to a sitting position. The room swirled around her for a moment, and both her head and stomach lurched. She clutched the bedsheets, taking deep, fortifying breaths until the sick feeling passed.

Jeez! What had Nezeral done to her, anyway? Her whole body felt weak and rubbery, like she'd had the stomach flu for a week. She pressed her fingertips to her temples again, rubbing them in slow circles, careful not to touch her painfully protruding bump. The pounding eased. Willow lifted her head.

The room that swam into focus was large and circular. Probably a castle tower, she thought, glancing at windows that revealed nothing but bare blue skies. That, or they were on a mountain somewhere. She pulled herself up using the bedpost and took wobbly steps to the nearest sill.

The sunshine burned her eyes. She squinted, ignored the accompanying pain in her head, and pushed open one of the glass casements. A warm, flower-scented breeze washed over her, ruffling her hair and caressing her skin.

Willow's gaze swept over a lush green landscape forested with leafy oaks and maples. For a moment, she thought she was back in Timorell. But then in the distance she saw a serrated line of snow-covered winter spruces rising behind the magical construct of summery trees.

She turned away from the window. That confirmed she wasn't in Timorell, anyway. She leaned against the sill and let her gaze roam the large room. It was like most of the other castle bedrooms she'd been in, but the furniture was dainty and elegant rather than large and ornate. She walked over to a richly brocaded couch and sat down, stretching her legs over its cushions. Willow laid her head against its armrest and that was when she noticed the ceiling, decorated with twining vines ringed with gold.

Wow. Nezeral had lifestyles-of-the-rich-and-famous taste. She smiled sardonically and reached over to scratch an itchy wrist. There was a dull scraping sound. She peered down at her arm, which still had its queen glow. Thin iron bands clasped her wrists.

She raised a tunic sleeve to touch one of the bands. Hot

wind blew against her face. She looked up. The wind had come from across the room.

"Good day, Princess."

Willow sat up quickly. An impossibly handsome and incredibly beautiful teenage boy stood before her.

The blue-garbed figure gave her a smile that was both obnoxious and charming. "I trust your *sleep* was refreshing." He sat down across from her on a matching brocaded chair.

Willow could only manage a dazed nod. His eyes mesmerized her – they glittered and shimmered like a turquoise sea, his black brows startling against his ivory skin and long silvery blaze of hair. He sprawled one leg over the armrest and leaned back, regarding her with a grin.

"I'm not quite what you were expecting, am I?"

This time Willow found her voice. "Are *you* Nezeral?" Even as she asked it, she knew it couldn't be true. He looked like he was seventeen! He was a kid just like her.

He rose from the chair. "At your service," he declared with a sweeping bow. His tunic swayed and the smell of ocean breezes swept across the room.

"But you're just ... How old are you, anyway?" She folded her arms protectively. He was staring again.

A mystified look crossed his face. "Is this of importance to you? My age?"

"You look as old as me."

"On Clarion we would be considered the same age. But

here, I am closer to five hundred."

Willow gawked. She knew that being immortal meant that you lived forever. But somehow her brain still couldn't see this gorgeous-looking teenage boy as a five-hundred-year-old being.

Trying to regain her equilibrium, she peeled back one of her sleeves, showing the iron bands attached to her wrists. "What are these for?"

Nezeral smiled again, but his face had lost its charm this time.

"Those bands are warding irons. They neutralize magic."

Dropping her banded wrist, Willow paled, remembering who she was up against. Nezeral wasn't a handsome teenage *boy* – he was a wicked faerie prince. She folded her arms again, trying not to look afraid.

I'm immune to iron, she reminded herself. *These bands won't ward a thing.*

Nezeral's confident demeanor, though, poked holes in her composure. What if Queen Cyrraena's magic *couldn't* cloak her thoughts? Or what if the iron were some special type of magic iron, and he really *had* warded her powers?

Willow peeked down at one of the exposed bands, testing if she could see its energy aura. There it was – the white glow. But did that mean she could manipulate it?

She looked back at Nezeral. He was staring at her, but with a new curiosity in his eyes. God! What had she almost done? Now that would've been real bright. Dissolving the iron band right in front of him.

"I would advise against that," he remarked dryly. "The burns can be quite nasty."

Willow thought for a second that he'd read her mind. But then she realized he'd just been reading her body language.

"So I guess this makes me your prisoner, then," she said, pretending acceptance. If she *could* use her powers, she didn't want *him* to know about it.

Nezeral's grin was friendly. "Prisoner is a bit heavy-handed, don't you think? Would you not prefer something less harsh, like shall we say ... guest?" He suddenly rose to his feet. "I know! Let's dine together and become better acquainted."

The smells of woodsmoke and roast chicken wafted through the room. Willow turned her head. A spitted chicken was dripping savory juices into the lit fireplace, and two chairs and a food-laden table had appeared.

Nezeral pulled Willow to her feet. She gasped as a sharp pain knifed through her head. She snatched her hand away. "Thank you, but I think I can manage."

Nezeral shrugged. He followed and pulled out a chair for her. "I really must apologize, my dear princess, for that lump on your head. My magic is so powerful on this pitiful realm that I often overdo my spells. You're not too queasy to eat, I hope?"

Willow said nothing. If he was really sorry, he would get rid of the lump. She reached for a soft pear slice, ignoring his patronizing smile. She shoved it into her mouth, chewing gustily just to prove to him exactly how *unqueasy* and *unfazed* she was by his powers and hyperactive spells.

Sitting across from her, Nezeral speared a wedge of pungent cheese and leaned back, regarding her with interest. "So, tell me, in which of the realms did Cyrraena manage to age you so quickly? Truthfully, I never felt a hint of her spell. The realm must have been distant."

Would knowing about Earth alert Nezeral to her iron immunity? But what else could she say? She didn't know the names of any other realms. "I was brought up on Earth," she finally answered, figuring it was better to look gutsy than afraid.

For the first time Nezeral seemed disconcerted. "But ... but that is a material realm. You would have had no powers whatsoever there." His white face registered shock and something else. Willow thought it might be fear.

Nezeral sat up straighter in his chair. She could practically hear his thoughts churning as he tried to figure out how this new development affected his plans.

"So how was it that Cyrraena trained you?" He casually offered her a warm bun. "Without magic, it would have been much like training a knight without a sword."

Willow accepted one of the buns and smiled. Nezeral was spooked by the no-magic thing. She decided to shock him a little more. "She didn't train me. I hadn't learned one thing about magic until yesterday."

"Yesterday ..." He gazed at her in disbelief. "You're lying," he growled, clenching a fist. He stood up and banged it on the table. "I don't believe you. This is Cyrraena's doing. Another attempt to mock me!" He shoved back his chair and roared into the ceiling. "You will pay for this, Cyrraena! Do you hear me?" Suddenly, a dark cloud of smoke engulfed him.

Shaken, Willow stared at the dissipating smoke. Nezeral *and* his chicken dinner had vanished from the room. She cleared her throat. Maybe egging him on like that hadn't been such a good idea. Ways to make Cyrraena pay, after all, probably involved Willow or the Game. She dropped the bun that was still in her hand and stood up. Maybe *she* should find Nezeral and see if she could calm him down.

She spun around, looking for a doorway, but saw only window casements and tapestry-covered stone walls. She marched over to a tapestry and lifted it to check underneath. Nothing but gray stone. She checked beneath the bed and the carpet. No trapdoors either. She leaned out over one of the tower windows, staring down at the fifty-foot drop. The only way she could get out of this place was if she grew her hair like Rapunzel.

She sank to the floor beneath the sill, her courage sinking with her. What was she going to do when Nezeral came back? A vast emptiness yawned in her mind. "Come on," she whispered. "Think. Think." But nothing came to her. No thoughts. No theories. No plans. She dropped her head to her knees and closed her eyes.

CHAPTER 24

A few miserable moments passed before Willow lifted her head. She'd forgotten about the bands.

Despite her fear, she held out her arms, ready to test them. A horrible thought stopped her, though. What if Nezeral could sense what she was doing the way Queen Morwenna could sense what Varian and Terrill had done? If she made the bands come off, he'd know and she would lose the advantage of surprise. She chewed her bottom lip. On the other hand, if she couldn't do it, then the surprise would be hers.

Willow let her eyes go out of focus until the aura of the bands blinded her. They shook around her wrists but held on. She concentrated harder, staring at the dense molecules. They writhed and squirmed like a swarm of insects. The band was moving, sliding ...

A balmy wind whipped hair into her face. Startled, Willow blinked away the magic, folding her hands back into her lap. Nezeral had returned, but he wasn't alone. He was grinning wolfishly, his fingers pressed over the eyes of a young woman Willow didn't recognize.

"Are you ready?" he said.

Willow stared at them as she climbed to her feet. She didn't like the trigger-happy edge to his voice or the way the woman's mouth trembled. No surprise could be a good surprise if Nezeral was behind it.

What was he up to? Willow peered hard at the woman.

Nezeral's hands started to pull away from the woman's head and Willow realized the cruel trick he was playing. Red hair. Wide brown eyes. Thin gold circlet on her head. Willow *did* recognize her – Princess Diantha, her mother. And she was about to meet her only child, except she didn't know it yet. Nezeral pushed her forward.

"I told you that an infant was merely a bother," he said. "Look, see what Cyrraena has done. She has saved you ever so much trouble. She has –"

Willow panicked, bolting forward. "Don't! Please don't!" She wasn't ready for this. She'd been so sure that her mother was lost to her forever. And now Diantha was standing in front of her with a growing look of horror on her face. Nezeral was playing a trick on Willow – maybe the woman wasn't even real.

He released the woman's arm. "Princess Diantha, meet your daughter," his smile was victorious as he spat out, "Princess *Willow*."

Nezeral stepped back and sprawled on one of the brocaded chairs, while Willow and Diantha stared at each other like statues.

Her mother wasn't as tall as Willow had expected. Only about chin level. But she was lovely, the portrait Willow had seen only a faint imitation of her beauty.

A knot twisted inside her. It wasn't a trick. It couldn't be.

Tears stung Willow's eyes. She could imagine what this must be like for her mother. Like having your kid snatched and then finding her years later, a grown stranger. Except it wasn't years later. Only four months had passed for Diantha.

"I'm sorry," Willow said, not knowing what else she could say.

"*No.*"

The word was low and harsh and didn't sound as if it could have come from Diantha. But the young woman drew herself up and glared at Willow. "You don't say that to me. Only *he* has to say that." She faced Nezeral. "You *will* say it. You will *choke* on it!"

"Come now, your scathing words do wound me. Even my great patience has its *limitations*." The last word was full of threat. Diantha paled. When Nezeral saw that he had had the proper effect, he smiled and rose from the chair.

"By your leave, miladies," he said, bowing deeply. "I shall allow your reunion to continue in private." He smirked at Diantha, then vanished from the room.

Diantha sighed. Whatever had given her that furious courage seemed to have left her. She looked worn and defeated, like a sad rag doll emptied of its stuffing. She sank down on the sofa and sobbed quietly into her elbow.

Pulling uncomfortably at a loose cuff thread, Willow looked away. She knew it wasn't her fault she'd grown up, but that didn't keep her from feeling guilty about it.

Diantha must have sensed her thoughts because she lifted her head. "Please forgive me," she rasped. "I swore he wouldn't make me cry again, and here I am, weepy as a waterfall." A shy smile wobbled onto her face as she held her hand out to Willow. "Come, sit beside me. Let me look at you."

Willow sat nervously on the edge of the couch, staring at her big booted feet, which, of course, looked embarrassingly gigantic next to her mother's tiny slippered ones. She tucked them beneath the couch.

A soft touch pulled her chin up and tentatively caressed her cheek. Diantha was studying her like a newborn, lifting her hands and checking to make sure she had all her fingers, tracing her nose and the shape of her face, feeling her hair and eyebrows, and even making her stand and twirl. "You are almost as tall as Alaric. I didn't expect that. You were such a tiny thing." Humor glinted in her eyes. "I assume you've met my father? He must have been heartened to see your Somerell blood so evident."

Willow laughed. Now that was an understatement. King Tarrant had all but renamed her Diantha. "On my first night, he announced to everyone that I was his new heir and that he wasn't going to allow me to be queened."

"Oh dear, that wouldn't have gone over very well with the court." Diantha's lips pursed into a tight smile as she reached for Willow's hand. "Is there any word," she whispered, her eyes suddenly earnest, "of your father ... my Alaric?"

Willow swallowed, her hand drifting to the slight bump in her tunic pocket. Didn't her mother know about his capture? She drew one of the White knights from her pocket, peering at the hard white eyes and long aquiline nose. Yes. This was the right one. Then she placed the little figure in her mother's quivering hand. "It happened just after your ... uh, disappearance. He and Queen Aleria were going to tell your family about you, but they were ambushed by your father's men. They all, umm, thought you were, you know ... dead."

Diantha nodded. "Nezeral told me," she admitted. "He took me out of the Game. He made it appear as if a White player had captured me by killing me with a knife. But it was just a ploy to anger my father into playing the Game. But I thought maybe ... I hoped that he'd lied about Alaric." She set the chess piece on a small side table, her fingertips lingering over the tiny helmeted head. When she looked back, her eyes were so full of sorrow that Willow couldn't bear to look at them.

Something had to be done. Willow's throat tightened with fury. The whole Game thing was just so senseless. So stupid! She jumped to her feet and began pacing the room. Beating Nezeral was taking on a new meaning. She just couldn't let him win!

"Does he ever sleep?" she asked, whirling to face Diantha. "Is there ever a time when he's vulnerable? When he could be attacked? And guards? Does he use guards?"

Diantha shook her head. "You must not ask me such things. He is listening." Suddenly, she started shrieking and writhing on the couch.

Willow struck at air. "Coward! You hear me, Nezeral? Leave her alone! Or are you too afraid to come back? Fight me face to face!"

Diantha was abruptly set free. She sat up, her terrified eyes flitting over the room. "Oh Willow," she whispered, "what have you done?"

"I ..." Willow began. But her mother rapidly faded away until Willow was staring at an empty couch.

The smell of dank seaweed alerted her to Nezeral's presence – and his anger. She closed her eyes, hoping some miraculous idea would spring fully formed into her head.

Nothing, of course, came to mind.

CHAPTER 25

"So, Princess, you are ready to battle me, are you?"

Willow stepped back. What was he going to do? Magic or no magic, Nezeral could beat her – and beat her badly. A growl rumbled from his throat. He shot an arm into the air and she flinched, expecting to be consumed in flames or something equally horrible.

Nezeral snorted. "Don't worry. I don't intend to destroy you – not yet. I have something I wish to show you first." He pointed past her, deliberately jerking his arm so that she flinched again.

Willow glared at him and turned to see what he meant.

A chessboard stood before them. It was even more ornate and fantastic-looking than the ones King Ulor and King Tarrant had used. The board, crafted from onyx and ivory-colored marble, stood on a pedestal as thick as a tree trunk. It was as large as a rec room pool table and the players were the length of her torso.

Nezeral brushed past her and looked over the board. "Well, well, it would seem that I may not have to destroy you after all. Your uncle is very close to doing it for me."

Willow felt any hope she had of living past her teens slide away. From the looks of the Game, Varian was at the back rank now, only two jumps behind King Ulor. She probably had one, maybe two days tops, before he caught up with him and pulled off a checkmate. And it was clear from what Nezeral had just said that a checkmate meant that all losing players, including herself, would turn to stone.

"So," said Nezeral softly, "I guess that just leaves it up to me to choose." There was no mockery in his tone. He was deadly serious and his eyes bore into hers with reptilian focus. "Ah, choices. We all make our choice. I think I must make mine."

Willow first felt a faint probe, as if someone had gently caressed her throat. It was a pleasant feeling, nothing to be afraid of. Nezeral's eyes reflected stars – she thought she could reach out and touch them. The pressure grew firmer, became a massage. She relaxed and imagined that she was floating.

Then something squeezed – and it squeezed hard.

Willow flailed, choking for breath. Too late, she realized what he meant to do. The "choice" he had made. He was strangling her magically. He had decided that it was better to kill her than wait for Varian to capture her.

She tried to speak, to scream, to beg, anything to make him stop, but the crushing force on her windpipe was too strong. She couldn't see properly – a murky brown haze outlined Nezeral. He was smiling, a thin feral grin that sickened her.

"No ..." she finally managed to gag out. She didn't want to die, not like this, not so ignobly. Nezeral's smile widened. The pressure worsened. Willow saw light everywhere, white, dazzling light. It hurt her eyes because she couldn't blink. Suddenly the light began to change, and broke apart into small particles.

No, not light, she realized. Auras!

Willow twisted her head frantically, trying to escape the pressure. She clawed at her neck, but there was nothing there. Blackness was beginning to edge in around her vision. Panicked, she thrust her banded wrists in front of her, fighting to stay conscious. The auras – she had to manipulate the auras.

She used whatever strength she had left to construct the image. Her eyes still couldn't close, but it didn't matter. She imagined the bands weren't around her wrists, but around Nezeral's. She imagined long chains growing out of the bands and bound them to the wall.

Suddenly, the pressure disappeared. Willow dropped to her knees, choking and gasping. Her throat was so raw it hurt to swallow. She collapsed, passing out even before she hit the floor.

Willow shivered, trying to shield herself from the cold breeze that had woken her up. She was confused and disoriented and her throat burned. A second later, everything came rushing back. Her eyes flew open. *Nezeral!*

She lifted her head and winced when she tried to move. Then she saw him. He was sitting on the floor in stony silence, watching her. Long, dangling chains bound him to the wall and iron bands circled his wrists.

Willow sat up. She kept her eyes glued to Nezeral's face. This could be a trick. Some kind of psychological cat-and-mouse game. But he didn't move or speak and the bands didn't pop off his wrists.

That's when Willow noticed that, except for the chess set, the room didn't have a single piece of furniture in it. She shivered again. Why was it so cold all of a sudden? An icy breeze against her back answered her. She turned around and saw that the breeze came from a window, the one she'd opened earlier.

Dazed, she struggled to stand, fighting the blackness that spotted her vision. Her throat ached terribly. She held her fingers against it as she made her way to the window.

Outside, the winter snow she'd left behind in Keldoran was doing its best to make up for lost time. It battered against the trees like a relentless army, obliterating the eden that Nezeral had created with magic. Billows of snow began to shroud the gardens below.

Willow shut the window. What did this mean? Had she won? Was the Game over?

She spun around to ask Nezeral, but all she could do was

croak. Gingerly, she touched her swollen neck. If pain was any indicator, it was definitely bruised. Willow took a deep breath and wrapped her hands around her neck. No one had actually taught her a healing spell, but she figured it worked along the same principles as any other spell. She unfocused her gaze, waiting for the aura lights to wink into existence. When they did, she closed her eyes, imagining her throat pain-free and healthy.

Her neck grew warm, then began to tingle. A thick wave of heat swept over her, and when she opened her eyes, her throat felt normal again.

When she spun around to face Nezeral, she was smiling. "Well, I guess there's just one thing I want to say to you. And that's ... checkmate!"

He regarded her with contempt. "Check, perhaps. But hardly *checkmate*. Look in your pocket."

Willow narrowed her eyes. Was he up to something again?

"Go on," he said, "look."

Willow slid her hand into her pocket. She knew what was in there. Her fingers wrapped around Brand and pulled him into the light. He hadn't changed. He was still a hunk of white marble.

"Your White knight, I believe."

Willow's heart thumped. What did this mean? Was the Game spell still functioning? She looked down at Brand again. Why hadn't he changed yet?

"That's right," Nezeral drawled. "The Game's still on.

And your time is running out. Varian will soon be succeeding where I have failed."

A queasy, stomach-sinking feeling gripped Willow. She remembered the lecture about intrinsic and extrinsic magic that Malvin had given her once, about how magic was either a part of the object or controlled by the mage. *Shoot!* It didn't matter that she'd trapped Nezeral's powers. The Game was intrinsic. It would just keep going until it was over.

"So what happens now?" She set Brand on the window sill. "Guess sending you back to Clarion won't solve my problems. Is there some sort of deal you want to make?"

"I don't need to make any deal. I just need to wait."

Willow frowned. "What do you mean? If I change to marble, you'll freeze to death up here."

Nezeral shook his head. "Cold doesn't bother me. Plus, gold is hidden throughout this castle. One of my human servants will free me for the right price." He rattled his chains and grinned.

"Not if I send you back to Clarion first." Willow didn't know if she could actually do that, but she'd say just about anything to wipe that smirk off his face.

"Can't do it. Not unless I agree, which I assure you, I won't."

Anger slammed into Willow like a fist. He was going to win. This selfish, rotten pig, who'd ripped apart her family – who'd tried to *murder* her – was going to win! The fury clenched her teeth together.

Her focus narrowed along his exposed throat. She saw his aura, dense and muddy as a stagnant swamp. It repulsed her, the way touching something icky would, but she ignored it, concentrating instead on the constriction of Nezeral's throat muscles and the shocked surprise in his widening eyes.

There! her mind cried. *How do you like* that*! And that!* She compressed his neck again and again, watching as he gasped, wheezed, and twisted his head in helpless desperation. He gagged. His face turned a dark red and his eyes rolled wildly in their bulging sockets. Maybe immortals could die after all. Like vampires. You just needed to get them when they were powerless. They certainly could suffer.

Something warm and wet ran down the sides of Willow's face. She wiped it away savagely. Those couldn't be tears. No way she'd be crying for *him*.

The tears, though, streamed down her neck and into her shirt collar. They blurred her vision and made her nose run. A sob burst from her lips.

She couldn't do it. She couldn't murder someone.

Even if that someone was Nezeral.

She sank to her knees, inhaling in quick, shuddery breaths and trying to block out the choking gasps coming from a few feet away.

Oh God, what was she going to do? Two kingdoms were counting on her and she was about to let everyone down.

Brand, her family, her new friends – everyone.

She sat back on the floor and buried her head in her knees. "I'm sorry," she whispered. "I tried. I really tried."

Pain welled up inside her. It wasn't fair. She beat her head again and again against her knees. She didn't want to die or be a chess piece. She just wanted to be a kid. A normal kid. Was that too much to ask? Just to be normal?

She froze. That was the one thing she'd forgotten. She *was* normal. In fact, she was the only freaking normal person in this whole realm.

Willow lifted her head. She'd been going about this all wrong, trying to play the Game by Nezeral's rules. She had to look at things the way the faerie queen had told her to – from her own unmagical perspective.

Nezeral cleared his throat to speak. "See, Cyrraena?" he croaked. "See what happens when you send infants to do a hero's job?"

His words mesmerized Willow. He didn't know it yet, but maybe, just maybe he had solved one of her problems.

CHAPTER 26

Willow looked Nezeral over. She'd been too busy trying to make sense of things to notice much about him since she woke. For all his composure, she figured that he must have been fighting pretty hard against those chains to make his wrists bleed like that. And his hair hung in loose strands as if he'd been whipping his head around too. So maybe he wasn't quite so cool and collected. Maybe he was just as scared as she was.

"What's *wrong* with you?" she blurted out. "Why are you doing this?" She'd heard Queen Cyrraena's side of things – now she wanted to hear his.

Anger flickered through Nezeral's eyes. "I am an upper realm immortal," he said arrogantly. "Nothing is wrong with *me*." He ran his fingers through his hair, brushing loose strands away from his face. "I will answer your other question, however, because it suits me to do so."

Wind howled outside the windows, sending chills through Willow. Without taking her gaze off Nezeral, she made a fire spring to life in the hearth behind her. She leaned forward to listen.

"Can you imagine what it's like to live forever?"

Willow shook her head.

"It's wondrous and marvelous and ... boring."

Boring? Willow gave Nezeral a skeptical frown. How could life as an all-powerful immortal being be *boring*?

"In my world," he continued, "every person is beautiful and perfect. No one grows old. There are no illnesses or deformities. Everyone has the self-same magical powers. Everyone *is* the same."

"Sounds pretty good to me," said Willow, curling her legs under her.

Nezeral flashed a scornful look that changed to a dry smile. "What do you think we do on Clarion to pass away the eons?"

Willow shrugged. Faeries were a mystery to her. She imagined, though, remembering Queen Cyrraena's beautiful Timorell, that they probably created great works of art or composed brilliant symphonies or something.

"We play Games," said Nezeral matter-of-factly.

"Play games? You mean like chess or Monopoly?" This was hardly the soul-stirring answer she'd been expecting.

"No, I mean Games of Life."

"Games of life?"

"Yes. On Clarion, we turn every aspect of our lives into Games. All the different fey kingdoms create elaborate magical Games and compete against each other. I am of the House of Jarlath, the reigning Game house of Clarion."

Nezeral leaned against the stone wall and casually crossed his legs at the ankles.

Willow didn't get it. What did any of this have to do with turning her and her family into chess pieces? She studied Nezeral. His handsome face was all angles – high-sculpted cheekbones and jutting chin. He looked like a teen model. Not some unfeeling monster. "Would you just get to the point and tell me why you're doing this?"

"Don't you understand? This is a new Game. If I succeed in getting the humans to play it to its conclusion, the council, which banned interaction with other realms, will have to lift the ban. New Games. New rules. New players. Don't you see? We will be the reigning Game house for eons to come."

What Queen Cyrraena had said about the prejudice against humans was frighteningly clear from Nezeral's words. Humans, to him, were expendable. Willow frowned. But still, the faerie queen had said that not all the fey felt this way. So why would they lift the realm traveling ban and create such havoc? "I still don't get it. If you make us play the Game to the end, why does that mean your council has to lift the ban?"

Nezeral cocked his head, strands of silver hair falling into his eyes. "When council makes rules, it usually adds clauses to amend them. Rule one: The fey are not allowed to realm travel. Clause one: Unless called to that realm by a being who lives there. Rule two: Once called to another realm, a fey may choose to cast Game spells on the beings that live there. Clause

MAGGIE L. WOOD –

two: If beings play a Game to its conclusion, the ban of traveling to that realm will be lifted. However ..." he smirked, "Clause two (a): If the beings find a way to thwart the Game, the fey must return back to his or her own realm. See, there are even clauses for you humans."

"But that's not fair!" cried Willow. "You faeries are *ten* times more powerful than us! You can't just come here and use us like we're your little toy soldiers or something. Where's the fun in *that*? The sportsmanship?"

"Fun?" said Nezeral, looking blank. "Sportsmanship? These are human concepts, not fey ones. We play Games for one reason and one reason only: *power*." His face grew imperious. "I am from the blood of the Ancients, the old gods who used to rule your Earthworld, and I will set things as they once were."

Willow cringed. So here it was, the *real* reason for his coming to Mistolear.

"Many of us wish to return to the old ways, when ruling the lower realms was our birthright. Of course, Earthworld and the other material realms are forever closed to us. But you Mistolearians have finally opened the way to the lower magical realms."

Sickened by his malice, Willow stood up. This whole Game scheme was about nothing more than gigantic egos and ignorance.

She focused on Nezeral's dirty brown aura. She supposed

that what she was about to do would, in a way, create a new type of Game. A Game that would promote knowledge and tolerance instead of ignorance and hatred.

The faerie prince paled. He could see she was readying her magic. "Wait. I answered your question. I believe you owe me the same courtesy."

Willow blinked at him, scattering his aura light. "I don't owe you anything," she snapped. "You should be glad just to be alive, and that *I'm* not the kind of person who can hurt someone who can't fight back."

Was that a sheepish look on his face? Willow squinted at him, not sure whether he was just putting on an act for her. "That was an unfortunate mistake," he said. "I let my anger get the better of me. For what it's worth, though, I would not have killed you."

"Yeah, right." He must have thought she was pretty stupid to buy into that one. She crossed her arms. "Okay, go ahead, ask your question."

"In fact, I have two questions. The first one is how is it that you were able to magic these?" He held up his wrists, indicating the iron bands. "No one can magic iron. So how is it that a lower realm mortal, who grew up in an altogether non-magical world, can have such power?" He studied her, his face greedy for an answer.

Willow knew what was going on inside his head. Ruler-of-the-universe dreams were shining through his turquoise eyes.

He still thought he was going to get out of this. And, if he could somehow acquire her iron immunity, so much the better.

"Honestly?" she lied. "I don't really know. No one does. Next question."

Nezeral hesitated, his cool demeanor switching into scared-and-vulnerable mode. "What do you mean to do with me?" he murmured. Suddenly, he was playing the part of shy teenage boy, uncertain about his future and hoping for mercy.

A kind smile spread over Willow's face. "I mean to give you a second chance."

Triumph broke through the vulnerable act and Nezeral let out a happy whoop. He held his wrists up. "You won't regret this, Princess. I may decide to remove you from the Game spell permanently. We shall join forces. With our powers united, we shall see no barriers."

Willow didn't say anything. She just nodded and watched the way his aura leapt with excitement. Already her mind was concentrating on the change. She observed how his aura brightened from dark shades of brown to deepest crimson to red and finally to a sweet, innocent pink.

When she refocused her eyes, the Nezeral that had once been was not to be found. His chains and iron bands lay empty on the floor. In his place, gurgling among his pile of clothing, was a kicking, squirming baby boy with a silky fine dusting of silver hair and eyes the carefree green-blue of a tropical bay.

Willow leaned over him, smiling, bringing his sweet pink

aura into view again. She wasn't the one who needed Nana's wish for a second chance.

She had to laugh as the baby rammed his tiny fist into his mouth, gumming it for all it was worth. With her magic, she diapered him and dressed him in snuggly pajamas, then changed his old clothing into a thick warm blanket. The baby squealed happily and waved his hands in the air.

Gently, Willow touched his plump cheek. "I still have to do something about that nasty old Game spell." She tucked his blankets tighter around his chin and stood up, staring at his round little head. At least he wouldn't be able to hurt anybody else – even if her Game spell idea didn't work out.

She turned to face the chess set. A storm outside had darkened the room and the tall, thin chess pieces cast fire-lit shadows that writhed and swirled. She peered at the board. She knew Nezeral's spell was too strong for her to break. But maybe she could alter it just a little.

Thinking about second chances had made her think about her computer. About how you could save a game and replay the same one over and over again until you got it right. And that made her wonder if the spell could be made to do the same thing.

White light glowed around the edges of the chess set. She could see the molecules, the way the magic had woven them into an impenetrable pattern. If she had attempted to destroy them, they would have resisted. Instead, she was only trying to rearrange them a bit. The spell would be exactly the same, with one slight difference. Her eyes narrowed, focused, and unfocused again. She knew exactly what she had to imagine.

There. Willow shook away her blurry vision and stared at what she'd done. The humongous chess set was gone and in its place was a gray Toshiba laptop, identical to the one she owned. The monitor showed a chess game in play mode and the pieces were set up in the exact same positions as on the other set.

She crossed her fingers, breathing a short prayer that her plan would work. Her heart seemed to pound in her ears as she touched a shaky hand to the keyboard. She clicked the exit button. The computer prompt asked if she wanted to save the game. Willow clicked "yes." The chess program closed without apocalyptic incident, and she quickly shut off the computer and vanished it and the evil faerie Game into thin air.

Instantly, fire engulfed her body. She gasped, crumpling to the floor, feeling as though some huge machine was siphoning the life out of her. Her body curled into a fetal position and her hands crossed protectively over her chest. It seemed to take forever for the magic's volcanic heat to drain from her, but finally it was over. Only a few seconds had passed.

Quivering from head to foot, Willow unclenched her body. She was wet and clammy and her eyes burned, but she was alive. *It worked!* The magic had drained out of her and she was just Willow again. She closed her eyes in relief, panting in rapid shallow breaths.

"Willow?"

That voice. Willow's eyes popped open. She knew that voice. "Brand," she said weakly. He was beside her in an instant, helping her to her feet.

"You did it! By the gods, Princess, you did it!" He laughed as he hugged her tight. Willow noticed that both of them had lost their Game glow. But then she couldn't think about that because his unexpected kiss was making her knees wobble. "There," he whispered. "Your lips have turned me back."

"Oh my God. You heard me?"

"Every word."

Willow blushed, remembering some of the more private things she had said to Brand's chess piece. A woman's squeal broke through her embarrassment.

"Alaric!"

Willow turned to see her mother standing in a doorway that must have materialized after Nezeral lost his power. Diantha raced across the room and flung herself into the arms of a tall fur-cloaked man with dark hair and a bewildered expression on his face. "Diantha," he said, blinking at her in surprise, "you are alive? The Game is ended, then? Are we free?"

Diantha could only nod as she nestled in his arms. Alaric smiled down at her and then looked over her head at Brand and Willow. "The explanation shall have to fall on you, Brand. My wife appears to be welded to my chest."

A playful backhand swatted his head as Diantha threw her arms up around his neck and drew him down for a kiss.

Willow blushed again. Those were her parents over there, and they were kissing! Not that it was gross or anything. Just weird.

Diantha whispered something into Alaric's ear. His arm slid bonelessly from her shoulder as he turned to stare at Willow, anger and disbelief warring across his face.

"This is ... our *child*? But ... but how? Who did this to her?"

Diantha shushed away his questions, leading him to Willow. "Willow," she said, beaming, "this is your father."

Shy smiles passed between them as Willow gazed into the clear icicle-blue of her father's eyes – identical to King Ulor's. The similarities between father and son ended there, though. Prince Alaric's chiseled features and tall muscular body carried no trace of King Ulor's heaviness.

His hand reached out to touch her face. "Is it to you, then, that we all owe our lives?"

Willow nodded, feeling the strength of his fingers against her cheek. She couldn't speak. Her voice was caught somewhere in her throat. This was her father. She had a father!

"Well met," he said, drawing her into his arms. "The bards will have another Farrandale to sing of." The cool, smooth leather of his tunic pressed against Willow's skin. He smelled like horse and leather.

Willow clung to him like a small child. It was over. Everything she'd been through in the past couple of weeks was finally over! Her mother's arm slipped around her back, and for the first time, the three of them embraced as a family – one big teary-eyed happy family.

A loud howl, though, shattered their peaceful silence. Every head turned to the small bundle on the floor and the small, swinging fist that punctuated each cry. Diantha's hand rose to her mouth. No words passed between them, but Willow knew her mother had figured out what she had done.

Speechless, and with her hand still pressed to her mouth, Diantha knelt beside the wailing baby, staring at him in misery. She didn't touch him.

Willow stood behind her and squeezed her shoulder. "If *we* bring him up," she said, "he won't be evil. We can teach him about what humans are like and about caring and stuff. But, you know, if you don't want to, we could find somebody else to take care of him."

Diantha didn't say anything. She stared at the baby and her hand slid up to her shoulder to hold Willow's. "Are you sure? Are you sure this is what you want – for us to raise him?"

"Yes." She'd never been more sure of anything in her whole life.

"Alaric?" Diantha's voice trembled with uncertainty. "Do you wish it as well?"

Alaric came to stand by them, staring down at the

squalling infant, his face thoughtful and sad. Finally, he spoke. "Aye, I do wish it." He picked up the baby, rocking him against his chest. The baby settled, his eyes closing. Alaric handed him to Diantha, who cradled him in her arms.

Willow smiled. They looked like a family. She clasped Brand's fingers and moved to join them. To join her family.

CHAPTER 27

Soon after the baby fell asleep, the faerie queen appeared in a blaze of golden light. She wore sun-colored robes, and her long russet hair spilled over her shoulders like a silken cloak. She stood before them, as grand as a goddess. "It appears, my netherchild, that you have chosen wisely."

Willow felt a rush of pure elation. She *had* chosen wisely. She glanced at Nezeral snuggled securely in Diantha's arms. No one had been hurt. No one had died. Everyone had gained something. Gallandra and Keldoran had their magic back. Prince Alaric and Princess Diantha had a baby, albeit not their own. And Nezeral would now grow up with a new understanding of humans. Everyone had benefited. No one was a loser.

Nana's face surfaced in her mind. No one, that is, except Nana and the poor boy pawn, Terrill Longbottom. They hadn't come out of the Game winners. They hadn't come out of it at all.

"I am no mage," interrupted Brand, "but is that spell truly strong enough to keep Nezeral an infant?" He frowned at the small bundle in Diantha's arms. "Is it not possible that he might break the spell?"

Queen Cyrraena shook her head. "No, Squire Lackwulf. The spell was cast with the magic of a whole kingdom inside your princess. It will not break. The Game is truly won." A victorious smile filled her face then, as if the win were hers. "Come now," she trilled. "Let us make ready for your return to Tulaan."

In the blink of an eye, she magicked everyone into rich fur-trimmed costumes that sparkled with jewels and the eye-catching golds and purples of the House of Farrandale. Elaborate golden crowns encircled the heads of Willow and her parents, and a squire's jaunty feathered cap rested dashingly low on Brand's forehead.

Thanks to the faerie queen, their return to Tulaan was warm, short, and comfortable. When they reached the city, the celebration was overwhelming. Willow's reception was surpassed only by Diantha's – no one had expected ever to see her again. When they reached the castle, the entire Farrandale and Somerell courts were waiting.

One family member, though, stood out from the rest. Her bright, orange-red hair was pulled severely into two tight braids and rolled at the sides. Her skin seemed whiter than the courtyard snow and her eyelashes and eyebrows were completely colorless. But her eyes made up for the lack of color. They were so intense they glowed like aqua-blue lights.

– CAPTURED –

Willow pulled away from her Keldorian grandparents and stared at the woman, who gave her a small, subdued smile and held out a gloved hand. Prince Alaric touched Willow's elbow and whispered in her ear. "Come. I'll introduce you to your Farrandale grandmother." The others moved aside as Willow and her father walked the short distance across the courtyard.

"Madam," he said, smiling at his mother and drawing Willow to stand in front of him, "your granddaughter, the princess Willow."

Queen Aleria's composure wavered but then she steadied herself, reaching out her hand to take hold of Willow's. "My dear, to have a granddaughter such as you – is a great honor."

Willow clasped Queen Aleria's outstretched hand. She couldn't say anything. She was too lost in their similarities. In how she and her grandmother stood eye to eye and how their long-limbed figures were almost identical. For the first time ever, Willow didn't feel like a clumsy giant.

"She takes after you, don't you think, Aleria?" said King Ulor, who'd had his long journey to Tulaan magically shortened by the faerie queen and was now hugging his wife's shoulders with youthful exuberance. "When she first came here, we had her wearing your shoes!"

Queen Aleria smiled and held Willow's hand palm to palm with her own. "It would seem, my lord, that you are correct."

Their long fingertips stretched to meet each other. It was

like holding her hand up to a mirror.

A loud cry ended their careful study. Willow dropped her hand and turned to search for her parents. The crowd had grown quiet again. Confused faces strained to catch a glimpse of the bundle in the prince's arms. Murmurs rose. *An infant? What was the prince doing with a new infant?*

"This child," announced Prince Alaric, "is the fey prince Nezeral." More murmurs. He raised a hand to quiet everyone. "My daughter has saved our world from tyranny. It was her choice to gift Nezeral with a second chance. And now it is our duty to make sure that her gift is not in vain. Princess Diantha and I have agreed to raise Nezeral as our own son."

Willow expected the crowd's silence to turn to dissent. Slowly, though, a cheer rose and it spread, growing louder. Pretty soon everyone was congratulating her again and clapping her back. She made her way, along with her family and Brand, to the foyer of the castle. Willow found Gemma and Malvin loitering on the front steps, waiting for their chance to greet her. "Now that's a neat trick you did there with Nezeral," said Gemma, beaming up at Willow. "Who'd have thought he'd make such a sweet babe?"

"Aye," agreed Malvin, "it was a most fitting defeat."

Gemma smiled and gave Brand a playful punch. "Master Brand, nice to see you're all loosened up again. Maybe we should have a nice game of chess sometime."

A loud groan came from Brand. "Not funny, Gemma. Not

funny in the least."

Malvin nudged her and asked shyly how she had defeated Nezeral. Willow gave him a rundown of what had happened.

"So your Earth mechanism was able to reverse the spell," said Malvin, eyes narrowed in scholarly contemplation. "Amazing. Who would have thought an intrinsic construct of such magical magnitude could be altered? I suppose, though, if the spell wasn't interfered with, it could be done."

"Well, I'd say that's plain," said Gemma, grinning. "If it couldn't be done, we wouldn't have Her Highness and Master Brand back now, would we?"

"I still say you should have blasted him," muttered Brand. He was having a hard time dealing with the fact that a heroic quest had ended with the villain being turned into a baby. "What if he grows up wicked again? Who's going to defeat him then? It's like taking home a baby dragon. All's well till he starts burning down your manor and eating all your livestock!"

Willow laughed but refused to be drawn into the argument. She linked arms with her friends and led them inside. "No more fights, because tonight we're gonna party!"

The banquet that night was magical. Literally. The chefs and musicians and entertainers had all had their magical powers restored, so it was unlike anything Willow had ever seen before. First a miniature, floating castle drifted to the center of the great banquet hall, hovered a moment in the air, and then settled gracefully to the floor. Each corner had a tower, and each tower was lit from within with sparkling lights.

The first tower held a boar's head that spouted fire, the second tower a great pike with three sections, each cooked differently, the third a roasted pig also breathing fire, and in the fourth and final tower, a beautiful redressed swan resting on a nest of golden twigs. For dessert, marzipan sugar spun into brightly colored birds flew to their plates, while tiny unicorn ice sculptures melted into strawberry sorbets.

The music transformed magically into each guest's favorite song. And when the jugglers, acrobats, and dancers performed, pixie lights lit the entire banquet hall. Real pixie lights – hundreds of little pixies flew over the room, sprinkling silvery dust on the performers.

When the dancing started, Brand was the first to claim Willow's hand, holding her close and spinning her around the room. Her father was her next partner, then Malvin. Toward midnight, when she was tired and flushed with pleasure, Queen Cyrraena reappeared.

"Might I steal a moment? I must speak to you."

Willow followed her out a side door into the snow-covered garden. It was quiet and peaceful but very cold. Willow shivered, rubbing her arms for warmth. "Want me to get us some cloaks?"

"Not necessary." The faerie queen passed her hand in front them. Willow's face broke into a smile as a giant bubble of summer suddenly encased the entire yard.

"Come. This won't take long." The queen led Willow down a warm, moonlit path to a secluded bench.

"Have you given any thought to your nurse's gift?"

Willow sat on the bench and looked up at the moon. "I know what Nana was trying to do. But I don't think I need to grow up again. I think I'm happy just the way I am." She looked at Queen Cyrraena to judge her reaction. The faerie queen, her beauty even more breathtaking by moonlight, was regarding her with what seemed like utter disinterest. It was hard to tell, though. Willow's newfound dealings with the fey had taught her not to be misled by their sometimes enigmatic responses.

"You do your nurse a great honor." Queen Cyrraena reached for Willow's hand. "Walk with me. I have something else to offer you."

"The council was much pleased with your dealings with Nezeral. For the first time ever, they have offered a lower realm mortal a council seat."

Willow stared at her, truly surprised. "Really? But isn't it a council of magic? Won't they care that I don't have my powers anymore?"

It was Queen Cyrraena's turn to stare. "What do you mean? You *do* have your powers. In fact, your powers are doubly potent, as your mother and grandmother Aleria are both master mages."

"Really? But the magic ... I felt it drain out of me." It had never even occurred to Willow that there might be some left.

"No. You felt everyone else's magic drain from you. Not your own."

Willow stopped walking and let her gaze unfocus. Immediately, a bright electric light appeared around the closed crocus buds that bordered her feet. It was true! She *was* a mage. A mage *and* a princess! She laughed aloud. As she and Queen Cyrraena walked along the narrow path, Willow opened the crocuses to the moonlight.

"So about this council seat ...?" Willow began, but Queen Cyrraena vanished as did her warm bubble of summer. Snow enveloped Willow's feet and goosebumped her shocked skin. Typical, she thought, hoisting her skirts and sprinting to the castle doorway. The faerie queen was always disappearing in the middle of a question.

Inside, with the door closed against the cold, Willow realized what a council seat meant. The council was held in Clarion ... She would have to go to Clarion. Would have to deal with even more faeries. And what about Nezeral's family? She doubted they'd be happy to see her after what she'd done to him.

A chill rushed up her spine. She stomped the snow from her feet, but not the fear from her heart. Cyrraena couldn't make her go to Clarion. *Could she?* The thought made Willow freeze in the hallway with a sudden conviction – the faerie queen of Timorell could not be trusted. And then another, more sinister idea formed. *Was this the start of a new Game?*

Gwen Turcotte walked along the narrow path. Willow

Maggie L. Wood's vibrant worlds collide in the second Divided Realms adventure

The Darkening

978-1-77080-072-4

Life in a magical realm is anything but normal for reluctant princess, Willow Farrandale, but she is doing her best to adjust. She enjoys spending time with her new friends, especially her sworn knight Brand – despite his infuriatingly old-fashioned rules about "proper courtship."

The peace does not last long, however, as a misstep in Clarion dooms Willow to play another faerie Game. Willow and Brand are thrown into the Goblin's Gauntlet, where a host of bloodthirsty creatures are on the hunt. Their only companions are two faerie siblings – the wily, inscrutable Dacia and the seductive Theon. Can Willow and Brand trust their "allies," or are the siblings playing their own sinister Game?

Coming in Spring 2012

The Divided Realms
Book 3

Following the nightmare of the Goblin's Gauntlet, Willow faces life with a broken spirit and a broken heart. She is easy prey for the seductive faerie prince, Theon Thornheart, who tempts her with a powerful, addictive elixir that warps her magic. Meanwhile, dark forces in Clarion set the stage for a new Game that will place humans, faeries, and goblins in a magical battle of wits. Does Willow have the strength to resist Theon's temptation and the ability to restore the balance of the realms?

ABOUT THE AUTHOR:

Maggie L. Wood grew up on Prince Edward Island. She later moved to London, Ontario, where she became a bookseller, and developed a passion for YA fiction and fantasy. Readers can visit www.maggielwood.com to read Maggie's blog and watch the book trailer for "**The Divided Realms**."